Cathy!
Dare to see
the beauty!

SCAR ME

BOOK TWO IN THE HAUNTED ROADS SERIES

INDIA R. ADAMS

Scar Me is Published by India's Productions

EDITOR
Kendra Gaither, Kendra's Editing and Book Services

COVER DESIGN
Jay Aheer, Simply Defined Art

PROOFREADER
Lyssa Dawn Personal Assistant and Proofreading Services

FORMATTING
Graphics Shed

AUTHOR WARNING

Very serious subjects of abuse are described, in detail, within these pages. If any reader has fear of sexual abuse triggers, please do not continue reading.

Dedicated to the ones who feel alone.
Know this—damaged souls are worth saving.

I don't think it's possible to hate someone you love...
I should.
I should tell...
I should scream!
But I can't.
I love him.

~Delilah~

CHAPTER ONE

Delilah

"Li-lah?"

The deep voice I could hear through a crowd of millions was scratchy and raw. Scared my ears were trying to trick my heart, I looked to the hospital bed where my husband had been in a coma for a month. Beautiful hazel eyes were staring at me. And just like that, everything but what that man needed was forgotten. All that had transpired while he slept didn't matter.

Maverick was awake.

Running to his side, I let a new sense of hope flow through me. "Maverick, I'm here. I'm right here." I adoringly touched his face. "Baby, I'm here."

His bearded face leaned into my touch. "Lilah—"

His eyes slammed shut as if pain were radiating through his whole body. Now conscious, his nerve endings could scream to his brain that he had been severely burned.

"Brother," Tucker, my brother, choked out before running out the door to fetch a doctor.

Maverick tried again, "Lilah... I have to tell you—" He grimaced when moving his legs. Those muscular limbs had been damaged by the ball of fire my husband was pulled from after slamming into the same tree that killed my high school boyfriend.

Kenny.

Even though two men I loved shared the same fate, they were complete opposites.

Maverick once asked me how deep is a woman's soul. The question came because he sensed how unsettled I was. The unknown of my past had him spooked and wondering how far down my secrets hid. He wondered if he would ever learn what had me scared in the night—what had me waking frightened. I think he was frightened, too. Maverick's intuition told him I wasn't experiencing a bad dream. Everything inside him screamed his wife wasn't waking from a nightmare but a memory.

Maverick was right.

Anyone who has been violated on a physical or mental level understands the unseen trauma, the broken and haunted road that leads to the hidden betrayal of the scarred. They understand the fear that sometimes keeps one quiet. Is it the judgment from others or of yourself? Is it the lack of hope or hope to dream? Is it the pain, the crippling notion that you will never be the same? Maybe it's a dangerous and sometimes deadly combination of it all that has you silent.

No matter what the poison, I still hear the memories of my ghosts, and I still feel the love that fooled me. And no matter what, I don't think it's possible to hate someone you love.

I should.

I should tell... I should scream! That's what the whispers in the night tell me, but I can't. To tell would change more than just one love. I love my family too much to be the cause of the carnage that might finally break the men I treasure. So, down the haunted road I go...

There's an indescribable responsibility when a dying parent has asked you to make a very special promise. My mother's lips were dry and cracked, and what hair had tried to grow back after her treatments was now matted due to her body still fighting a pointless battle. Her skin was pale, but she was still the most beautiful woman in the world to me.

Lying in her hospital bed, she had asked my father and brother to leave us alone. I carefully crawled past the wires and tubes the doctor had told this little five-year-old to watch for, not knowing my mother was wanting to say goodbye to me the best way she knew how. Pointing me toward a future without her, my mother's gracious heart never meant to steer me wrong, never meant to curse me. Since her days were numbered and her mind was trying to heal the hearts that were breaking for her coming death, my mother made a mistake...

Her raspy, tired voice said to me, "Your father and brother will do their best to guide you, so trust them." Snuggled to her, I nodded, not understanding. She continued, "But, sometimes, men need the woman of the house to take care of *them*. Keep them happy. Keep them from the darkness. It may take some sacrifices, but that's what true women do. We keep our men in the light, so God can reach them..."

As I got older and thought I understood what my mother meant, those words guided every decision I made, including the horrid ones...

After my mother was buried in the ground, I watched my father wither away to half the man he mentally was. To watch that happen was like witnessing the ground fall from underneath my feet. I knew I was losing him to the darkness my mother spoke of, but I didn't know how to stop it from happening. Feeling helpless, I clung to the only one still standing.

With my brother helping to raise me, I felt I was acquiring an unwritten list of 'I owe yous' with every sacrifice he eagerly made for the cause. Tucker fought for me, bled for me, and loved me with all that his young soul had to offer. This young man, willing to move mountains for me, made me want to become the most responsible human-being possible. So, I did what I could at my age: behaved at school, respected my teachers, and never got into trouble.

As time passed, my father began to smile again. A simple smile said he was aligning himself with Tucker's force of unity. That led us to really find our way through the lonely beaten path of surviving. We were undoubtedly damaged, to the point of never being the same, but still breathing. If you have that—the ability to take another breath —you have a beginning to another new beginning of sorts.

Cooking delicious meals and tending to our home, it began to appear simple to do what my mother asked of me—keep my boys, my father and brother—happy. I didn't see the impossible task, the huge undertaking I was attempting. I couldn't comprehend that filling their bellies was not the same as healing their spirits. The meals from my heart were a foundation, a way to support them, but I didn't learn until later that Mom *should* have said, "To each is his own, and his own must make wise decisions to fulfill his *own* heart. And, no matter what, never try to fill a void that's not yours nor one you created."

Yes, how *those* words would have guided me into recognizing the young man entering my world... Kenny. Instead of seeing a spooked young man who was cautious of every step he took, I saw a warrior fighting through unspoken pain. His fierce ways had him battling through the sorrow of missing a piece of him. Like Tucker, he was ready to fight the world, so that not one more loved aspect of his life could be stolen. That somehow made Kenny perfect for us. Another guardian to protect what we had left after losing Mama. He was like Viola, our childhood friend who understood how our life had already had deadly twists and turns. Hers was even worse—both parents gone without warning; a plane crash—but at least their deaths brought back Diesel. He was an older brother she had never been told about, due to a family fall-out we didn't learn about 'til we were much older. I'm thankful we had been spared the gruesome details of that awful family feud.

Even though Tucker or I didn't yet know of Kenny's hardships, it shined through every sad expression he attempted to hide with a smile. What told me how aware of the pain he truly was, were his soulful eyes. They were a marvelous green with an impeccable quizzical stare, studying me as if I were a mystery that he was determined to solve. The deep-set, studious eyes didn't frighten me; they made me feel as if he understood what I didn't have the strength to say out loud; I missed my mom.

I sensed Kenny had someone he missed, too, so he fit with my brother and I like an odd puzzle that only the damaged could understand. Kenny's smile and embrace had me trusting him, another brother I could turn to, count on, every time. At first, he seemed so sturdy that I wondered what I had done to deserve such devotion. I would soon learn that everything has a price, and that mine would be hefty.

A slight crack in Kenny's persona appeared after an alarming phone call during dinner one night. My brother, father, and I rushed to Kenny's house to see sheriff cruisers already parked in the yard. In the back of one was his mother's boyfriend. Sternly, my dad told me to wait in his truck with the doors locked.

I was glued to the window, desperate for a glimpse that Kenny was okay; that part of what kept me strong hadn't crumbled. As lights from the ambulance blinked, I kept thinking of all the history Kenny and I had. All the fights against boys being cruel to me, especially the first one. All the laughs, movie nights, and fishing at the lake...

Loyalty had me disobeying my father and quietly sneaking inside Kenny's home. Making my way through the destroyed living room, I was careful not to trip on overturned furniture. Searching for Kenny, I saw a picture hanging in the hallway. In the frame, there was a little girl with blond hair, curls at the bottom, and a set of green eyes that looked identical to Kenny's.

Following the deep voices of my brother and father, discussing the packing of Kenny's belongings, I found Kenny sitting on his bedroom floor, completely broken. Exactly what I had feared. He was leaning against a wall as if that's where he had landed after a hard punch to the face. It pained me to see the one who had endlessly fought for my honor now beaten to the ground. His home life had swallowed him whole and spit out a terrified soul.

When Kenny saw me, he slowly lifted his arm, reaching out for me. That delicately simple, silent plea started the change of our roles to one another. I was blind to it at the time, as most inexperienced young women are, but the blood on his hand had my nurturing ways stepping forward. I felt the need to protect him, care for him, just as he had done so many times for me.

Sometimes, the line between loyalty and responsibility of oneself becomes blurred.

Kneeling in front of him, I held his hand tightly. His injured lips tried to make words, but when none could be formed, I silenced him. "It's over now. We won't leave you alone anymore."

His tortured eyes stared at me for some time before he nodded and agreed to come home with me. Not letting him go, we climbed into the rear seat of my father's crew cab dually.

Kenny became more dependent after that, and I was far too naïve to see the potential harm in being someone's crutch. To compound my blindness, my father and brother were incredibly relieved and pleased, thanking me for supporting Kenny, saying I was really helping him recover. They were the rescuers, and I was the healer—the one able to make their mission complete.

Bringing my brother and dad tranquility brought me such inner joy because I was fulfilling my mother's wish. I quickly hungered for more of that internal, magical sense of self-worth. That is how I became the advocate for Kenny's inner peace. That is how and why I decided to do whatever was necessary to keep him stable.

Simple maybe, but painfully true.

I couldn't even comprehend why Viola disapproved of how attached Kenny had become. "Viola," I explained, "I don't even know what *co-dependent* means."

The blonde, hot-headed bombshell sneered. "That's evident, Pretty D, but you're living as an active member of the Co-dependent

Society. Listen, I'm not trying to upset you. Just know I love you and plan on watching your naïve, wide-open heart."

Ignorantly, I believed she was too rough-edged to care for a man like I could. So, against her solid advice, I remained unconditionally patient with Kenny, and soon, I felt that patience had paid off. Kenny became himself again, and he and my brother returned to being *complete* pains in my ass. When I turned on my hairdryer and ended up looking like a melting Pillsbury Dough Boy, I acted livid but was truly relieved that a normalcy was present again. When I peed in my toilet, not aware of the saran wrap covering the opening and got urine on my brand new cowgirl boots, I faked being enraged, yet was so pleased I had saved Kenny. I even recruited some of my dad's employees to keep the fun times going: closet shelves and bed collapsing. Before I knew it, Tuck and Kenny were back to being each other's wingmen, hunting down the ladies as normal high school boys do. Proud of my accomplishments—and my brother doing my laundry—I would snuggle into a chair in my room and read novels, a favorite pastime.

Since it was Tuck's last year of high school, Dad caved and let us go to Daytona for a couple days of our spring break. At first, Dad had been so against it, he refused to budge with his answer "no way in hell..." until Viola convinced her brother, Diesel, to have a chat with him. Diesel had also been reluctant of our Spring Break vacay in the beginning but also finally caved. And since he claimed to already be going to hell, he had bought us alcohol. "Can you morons at least keep this shit on the *el* down low-o?"

Viola saluted him, and with a loaded trunk, we headed to our much-needed vacation. Yep, my junior year of high school, Tucker's beautiful black mustang sped us around town, taking every corner with screeching tires—much to the dislike of elderly locals—and now was racing Kenny, Viola, and myself to Florida's famous city, Daytona

Beach. With windows down, my golden brown hair blew wild in the back seat.

Sitting next to me, Viola leaned forward between Tucker and Kenny's seats and reached for the console. Tuck swatted at her. "*My* radio."

She bit his ear then growled, "Then turn it the fuck up." As she pulled away to sit back down, his mouth hungrily opened and went after her—to kiss or eat her, I wasn't sure—but she comically bitched slapped him. "Keep your eyes on the road, Nascar Bandit." Tussling his thick brown hair, she sat back and winked one of her gorgeous blue eyes.

I loved how she managed to bring out his playful side. Dad said Tuck always looked angry. Maybe he had a lot to be angry about. But not on this day. Music blared goodness to our free, teenage souls. Tucker laughed, his brown eyes—that we both got from our mom—proudly watching me from over his shoulder as I danced in celebration. I could literally feel his speakers pounding out "This Time" by Bryan Adams.

Kenny yelled from the front passenger seat, "What is this old shit we're listening to?"

Viola hissed. "I'll be sure to tell my brother what you think of his classics."

Kenny ran fingers through his dark blond hair. "Great. A pissed off biker in Daytona. Just what I've always wanted."

Yes, Diesel keeping an eye on us was part of the deal with my dad. Knowing I was in safe hands, my dad rented us teenagers a hotel room for a few days. I think he did it because, in a few months, my brother was to leave high school and us behind. Tucker was almost two years older than me. It was time for him to go and experience the college life. I think my dad knew it had the rest us all on edge. Viola and I had never been without Tuck. Years ago, he made us a promise to always be with us, one he took seriously.

After we checked into the hotel and settled into our room, we filled up travel cups to be on the 'el down-low-o', and with our beverage of choice, we headed out to walk the strip. The sun blazed down on all the celebrating people, everywhere—outside restaurants and bars—as we strolled down the sidewalks. Horns honked, young people hung from open car windows, and we all screamed in some sort of 'we're here to get crazy and forget all our problems' mentality.

Clearly, I wasn't the only one desperate for an unspoken freedom. "I'm blown away by everyone wanting to have fun."

Walking by my side, Kenny said, "And it ain't even night time yet. So, stay close, okay?" Just Kenny mentioning I may need his protection had me stepping closer to him.

"Yeah," Tucker roughly threw his arm around Viola's neck, "no wandering off."

She punched his gut. "I don't wander. I strut with purpose. Questions?"

A rumble of motorcycle engines got louder as they cruised up behind us. "Hey, dumbass. Taking care of my sister?"

I spun around. "Diesel!"

The four of us slowed our walking so the bikes could catch up. Due to the punch Viola had just delivered, Tucker held his stomach, moaning to Viola's brother, "Impossible task."

Looking menacing and rugged yet somehow charming with his *you-know-you-wish-you-could-taste-this* seductive smile, Diesel was riding his jet black Harley. A woman sat behind him with her thighs possessively clenching his hips. Diesel's eyes popped wide. "Damn, you're happy as hell! I didn't even know your voice could get that high."

Feeling giddy, I squealed, "This place is awesome!"

Once his bike caught up to us, he coasted due to very slow moving traffic. We walked alongside him. A few bikes rode in front of Diesel, a bunch more behind. His friends, who I'd never met before, were a leather and blue-jeaned up group of long-bearded, rough-looking characters quietly watching our surroundings.

In prayer, I put my hands together. "Diesel, tell me you're taking me for a ride later."

"If you're still standing after your first day of spring break, you got it, gorgeous."

His sister shook her hips while circling me. "She'll be standing and dancin'."

"V," her brother warned.

Viola always graced a sexy flare; this behavior was no different, so I wondered why her brother was irritated. Feeling like maybe pushing myself on Diesel was the cause, I tried to back out of the promised ride. "Hey, don't worry about the ride. You probably have plans—"

Kenny put his arm around my shoulders. "Don't worry, Diesel. I won't take my eye off her. Stick to your plans."

Viola suddenly stopped dancing and faced her brother with a glare. He growled, "I hear ya." He lifted his chin to me. "I'll call you in a bit for a ride."

As if satisfied, V went right back to dancing, wiggling her hips without missing a beat.

Watching her, Diesel leaned his head back and busted out laughing. "Oh, Little Man, you better keep your promise. She better not have a mark on her or it's your ass I'm comin' for."

"V!" Tuck yelled. "Stop bein' sexy and causing problems."

She didn't stop. In fact, she started twerking against his thigh. "Bite me, *Little Man*."

I remember when Diesel called my brother Little Man the first day we met him. It was at his parents' funeral. On that godawful day, this motorcycle man entered our lives and became a hero of ours.

Tucker answered Viola. "Bite you? Your *boyfriend* may disapprove."

Traffic started moving again so Diesel pulled away, laughing. "Bryce. What a joke."

To Diesel—a man who appeared to have the ability to kill you in mere seconds with only his hands—a skinny sweet teenager who wore glasses was a bit comical, especially when knowing this nerd's girlfriend was over the top sexy Viola.

As they passed us, each biker gave a head nod to Viola in some sort of unspoken greeting or goodbye. Watching the bikes turn off the strip, I noticed a lot of them were with women sitting behind them. Viola flipped off one girl in particular and warned, "Watch your step," as the girl rode by on the back of another bike, glaring disapprovingly at us. The biker driving didn't say anything to V to rebuke her comment; he just smirked, stunning blue eyes sparkling.

I asked Viola, "You know her?"

V shrugged it off. "You could say that." Then she pointed at a bar. "Let's go inside that one."

Viola and I were feminine but never small or extremely delicate. We resembled women—not the sixteen-year-olds we were. Our height, boobs, and large hips and ass to match had me believing that's why we were able to waltz into the bar without being carded. The fact that Tuck and Kenny got in with no questions either was lost on me.

Within moments, we were playing pool in a filthy, smoky bar as if adults, and I loved it! The only thing I didn't love was how annoyed Viola was every time I had to say 'excuse me to hint for Kenny to give me more room to maneuver my pool stick. So used to Kenny glued to my side, I obliviously took in the scenery. In all the novels I had read, I learned about one-night stands that had taken place between lonely souls meeting in such a questionable dwelling as the one I was in. Even though I couldn't fathom how a 'happily ever after' could come from such an encounter, I wanted to witness it in real life. But what I actually saw were bar stools that appeared as shady as the drunk men sitting on them. Reading about the lusty heady affairs and actually seeing the lonely people needing affections were clearly two different events in real life.

"I'm done with suffocating," V glared at Kenny, "and this pool game. Pretty D, let's get a beverage." She eyed Tuck with judgment. "Or two." As soon as the boys went to follow us, V snapped, "Stop hovering!"

Tucker snapped back, "Stop being a bitch."

Her face paled slightly. "I'm not being a bitch. I'm being independent."

Tuck rubbed the back of his neck. "Damn. Sorry. I'm just not used to you," he gestured around, "in a *bar*. Do you know how many men already have you naked in their head?"

She smirked. "Most of them. Does that fact bother you?"

He winced, readjusting his stance. "*Pfft.* No."

She lifted a brow in challenge.

"It's just... I don't trust them."

As if satisfied with him being uncomfortable, she pointed to the bar. "Jesus, Tuck, we will only be ten feet away."

Kenny grumbled, "Not a good idea."

"Didn't ask you," V snipped. Then she waited for Tucker's permission, which surprised me.

Tuck pointed at her with his pool stick. "But no starting a bar fight *I* will have to finish."

With fake hurt feelings on grand display, V gasped, "Moi?" then grabbed my hand, dragging me toward the bar, whispering, "Let's see how fast we can cause problems."

Maybe it was because we were on spring break, but that idea didn't sound half bad. "I'm in."

CHAPTER TWO

When alcohol shots were delivered—ones we never ordered—and were already paid for, I was shocked, informing the female bartender that she was mistaken. Viola ignored me and asked the bartender to point out our gift-giver, then mumbled to me, "Follow my lead." She held up her shot, winked at the scary looking individual smiling at us, then slammed the beverage down her throat.

I did as told, mimicking her.

Then I coughed and gagged, making facial expressions that were beyond unattractive. Yet, within minutes, the bartender returned, laughing. "Delivery."

Apparently, winks and gagging equaled free drinks. *Noted.*

Viola told her, "Thanks, doll, but this will be our last shot. Only beers from here on out."

"Smart move," said the bartender as she walked away, only to return. "Delivery..."

With our arms full of beers, we leaned our backs against the bar, me completely stunned. "How much do these guys think we can drink before we pass out?"

"Think about it, Pretty D."

"Eww." I shook off a shudder of disgust, understanding unconsciousness wasn't a rejection in these strangers' books. I studied all the beers in my arms. "All right, so why do you say we have to keep an eye on these bottles?"

"The bartender has to open each beer since they're paid for, and smart girls never leave open beverages unattended. Roofies suck."

Scanning my surroundings a little more seriously, I suddenly felt like prey being hunted. "Thanks for the heads up."

Two bikers approached us. One chuckled, gesturing to the four beers against Viola's chest. "Need a beer?"

"Got it covered, thanks."

The other biker said, "We thought you pretty ladies might want to dance."

Viola started saying, "No," but I figured if Diesel was trustworthy, these bikers must be, too, so I yelled, "Yes!"

"Shit," uttered Viola as she peered around to see Tuck and Kenny already shaking their heads. V unapologetically mouthed "oops" while we headed to the dance floor, arms still full of beers. I didn't know why V was laughing, yelling at them across the bar, "I guess it's time to get this party started!" We were just dancing. It was great!

Beer bounced in and out of our bottles with every sexy move V and I made. I was cheering and laughing until I felt wandering hands begin to, well, *wander*. Before I could even set my dance partner straight, V had all her bottles balanced in one arm and her fist swinging through the air. *Wham!*

She punched him!

I yelled, "Holly shi—" but couldn't finish. Tucker was pulling me —and a laughing Viola—in one direction while Kenny and some other guy were pulling our handsy dance partners in another. The guy helping Kenny had on a leather vest, like my dance partner, but was much younger, and he was scanning my body with intent. It didn't feel like an invasion though. See through electric blue eyes studied me as if checking for damage.

Blue eyes... My intoxicated mind announced I recognized him, but there was no time to ask who he was. Other friends of the handsy bikers weren't particularly interested in their buddies being manhandled by any babysitters of mine, so an exhilarating bar fight took flight. Not pretty, but *definitely* out of a book I'd read.

Bouncing off bodies, I laughed watching Viola try to drink her beers in a rush. "Pretty D," she wiped her chin, "we're about to get kicked out of this joint so down the hatch." After some more guzzling, she sang out, "One down." She ditched the bottle on a nearby table preventing her fall and tilted the next one, her lips extended trying to suck up every drop while being jolted with the surrounding fight.

In the midst of the chaos, I, again, followed her lead, downing my beverages as fast as I could. Never having slammed beers before, my gut was becoming a fizzed war zone. Viola and I were choking on laughter—and beer possibly coming back up—when I noticed the electric blue-eyed guy again, now punching strangers. His vest read *Prospect* and *Redemption Ryders*.

Tucker grabbed my hand and a still laughing Viola's. "Ditch the beers, damn it!"

V balked, "But I winked for these!"

He tossed them to a table, not caring as they rolled. "I'll buy you more." Tuck yelled to Kenny—who was in mid-swing, "Got'em! Let's roll!" Kenny's fist landed, and then the five of us ran out the door and down an alley.

Blocks away, I heard sirens. We stopped to catch our breath. Viola told the *Prospect,* "We're good. Thanks for the back-up."

After his eyes raced to mine, he gave a one-fingered salute to Viola and took off in another direction. It was the biker that V had flipped off his girl. I was about to ask what that was about, but Tucker was full of worry. "You okay?"

Nodding, I smiled, feeling euphoric. "I actually think so. Or maybe I'm drunk." For once, I was caught up in the thrill of a scene. "That was right out of a book!"

With hands resting on knees and lungs panting, Kenny looked to

Tucker and Viola. Then they all begun to laugh! Tucker yelled, "I think she liked it!"

Viola howled, "Pretty D's got a wild side!"

"This shouldn't be funny!" I hollered in excitement.

Kenny proclaimed, "That *was* fun, darlin'. You can admit it to us."

Tuck started rolling his shoulders, looking around. "Let's do it again."

Apparently game, V started thumbing her nose like a boxer. "I'll wink—" she accusingly glared at Tucker, "finish my beer this time, and let the games begin."

We had just used up one of our nine lives, but Tuck, Kenny, and Viola wanted more. If the bikers hadn't been surprisingly annihilated with consumption by midafternoon, and we didn't have some lone *prospect* to help us, that could have had a horrifically different outcome.

Kenny pointed to the bars surrounding us. "Delilah, smile at a guy. That'll start more shit."

V offered, "I can shake my ass—"

"No!" yelled my brother.

"Y'all are insane!" I cheered, buzzed from alcohol and misbehaving.

Walking to the next dive bar, the breeze was refreshing and clearing my head. My chest felt lighter and my lungs felt fuller. It was a bewildering free sensation as if my newfound wild side was creating a drug inside my body, opening me up to a whole new world.

Once inside the questionable establishment, Tuck asked, "Can you two behave this time?"

V pulled me to her. "Nope." With my back to her chest, she started swaying her hips, moving mine with hers. "But I can promise not to dance with anyone other than your sister."

Wanting to move to the music, I let my head fall back to Viola's shoulder as I started willingly moving with her. Kenny peered around at the patrons—who were now staring at me and V—and mumbled, "I take it our goal is to keep the cops busy tonight?"

Such words were a reminder that, no matter what town we were in, Tucker and Kenny were two loose cannons and a lot of work to maintain, and we didn't have a biker friend as back-up this time. Viola, enjoying the ruckus too much, was no help to prevent another volcanic eruption. "No. No more fights. Just dancing."

Still swaying with me in her arms, Viola shooed the boys off. "I promise to behave." She grabbed my hand and spun me around, landing my back to her front again. We swayed to the music "I hope you dance" by Lee Ann Womack. Watching the boys walk away, Viola told me, "I hope you're like this song someday, Pretty D. I hope, when you get the chance, you dance."

I grinned. "Am I too reserved for you?"

"No, just too controlled. Always mindful."

"And that's a bad thing?"

"If you're missin' out, it sure is."

Still swaying to the music, we observed Tucker and Kenny on the hunt. When Tuck approached a girl, Viola's chin rested on my shoulder and she sighed.

Wondering when Viola was going to dance and admit to being in love with my brother, I teased, "Thinking of Bryce?"

Absentmindedly, she uttered, "Uh-huh," staring at Tucker now dancing with the girl all-too-happy for his attention. This scene, in a book, may have been described as *a woman with a dark past who was longing for a man to fill a deep, tortuous hole in her heart,* when in reality, I think she was a simple bar fly not caring that she was headed for a one-night stand.

Kenny danced with some girl who an author may have described as *a young girl who wanted to be set free, and was in a bar unbeknownst to her father...* Oh, wait, that was me.

I turned in Viola's arms, still dancing. "Why are you with Bryce?"

She exhaled, looking to our moving feet. "Conversation for another day."

"Understood." I delivered her a Cheshire grin. "And tonight?"

Her eyes slowly closed as if being drugged. "Tonight... young and *free*."

Maybe energy is easy to read because no guys approached us. Viola and I got to swivel our hips and love being best friends, trying to shed the invisible weight we felt at home. Her weight was apparently from Bryce, and mine from the two loose bulls in an overpriced China shop. In fact, there were no interferences until V cooed, "Ohhh, Pretty D, there's the book guy you're always describing."

A very tall, young man with dark hair, who was incredibly fit was with shoulders that screamed, *"You can rest your little head here, sweetheart, and I'll keep you safe, forever."* Any characteristics that I had conjured up in my mind—what handsome ruggedness would qualify to stir the female in me—had been surpassed with this specimen of a young man.

Admiring the eye candy, I grabbed my chest. "You know me well, V."

He was dancing with a woman who was *clearly* older than him.

Viola said, "If our guard dogs were on a proper leash, we could introduce you so you could finally experience the enchanted evening that only exists in those magical pages you read." She spun me around before having me face him again. "Do you think he would be a great first kiss?"

I sadly exhaled, not knowing that the young man who'd just captured my attention would one day capture my heart. He had yet to grow the goatee that would soon tickle me during delicious kisses, but the hypnotic hazel eyes that belonged to the man I would someday love were clear.

Watching his dance partner, I whined, "I envy that woman," not knowing I would someday marry the one she was holding.

Viola jolted before grabbing her cell phone from her back pocket. After reading the screen, she smiled. "Well, let her envy you on the back of a Harley. My brother is ready. Let's roll." She snapped a pic of the hot guy gave Tucker an expression that was a bit evilly sexy, and then put up a peace sign while leading me toward the exit of the bar. Tucker's eyes widened with panic before he heard an army of Harleys rolling up outside. The girl talking to him palmed his face to gather his attention again, but Tuck stared at Viola. She rolled her eyes as we walked out the door.

I was surprised to see it was now night time. And I was surprised to see our biker accomplice—*prospect*—on a bike further down the row of Diesel's friends. He no longer had a girl sitting behind him and was staring at me.

I pointed. "Hey, isn't that—" But I was interrupted by Diesel.

He was sitting on his bike next to the curb, studying V. "What's got your *el* panty-os all bunched up?"

By my elbow, she led me to his bike—that no longer had a girl on the back, either. In fact, none of the bikers did. "Not a damn thing," replied Viola. Leaving me, V headed to the bike behind her brother's. She took the helmet offered by the leather-vested driver and strad-dled the bike, behind him, as if an everyday practice.

After strapping on a helmet of my own, I timidly slid behind Diesel. "Thank you for this. So. Excited."

"It's been a few years, hasn't it?"

I wrapped my arms around his waist and hugged tight. "Yep. Feel guilty?"

He revved his engine. "Does it help that I ditched a hot piece of ass for you?"

"Don't pretend she's not going to hunt you down later."

He laughed really hard. "Delilah is one smart little girl." He lifted his chin before the bikes in front of him rolled forward.

I yelled over the engines, "Hey, one of your friends was at the last bar we were at."

"Yeah? What a coincidence."

As my brain cleared more and more of alcohol, my suspicions rose. "Diesel, why *do* you keep me from this bike world of yours? It's clearly more than I thought it was."

He heavily exhaled in my arms. "Trying to protect you, precious."

I wondered how anything he was involved in could ever bring me danger. He adored V and me, desperately so.

Driving down the road, I got to view Daytona from a whole different perspective. Night lights were on, and the city had definitely come to life. Even more people were strolling the strip. With all the congested traffic, it was impossible to drive fast and I was thankful. The vibrations the bike offered were exhilarating, rumbling through my whole body. I loved how there were no barriers around me yet I was unapproachable. Everything felt more real without a piece of glass to look through, like when in a car. And I knew no questionable character would get handsy with Diesel present. The air even seemed more vibrant. I didn't want to lose the sensations I didn't know to appreciate on my prior rides with Diesel. I leaned my head to his shoulder, thankful for the man who kept my dear friend from moving away years ago.

With only brotherly intentions, his hand patted my thigh. "You hungry, baby?"

"Staaaaaaarving."

Diesel's hand went into the air, made some sort of signal, then the bikes changed course. Realizing his bike, the one *not* up front, was the one actually leading this group, upped my growing suspicions. When Diesel had been in court, fighting for custody of Viola, the judge said Diesel could not raise V in the motorcycle club environment. I was told he walked away from that way of life. But all these signs were telling me only a façade had been set into place. I also suspected my father knew the truth, and that's why I was allowed to come to Daytona.

Parked and off the bike, and now on a sidewalk, Diesel's stained finger—from working on his bike's engine—pointed to the vacant spot in front of him. He was as tall as my dad, same as Tuck. Diesel's dominant presence had me easily falling in line, going to where he wanted me. Not even V questioned his silent order for her to do the same.

With her brother looming over us, Viola and I were taken to an open bar on the beach for some much-needed grub. Wooden picnic tables were being overtaken by bikers while a band played old rock-n-roll. The bartender seemed very familiar with Diesel's friends as she observed. She even knowingly winked at Diesel. "Hello, *stranger*."

Diesel delivered a panty-dropping, sexy, crooked smile, his deep-seated eyes gleaming approval. "Gorgeous, do I get to see you on this trip?"

Seeing how she was lustily staring at him, I came to the conclusion that "seeing" him meant sex. The bartender eyed me and Viola. "Looks like your hands are already full."

"Yes, but no. This is my sister and her friend who are in desperate need of your grouper specials. Once they're fed, there's another hunger needin' quenched."

Her eyes went half-hooded as she replied, "Then yes to both. Sandwiches... and tonight."

"What time you get off?"

"That depends when I get your hands on me."

He chuckled a low purring rumble then lifted his chin, waiting for her answer.

She wiped the bar with a used-to-be white towel. "About two-thirty."

"Perfect." He gestured to the filling tables. "Need pitchers of beer."

She tilted her head. "You doubtin' my smarts?"

He growled hungrily then guided us to a table where some spots had been saved. I whispered over my shoulder to Diesel, "I thought you *already* had a date for tonight?"

"Plans changed. She's a wildcat." Viola and I eyed him with

scrutiny. Diesel shrugged. "Never sleep with a man who doesn't treasure you, and you'll never be traded when somthin' tastier presents itself."

I shivered because that was such a cold statement. True, but uncomfortably cold.

With his hands on our backs, Diesel nudged. "Sit. Eat. Drink. Then you two can dance all you want with proper protection. Dumbass apparently needs another year of maturing before he can handle your sass." He swatted V's butt before she sat next to me. Then he lectured me as he squeezed between us. "Don't be corrupted by this one."

"Too late, I'm afraid."

That had his laughter roaring. "Well, shit. More greys for Diesel."

A waitress brought out pitchers of beer and mugs for Diesel's friends and set them on the table. Diesel's late-night date reached over his shoulder with four ice-cold mugs and another pitcher of beer. She let her breast touch his back as she filled our mugs. She had his full attention until one of his friends held up a cell phone and lifted his chin in question.

Diesel eyed V and I then shook his head. "Later."

I didn't ask. He said he was trying to protect me, so I planned on staying out of his business.

As V and I stuffed our faces, Diesel admired. "I love that you girls ain't afraid to eat in front of men."

I licked the tartar sauce dripping down my hand from the best grouper sandwich in the whole world. "Diesel, will you marry me? A man who can find food like this is *the one*."

"I'm not into robbin' the cradle, pretty girl. Talk to me in twenty years."

Viola commented, "But then you'll be beyond old as dirt."

"Zip it," he told his sister while scowling at my display of starvation. "When the hell did Little Man feed you last?"

Viola washed down her mouthful with some beer. "Hasn't yet. You should beat his ass."

He smirked at her. "For not feeding you, or for hanging with some bitch for the night?"

V growled, "I don't give a fuck what Tuck does. I have a boyfriend." When the rest of the bikers started laughing, she sneered. "Bryce is not a joke."

Speaking of other halves... "Where're all the women that were with you guys earlier?"

Diesel answered, "Gettin' all dolled up for an event we got goin' tonight."

I eyed the bartender, wondering if she knew she was the second treat of the evening, but jumped when V slammed down her beer. "We're being dumped by another set of babysitters?"

Diesel filled her mug. "You'll be fed and buzzed, ready for bed, so what's it matter, little girl?" He lifted his chin to someone at a table behind me. "Besides, you'll have one babysitter present in the room 'til Twiddle Dee and Dumber get back."

I peered over my shoulder and saw eyes that had been becoming more familiar as the night went on. "Oh, yes. The one who just so happened to be at a bar when needed by yours truly."

Surrounding bikers chuckled.

Prospect had dark hair and an *I'm-all-the-trouble-you-can-handle* wicked smile forming. He was practically a younger version of Diesel. Trouble had *never* looked so good.

"No." Diesel scolded me like a pup who just pissed on the floor. "He's twenty-one."

I internally pouted as I realized, between my dream book guy and the hot biker, my hormones were in overdrive for the evening. Turning back around, I noticed a patch falling off the front of Diesel's vest. I went to fix it, but it fell into my hand, exposing another one still on his vest.

Diesel exhaled as he put his beer down, eyeing his sister. "Ya just had to come to Daytona, yeah?"

Still in her foul mood, she complained, "Like you were going to let me come without a proper escort." She softened when seeing me sitting, stunned, eyes locked on his covered pec. "I need you to be cool about this, okay? I need just over one more year 'til the courts can't interfere."

The exposed patch read: *President.*

CHAPTER THREE

The band continued to play old rock-n-roll, but my ears couldn't hear. They were bussing with adrenaline. "I feel like such an idiot for," I gazed around, "thinking all these guys were just your biker buddies."

Diesel dropped the fake patch in a full mug of beer then put an arm around my shoulders. "They are, in a sense, but we're a bit tighter than just that. These are my brothers, by choice, and when the courts asked me to walk away, well, it wasn't an option."

"This is what you tried to protect me from?"

He sighed. "Other clubs are always looking for weaknesses. You on the back of my bike can potentially make you a target." He looked at his sister. "Wish someone would've taken no for an answer."

Viola looked away, regret in her eyes. "Shit. Sorry, bro."

I told Diesel, "So, you felt it was needed to lie to me."

"Yes. You're family, one I protect. Would you lie to Tucker, to protect him?"

I looked him straight in the eyes. "Yes, and I will lie for you. No one will learn the truth from me."

His smile was grand. "I appreciate that, more than you know." He kissed my forehead.

———

Our hotel room was one palm tree design bleeding into another. Even the lamp sitting on the nightstand between the two queen-sized beds was a freaking palm tree. The smell was a tad alarming, but we were right on the beach, third floor with a spectacular view, so no bitching was allowed. I was excited to see the sun rise over the water the next morning, but for now, the drapes were closed and we were with our hot babysitter—AKA Artist.

While working the remote control, Viola grumbled from the bed we were to share. "I can't believe Tuck and Kenny are getting those bitches drunk with *our* alcohol." When we had returned to our room, we noticed the boys had been there and must've left with full arms. *Bastards.* V whined, "This is *not* how I envisioned our Daytona vacay."

Artist leaned back in his chair. "No complaints here. I'm in a hotel room with two beautiful girls."

V chuckled. "Two jailbaits that can get you in more trouble than your worst nightmares."

Seemingly bored himself, he flicked a lighter on and off. "Straight up truth right there."

"Soooo," V tossed the remote and rose to her knees, "will you get us some beer?"

"Boss man said you had to stay in this room." He stood. "He *didn't* say no more alcohol. And I, for one, am parched! There's a store right next door."

Viola jumped up and down on our bed, "Just for that," causing me to bounce next to her, "I'll convince Pretty D to give you her first kiss!"

"Wh-at?" I shrieked, practically flopping off the mattress.

He rushed into the hallway, "Be right back," then slammed the door behind him.

"Viola!"

She plopped onto her belly. "Relax. I would *never* sell you for a twelve pack."

I exhaled.

"Now, if he brings back a case, you best pucker up."

"Viola!"

She giggled then purred, "He's eye-candy, ain't he?"

After a moment of pause, I rolled my eyes. "Who'm I kidding. I'd kiss him even if he only brought back plagued water."

V howled out laughter. "*Love* this wild side!"

"So, ya gonna make it happen?"

Her jaw dropped in dismay. "You're serious."

I nodded emphatically. "How many chances will I get to be alone in a hotel room with a guy other than Kenny and Tuck, neither one kissable?"

"So fucking true." She tapped her chin. "Art is going to get shredded by my brother—"

"Only if Diesel finds out. My lips will be sealed—well, after the kiss."

"Or during!" She rolled over and kicked her bare feet into the air.

We kept laughing until her cell phone lit up. It was from Tuck: *U at the room?*

V sat up and typed: *Yep. No booze thieves or skanks allowed.* Then she told me, "He needs to find another room to get laid in."

Internal shudder. "Eww."

"Nothing is *eww* about your brother, Pretty D."

"Except who he will be sleeping with tonight?"

Just then, Tuck texted: *Damn, wuz jus makin sur u 2 wer safe. Hav a place for her.*

I pitied the phone V angrily typed on: *I can handle my own. U can get to fuck'n*

Why u hatin on me tonight?

A mournful expression appeared. "God, I'm a bitch to him." Eyes watering, she typed: *Sorry. Mean it.*

I fuckin love u, girl.

She stared at the phone and whispered, "Not the way I want you to."

My eyes started welling for her. I leaned my head to her shoulder. "Oh, V. I'm sorry you hurt this bad for him. I wish you'd let me to talk to him."

"Oh, God, no. Never would I want such a stallion out of pity. I want him to desire me like he does over half the female population of our town."

I respected her pride. "Does it help that our town is small?"

Her phone alerted another text: *Nothi'n to say?*

She sighed. *luv u too*

Better. Later. Don't wait up.

Viola closed her eyes to the ceiling and chanted, "Don't be a jealous bitch. Don't be a jealous bitch." Artist walked back in with a case of beer. Viola got up and followed him to the little palm tree table in between two leaf-patterned chairs.

He watched as V ripped into the box, grabbed a beer, and downed the whole thing. With a smirk, he sarcastically said, "Drowning out thoughts of Bryce?"

After she swallowed, she softly said, "Please don't know me so well tonight."

I was shocked she claimed this guy, whom I'd never met before, knew her well. I was also surprised to see sympathy cross his face as if he cared about her wellbeing. "All right, girl. I'm done pickin' on ya. Tucker's a blind fucker." He pulled something out of his back pocket and held it up. "Cards?"

V stared at the freshly bought deck. "You're officially my hero."

He winked at her and grabbed another chair.

Sitting around the small table, bottled beers were being *popped* open. I was in the middle chair facing the palm tree-curtained sliding glass doors. Viola was to my right, and Artist was to my left, closer to the AC unit cooling the room.

Artist said, "Okay, here's the rules—"

"Strip poker," announced V.

Artist lifted a brow. "And die by the hands of your brother? No thanks."

"The winner gets to kiss Delilah."

"One game, but that's all."

She smirked. "Figured you see it my way."

"When is it *not* your way?"

"Good point."

As Artist shuffled cards, I teased, "What about the girl on the back of your bike?"

"I ain't married." Artist's eyes met mine as he shrugged. "What about her?"

I stared at him.

A side-smile appeared. "What does it matter?"

"Apparently, it doesn't." I figured I should get to know who I was soon to kiss. "So, how'd you get your name, Artist? I'm presuming it wasn't from your mama?"

"Damn, your voice is sultry up close." I opened my mouth to ask what the hell that meant but he kept shuffling. "Uh... Your presumption is correct. Viola gave me this road name."

V? "What?" I looked at her.

She sipped her beer. "He creates masterpieces. It fits."

I asked him, "You paint?"

"No. Viola claims some of my thoughts to be artful. Now, I'm stuck with this name."

Viola's brows did a dance. "Hot, right?"

I faked dabbing sweat from my forehead. "Damn straight."

She winked at him. "Told you it's hotter than Killer or some shit." She told me, "We sometimes call him Art for short."

"I like it." I grabbed my beer. "And I think I like you, *Art*. Hope you deal yourself a winning hand."

Shuffling cards exploded from his hands.

Gathering and *re*shuffling, he asked, "Why'm I suddenly feeling nervous?"

V tossed a bottle cap into the palm tree wastebasket. "Because you're a guy, in a room, with two underage girls, who you're illegally giving alcohol to, and this scenario—us about to shed our clothing—has potential to be deadly for you—or, at least, another illegal activity to add to your growing pile."

"Oh, that's right." He dealt out cards. "Thanks for the reminder."

I picked up the five dealt cards and examined them. "With all you're up against tonight, I'm surprised you're daring enough to sit next to me. Not insisting on V in between us."

He organized his cards. "Behave."

"Not sure if you've noticed, but I'm a young woman, on spring break, in the great town of Daytona—where *no one* behaves."

His chest rumbled with laughter and temptation. "To argue with that valid point would make me a fool."

With enough beers in my system, it was easier than I thought it would be to remove clothing in front of a guy, one I had just recently met. The only real problem was that Art and I were *losing*. He was down to his jeans—not exactly a horrible sight—and I was in my bra and jeans. Meanwhile, Viola was fully clothed. The bitch had only lost one earing and a hair tie, which Art claimed to be a cheater's move. She claimed he needed to "bite her" and "shut the fuck up".

With my bare foot, I kicked her under the table. She yelled, "Oww! Why'd you do that?"

"Because I don't want to kiss *you!*"

Artist sat up straight in his chair. "You weren't joking?"

My intoxicated face scrunched as if that notion was absurd. "No."

He laid a hand on his chest. "Aw, girl. Damn. I'm sorry. I thought we were just playin'." My expression must have shown the ego hit I was experiencing because he said, "No, don't take what I'm saying wrong."

I closed my eyes, wishing to die on the spot. I was offering myself, so easily, and now felt like a cheap hussy. "I'm sorry. I had no idea you wouldn't find me attractive."

To my bafflement, my appearance had always caused problems for Kenny and Tucker. Even modeling agencies knocked on my door. So, Art finding me ugly wasn't close to being on my radar 'til now.

Big hands rested on my thighs, causing me to open my eyes. Art was now on his knees in front of me. "You're gorgeous, no joke. In fact, I've been trying to remind myself for some time—" he shook his head to clear it, "—uh, I mean *all night*, that you're a no go."

"Why?"

From the floor, he examined me. "Even though your body's curves scream 'I'm all woman', you're only sixteen."

"How do you know that?"

His eyes widened. "How do I know that? How do *I* know that? Uh…" He studied something Viola was doing behind me. Not sure when she had stood up, my eyes raced over my shoulder only to see her hand leave her chest to fix her hair. Art quickly said, "You're friends with V, so I *assumed* you two are about the same age."

Made sense, so I replied, "If it helps, I'm almost seventeen. But I *feel* much older."

"That's clear, and you act more confident than most women I date."

"Still doesn't help the jailbait issue, eh?"

He sat back on his heels, his hands sliding from my thighs. "Exactly, I'm too old for you—"

"Art, spare us the lecture." Viola plopped into her chair. "She's not asking for sex."

"Either way, your brother will own my balls!"

She nonchalantly waved her hand. "You're a prospect. He already does."

Feeling frustrated, I sighed. "This is *so* not how I wanted my first kiss to go."

Artist's firm muscles loosened as his bare chest caved. "You've never been kissed?"

This fact annoyed me. "Nope."

"Bullshit."

Viola snickered. "Have you not met her brother or his best friend?" She said best friend with disdain. I couldn't help but suspect V was secretly hoping for me to have someone as a buffer between Kenny and me.

Her plan almost worked...

Artist tapped the side of my calf. "So, you're really not with Kenny?"

Playing with his own words, I smirked. "What does it matter?"

That won me another tap to the calf.

My head tilted. *Art doesn't even know us. Why would he assume* — "Does it seem like that? That Kenny and I are," I thought of where Kenny was at the moment, "a thing?" Because it couldn't have been labeled as a relationship.

As if uncomfortable, he nodded while staring at me in question. "A tad. Yeah."

I gestured to the door. "But, Kenny's off with some girl." He shrugged as if that point had no merit. Thinking of Diesel's actions—setting up a date even though he had one already on the schedule—I replied, "No. Kenny and I are not an item. He's like a brother to me."

Art smirked. "Does *he* know that?"

Viola forced a laugh then mumbled, "Tell me about it."

"Wait, Art." I was confused. "you've only been around Kenny and I like twice."

Art shook his head. "Never mind. It don't matter. You're not available to me."

Under my breath, I said, "But I want to be."

"Yeah?"

Intimidated at being so raw and honest, because wanting someone had never happened by this point in my life, I only nodded.

He set his shoulders back then gestured between us. "How about we make a deal?"

Very intrigued, I, of course, faked boredom. "Make it worth my while, and we'll see."

"Come your eighteenth birthday, if you're still available, *I'll* claim you."

I didn't think that was an offer for a relationship, and I didn't give a damn. Heat rushed through my veins like a hot bath soothing a frigid chill on a winter's night.

V moaned with a need of her own.

I said, "Claim? Bit barbaric. Especially with a stranger, yes?"

The "man" side of Artist presented himself, loud and clear. He lifted back to his knees, putting his body between my legs. His hands easily gripping my large thighs as if he'd longed to, his voice lowered and his jaw tightened. "Yes, because that's exactly what it would feel like by the time I'd be done with you."

A hot-as-hell *biker* had just promised to savagely take my virginity. Twisted, maybe, but my body went slack as I wondered if I could make it through a year of waiting.

He proudly smirked at my stunned silence. "I see I've made my point."

I couldn't help it; I lifted a brow. "I'll let you know after the *claiming.*"

Art stared at me up and down, his eyes locking onto the area between my legs before closing as he sucked in air. He quickly reached to the table, grabbed his beer, and tilted his head back, guzzling the beer down his throat as if he had spent a month without water. I watched him, his body still between my legs, as his throat muscles worked vigorously.

My hand slowly reached out. Not sure what I was doing, I let a finger touch a muscle cord in his neck. He pulled the bottle from his lips but didn't move from my touch. Only his eyes came back to see me as my finger descended to his collarbone.

With his mouth positively gaping, he choked out. "Mercy."

I met his eyes as I retracted my hand, answering his plea. "Sorry."

"Don't apologize for being a sexy flirt."

"Is that what I just did? Wasn't even sure I would be any good at it."

He wiped his mouth. "Fear not, beautiful. Flirt, you can."

He smelled like a leather and a spice cologne that must have been titled Artist, and I was going to be damned if I didn't get a taste. "So... the kiss still off the table? Since I have a year to wait?"

Slowly, a mischievous grin formed. "Nah, ain't saying that."

I matched his grin with one of my own and tightened my thighs around him. "Ya sure? It's a lot of pressure. I've already been waiting almost seventeen years. If you suck at it, that would be shameful for you."

He moved in closer. "I don't scare easily."

I relaxed my legs, giving him room. "Good to know."

Viola gawked at our open teasing and numbly said, "I asked Tucker to claim me."

I didn't take my eyes from Art but asked, "Is this before or after you asked him to steal you?"

Viola kept watching us as if imagining her and Tuck. "Before."

"So, before Bryce."

She shook her head as if to break free of her imagination. "Actually, the same day. I gave him one last chance before saying yes to Bryce."

I touched Art's arm. "He didn't take it?"

Art tightened his hold on me. "Dumbass."

Longing for something I'd never had, I warned Art, "Not so sure you're any smarter. How many chances you think I'm going to give you?"

He licked his lips then spoke with a confident tone, "V, mind looking away for a minute."

My heart started to flutter uncontrollably. I was about to get my first kiss. My hands found his ribs, silently begging him to make good on his promise.

"Fuck no," rambled Viola. "I've got a kinky side. I'm watching."

I didn't care what she did or didn't do. I couldn't stop staring at Artist, so excited for what was to come. Being the entertainment didn't seem to be an issue for Artist, either. He scooted closer to me, his waist and hips taking up the remaining space between my thighs, amping up an unexpected yearning inside me. His hands moved to my hips. "You okay with Viola watching?" Hungry, so hungry to know what it felt like to have lips touch mine, I nodded, my mouth slightly open from being breathless. I noticed his breathing started racing, too. He growled, "V, if I can't easily walk away from her, I'm beating your ass."

"Deal. Get kissing. Been a long time coming."

She was right. I had waited so long. And, now, I was entranced with Art staring at my lips. He leaned forward... *Warm*, soft, full lips pressed to mine, causing my whole body to internally melt with delight... and relief.

It's amazing how a simple touch can be felt in more than one place. That's what this kiss was like. One sensation that built into more sensations and wants. My eyes closed. I may have moaned or whimpered when one of Art's hands moved from my hip to clutch the back of my head and pull me closer, deliciously and expertly opening my mouth. And I may have moaned or whimpered as his other arm wrapped around me, forcing my chest to his heated bare one.

A couple gentle swipes from Art's tongue landed on mine before the kiss deepened. His masculine taste and smell were more intoxicating than the beer that had been giving me a buzz all night. My arms wrapped around his shoulders and neck, trying to get impossibly closer. When his hands raced back to my hips and he roughly tugged me to the edge of the chair, he froze.

I mean, *froze*.

His tongue, everything stopped moving. I opened my eyes, yanked from the moment. His blue eyes were wide, staring into mine as his tongue started to slip from my mouth. My lips tried to close, preventing his escape, but he pulled away, gasping for air. "Sorry."

I reached for him, "What? Why? For what?" but missed.

He somewhat stumbled backward, finding his seat. "T-Too far. I was taking it too far." As he hid his lower half under the table, he licked his lips. "My God. You taste better than I had imagined."

Too mystified to hear what he was saying, my fingers reached up and touched my wet lips.

Viola stuttered, "T-That was the most liberating and intense kiss I have *ever* seen. Movies included." My tongue darted out to taste what was left of Artist. Panting, Artist watched my mouth, gripping the arms of his chair. Viola giggled. "Do I need to leave the room? I'm only willing to witness so much."

I nodded.

Art, still staring at my mouth, shook his head. "V, I will pay you a hundred bucks if you stay and force me to behave."

My body begged me to up the ante. "Two hundred if you leave."

Viola stood.

Art closed his eyes, appearing incredibly stressed. "Name your price or be my friend."

She slowly sat back down. "Jesus. Art, you look like a tortured soul. 'Kay, I'm staying."

After a long minute, his eyes finally opened, finding me. He swallowed. "I've never wanted someone more... than I want you right now."

Viola dramatically slammed her head to her arms resting on the table, breaking the trance Art and I were in. I started laughing. "You okay?"

Her voice was muffled against the table as she whined, "I want someone to want to eat me alive like," without lifting her head, she blindly pointed to Art, "like he wants to eat you."

Now, Art was laughing. "That obvious, huh?"

She nodded, still in her arms. "So fucking hot. I'm so wet, it's a good thing I have pants on or I'd slip off this fucking palm tree and onto the floor."

Art smiled at me but teased V, "There's a whole gang of bikers for you to choose from, so stop bitching."

Still without lifting her head, she raised a hand and flipped him off. "You know there's only one dumbass for me."

The heated moment was over. As much as I already missed it, I was so appreciative. Art watched as I leaned forward and grabbed his hand. I gave it a shake. "Hey, I never thanked you."

His fingers squeezed mine. "For the kiss?"

"No, ya confident bastard." I laughed. "For having our backs at that bar."

In thought, he examined my long fingers. "The kiss meant nothing, huh?"

Trying to deny it, my head bobbed from shoulder to shoulder, forcing a surrender. "Okay, the kiss, too, but seriously, that bar fight could've got ugly, so thank you for helping us."

His eyes met mine. "Any time."

After a pause of regret for the now-passed dreamy moment, I asked, "Back to the game?"

Art leaned back in his chair and faked a stretch. "Still trying to get me naked, I see. Don't blame ya."

I picked up my cards. "If V doesn't ease up on her winnings, I will be in my skivvies in no time."

He examined his cards in his hand. "Dear God, V, don't ease up."

"Hell no, Art, I enjoy watching you suffer. Stripping Pretty D is high on my list."

"Sassy bitch."

She laid down her winning cards, facing up. "Just for that comment, hand over your jeans. Hope you're wearing underwear."

I balked. "Why?"

She nodded at me with quizzical eyes. "Ya know what? You're right. Why am I shorting myself like that?" She picked up her phone and started the song, "Like A Wrecking Ball" by Eric Church. "Art, make it good."

He stood from his chair, mumbling as he unbuckled his jeans. "Make it good she says. My *naked* body is gonna be found on the side of the road by the time Diesel is done with me. Make it good." With no sexy dance to please the ogling eyes, he yanked down his jeans... and was, unfortunately, wearing boxers.

"Damn!" complained Viola. "No free ballin' tonight." She grabbed the cards and started shuffling.

Art tossed his jeans on the floor and sat down, grabbing another beer, his muscles flexing and moving accordingly. I wiped my mouth *before* guzzling my beer. He smacked my knee. "I thought I told you to behave."

"I thought I already explained that's not happening."

He picked up the five cards offered by V, "Well, fuck me runnin'—" before leering at her. "Are you cheating? I ain't got shit. Again."

She fake-winced. "Sucks for you. I'm absolutely going to kill this hand."

I studied my pair of threes then laid down my pathetic hand. "What am I taking off?"

Understanding me already folding, she changed the song on her cell to "Cryin'" by Aerosmith. "Jeans, baby. And make him squirm for being such a little bitch."

Alarm raced across his handsome face. "No. Don't make me suffer, D-D-D-Delilah—"

Not wasting one more second of my freedom, I seductively slid from my chair.

With my hips swaying to the beat, my hands slowly traveled down my stomach. Viola sang about Art needing someone he couldn't resist. As my fingers fiddled with the jean button, I teasingly turned away from the man who was focused on only one thing in the room: me. Sliding my thumbs into the waistband of my jeans, I gazed over my shoulder. Art's eyes were locked onto my ass, perfectly, for my next move. V was loving it! "Oh yeah, show Artist how his world will *never* be the same." Torturously slow, I pulled down my jeans, one-ass-cheek-at-a-time-popping-out kind of slow. And, if that wasn't enough of a slut move for my very first striptease, I bent over as I pushed my jeans down to my knees.

V chuckled. "Uh, Art?"

"Huh?"

"Your beer is on the floor."

"Huh?"

"Yeah. Slipped right out of your hand."

Breaking his stare from my G-string'd butt, he looked down, below where his hand was hanging off the chair. "Oh shit!" He rushed to pick up the beer bottle spilling onto the ugly carpet.

I kicked my jeans onto the floor then sat, very proud of myself while Aerosmith sang out about sweet miseries.

What a night it was.

By the time Tucker and Kenny returned, hair tussled and clothes disheveled—and heavily intoxicated—Art, myself, and Viola were all in our skivvies playing cards. Tucker stood motionless, studying Viola in her bra and G-string only. Her feet were propped up on the table, her long smooth legs extended, and she looked sexy as could be.

He half-growled, half-slurred, "Wha' th' fuck?"

Over her cards, she winked at him. "Have a good night, Tucky Ducky? *We* sure did."

For reasons unbeknownst to him then, Tucker grabbed his stomach, looking confused and a tad nauseous. Alarm racing across her face, Viola stopped being a smart ass in an instant and rushed to him. "You going to be sick?"

She touched his now sweaty face as he nodded. "I-I think so."

V yanked his arm over her shoulders and slipped hers around his waist, guiding him to the bathroom. Passing his duffle, she quickly grabbed a pair of his underwear. "Come on. Maybe a shower will help."

He staggered into the bathroom, smelling her hair. "I don't know what happened. I was fine a second ago..." The door shut, and I couldn't help but think of the girl Tucker just had sex with. Did she think she snared a fine catch? Did she think he would be back for more? If she did, she was mistaken. Viola may have asked Tuck to steal her, but she had already, at such a young age, stolen him. He was just too much of a dumbass to know it yet.

With my feet resting on Artist's knees, I observed Kenny. Rooted to a spot in the middle of the hotel room, staring at my bare legs, Kenny was so pale that I slowly retracted my feet from Art and stood. "Kenny, you okay?"

His eyes blinked before he looked at me, saying nothing.

Sometimes Kenny had appeared to get tired and distant at night, so I approached him slowly, gently taking a hold of his hand, denying the fear I felt somewhere deep. I was too young to understand my natural survival instincts were kicking in—that I was sensing the danger lurking from within my friend. Nope. Quietly, I said, "Kenny?"

In almost a numb way, he whispered, "Can you put some clothes on... Please?"

I internally cringed, suddenly feeling dirty. Those words robbed me of the joyous teenage freedom I was rejoicing in. So far, my night had been harmless, wonderfully adventurous, and promised a fun future. Now, I felt I had cheapened myself, standing there with barely any clothes on. The shower's water was already running, cleansing my brother while I stepped into invisible dirt that would cling to me for years.

From his chair, Art watched me reach for my shirt. He asked, "Do *you* want the card game to end?" I wish I hadn't been too naïve to understand what he meant. I had a choice I couldn't acknowledge.

Instead, out of guilt for Kenny always fighting for my honor and the need to keep his inner peace intact, I pulled the shirt over my head, saying goodnight to the evening I didn't want to end.

"Wow," uttered Artist.

I picked my jeans off the floor. "What?"

"I've never witnessed stolen freedom before."

That had me going eerily still, thinking of V's claim he had a way with words.

Art nodded, reading me like a novel on my bookshelf. "Yeah, that light I've spent the evening with has just been snuffed out."

Light.

I faced Art to tell him I didn't want to stop shining but heard a weak plea. "Delilah... *Please?*"

Kenny needed me. I closed my eyes and inhaled... then stepped into my jeans, silently apologizing to Art. With an exhale laced with wisdom, he stood, casually saying, "You have nothing to be sorry for. No outsiders need to judge." He eyed Kenny and told me with a smile, "We shared some laughs. No crime in that, right?"

Remembering the kiss and what we had to wait a year for, I pulled up my jeans and giggled. "No felonies to report." *Unfortunately.* My stomach fluttered again at the thought of being claimed.

Artist hungrily grumbled, "One year," as he grabbed his jeans and slipped thick thighs inside them. Buckling his button, he quietly asked, "That normal?"

I glanced to where he was gesturing. Kenny was now sitting on a bed, utterly dazed.

Memories of Kenny when he was younger, before my dad monetarily and emotionally provided for him, pelted my heart. When this boy entered our world, he had been cruelly underfed. Bones poked out from underneath the clothing that had expired long ago. Kenny had anger issues, and from what we could tell, many reasons why; abuse was only one of those reasons. His mother chose boyfriends and drugs over him, and she never asked for her child back once my dad stepped in and permanently took him under our roof. In high school, his nightly mental delusions started getting worse.

Not wanting to share Kenny's personal story, I went to care for my friend while telling Art, "He's just drunk." I pulled back the covers then tugged Kenny's sneakers. Bright pink lipstick on his collar spoke of his conquest of the evening, so I grabbed the hem. "Lift your arms for me." He did. I pulled the dirty shirt off him before guiding his body to lie down.

As I covered Kenny, he whispered, "Delilah?"

I endearingly wiped his hair from his forehead. "Yes, it's me. Get some rest, okay?"

He reached for my wrist. "Don't run. Stay here."

My brows bunched but I nodded. "Not going anywhere."

Kenny's eyes closed, so I gently pulled my arm from his grasp.

When I turned around, Artist had his shirt in his hands. "You sure you're sixteen?"

Feeling as old as a grandma, I replied, "Almost seventeen, remember?"

Art put on his shirt then gestured to the bathroom. "You both act lost somewhere between starving young women and nurturing mothers. Viola practically takes care of the whole club. You... you..." He took a hungry step forward, eyeing me from head to toe, before stopping himself. Instead, he grabbed his biker boots then sat back in his chair to put them on. He chuckled. "I'm going to beat Viola's ass. You got me spinning like a schoolboy."

As he laced his boots, I stared at him, wondering how one kiss could make me feel so attracted and so connected to someone I just met. Were my romance novels right? Love at first sight?

"Stop staring at me like that, Delilah. It's making me want to stay."

Fresh air blew through my lungs as my self-esteem gathered traction. "Not easy to walk away from me?"

Artist sighed in surrender, sitting back in his chair. "I don't even want you crawling into bed," he pointed to Kenny, "with him tonight."

"I'm sleeping with V."

"That's not what he wants."

"Already being the jealous guy?" A wicked smile from Ego Land found its way to my face. "Be careful, I might like it."

Not admitting to my suspicion, he stood. "I need to go."

"Why the rush? Got a hot date?" A ping of pain hit me right in the chest when he didn't say anything, and I remembered his bike companion. "Oh, that girl that's *not* your wife." I attempted to sound unaffected. "Not like we're engaged either, after one kiss."

"Nope. We're not."

"She, uh, your girlfriend?"

"Nope. Don't have one."

"Oh, good."

"Good?"

"Hate for my first kiss to be tainted by a cheater."

With regret for how this night was ending, him about to go hook up elsewhere, I started walking him to the door, my feet dragging across the nasty green carpet. What choice did I have? He was a biker. To think he would behave any differently was absurd.

Art's head hung forward. "You look sad."

I wrung my anxious hands. "No, I'm good."

He elbowed my arm. "Tonight was all in the name of fun, right?"

I chewed on the inside of my mouth. "Fun. Yep."

Still headed for the door, he grabbed my hand. "Why you lyin' to me?"

My fingers laced with his in a rush. "What makes you think I am?"

He observed me then sarcastically said, "Huh. No idea." He tugged on my hand. "Do you really want to try for something in a year?"

My whole body cringed. "Please don't ask me that when I know where you're headed."

He stopped walking and leaned his head away to peer at me out of the corner of his eye. "You just claimed I have no right to be jealous over Kenny. What gives?"

I looked at our joined hands. "Point made." My toes nervously gripped at the short carpet. "We each crawl in bed with someone else tonight."

He growled. "You tryin' to get me started? 'Cause it's working. Watch it."

The bit of relief that I could cause him to feel a sting, like the one still attacking my chest, had me utterly confused because it was wrong. But it felt so good.

A finger from his free hand lifted my chin, and a deep voice demanded, "Tell me what you want."

I swallowed and lost the use of my tongue.

"You poked this bear. Now, tell me why. What. Do. You. Want?"

I raced out the foolish words before I could stop myself. "You to take a cold shower instead of meeting up with whoever she is."

He studied me for a moment... then asked, "Feeling this strong in one night?"

My brows bunched. "Isn't the same for you?"

"Not exactly."

"Harsh."

"Hear me out. I don't fall easily, and I don't fall fast. In fact, I've only fallen once."

Jealousy knocked on my naïve door again. "She must've been really special."

His thumb caressed my cheek. "Yeah. And then some."

The toes playing with the carpet ran over his steel-toed boot. "Maybe you will be that lucky twice?"

Looking deep into my eyes, he smiled. "Not sure if it's needed, and I'm not sure I'm lucky at all."

I laid my hand on top of his still touching my face, and I whispered truth, "I hope you are. I hope I am, too."

"But you haven't been in love yet. How do you know you will need two chances?"

Thinking of my dad losing my mom, my chest tightened. "I've seen heartache, ones never expected. Life happens. So, I know it could happen to me. I could lose the love of my life through disease or a freak accident."

"I wish I didn't know exactly what you mean."

"You've already lost someone?"

He nodded.

"When?" *When was your world turned upside down, never to truly recover?*

"When I was very young."

His voice had been so strained that I knew what he meant. "Family."

"Been on my own for a long time."

I thought of Diesel's biker friends and how he called them brothers by choice. "Is that why you want to be with Diesel's, er, club?"

He sighed, still staring at me. "It would be nice to belong," he paused, "somewhere."

My hand tightened on his. "I'm sorry."

After a moment of silence, Art told me, "Whatever man wins your love, Delilah, will be happy for it, however long it lasts."

"You really believe that?"

His thumb caressed me again, his voice almost a whisper. "Wholeheartedly."

Pushing my doubts aside for a second, I timidly asked, "Wanna back-up your statement?"

That won me a smile. "How do you suggest I do that exactly?"

"Date me."

"I can't date you."

"Why?"

"That would land me in jail."

"Only if we had sex."

"I'm not ashamed to say, after that striptease earlier, us dating would equal me begging for sex, and doing my best to convince you to let me between those—" His eyes closed as he inhaled. "You're sixteen. I'm a goddamned perv."

My hand shook his. "I never get carded. I know I look older, not twelve, so ease up on yourself."

He groaned, "And your voice, so mature." His eyes opened and sparkled at me. "Thank you for trying to make me feel better about robbin' the cradle."

I swallowed. "So, you will date me when I'm eighteen?"

"I already made that offer for a year from now."

"But, until then—" My eyes raced to the floor.

"Oh." He grabbed his chest. "You askin' for me to go solo for a whole year? No girls? Like... at *all*?"

Even though I slightly tugged away, Art wouldn't release my hand, so I answered with a shrug, not gutsy enough to speak any more of my immaturity.

"That's a fucking tall order, beautiful, so I need to hear it from you."

I had never been in a relationship. I had no experience with offering up what felt like demands. And, until that moment, I hadn't realized how much I didn't believe I deserved my words to be heard, no matter how confident I acted on the outside.

Still, with my hand firmly in his grip, he put an arm around my waist, gently wrenching my arm behind me, then pulled my body flush with his. The aggressiveness stole my breath; his next words, even more so. "Try to always find the nerve to speak what you want, what you deserve." I opened my mouth again but still couldn't muster up the words. His arm gently jolted me. "What's the worst thing that could happen? I tell you no?"

I wiggled my bottom jaw. *You telling me no would suck.*

He kissed that nervous jaw of mine. "Talk to me. Scream if you have to."

I rushed out, "Wait for me."

He smiled. "Was that so hard?" I nodded, causing him to chuckle. "At least, now I know. Now, I have a chance to react."

That statement stunned me a little because it made me think of how many relationships didn't stand a chance because they were too afraid to simply talk. "Then," I said, "react to this." I didn't want to but knew I sounded desperate. "I'll be worth the wait, I swear."

With his free hand, he pointed to the table. "That kiss already sealed that promise."

"Then, no other girls?" I knew I was outmatched, that he was right. He was too old for me, but I was still starving like he told me I was. I had pent up frustrations I couldn't understand. Feeling so confused, I pulled from him and put my back to the door to face him, my palms against the cold wood. Did I think I was going to hold him hostage? I don't think any thoughts were clear, only the desperation that had me under its spell.

We were the same height, but his shoulders were much wider than mine, stronger, yet I didn't move. And I didn't say anything because I didn't know what the hell to say, but I didn't want the spark he lit to die. I feared, if he walked out the door, that's exactly what would happen. My eyes welled up, even though I begged them not to.

His face softened, then his fingers affectionately pushed my hair behind my ear. My breathing raced again as I stared back and forth from his eyes to full lips. Art closed his beautiful blue eyes as he inhaled and leaned back. "*Fuck,* this is going to be the longest, most torturous year of my life."

I almost fell into him. That was a yes, a much-needed approval that I would be worth the wait. Warm hands clutched my face, tilting it to see into my eyes.

As if announcing the beginning of a torturous year to come, the shower turned off. In mere seconds, Art and I would have to start lying, to everyone.

I asked, "Do you live in my town?"

He softly spoke, "I do."

"Will I get to see you?"

Bright, straight teeth appeared under his smile. "You honestly think I can stay away from you?"

Knowing how small towns work—everybody knows everybody's business—I was very aware that this biker had a challenge in front of him, one he may bail on, and that was terrorizing me. I panted and, with a soft despairing tone, begged, "Please kiss me. Just one more before reality kicks in."

In a rush, he brought his lips toward mine but then stopped, leaving them to hover. He swallowed. "Do you know how to tell when someone *really* cares for you?" This was not the action I was hoping for, so I just stared at him, a little stumped. His smile faded. "They don't always give you what you *think* you need." Then, as gently as a masculine man could, Art kissed my forehead, showing absolute discipline.

Such a simple yet epic gesture had me sighing. "Thank you." I felt even more fulfilled than from the kiss he'd given me earlier. At that moment, I felt... cherished. Artist was almost a stranger. I had only met him that night, but he touched me deeply. He taught a young woman a strong lesson of self-worth. The lesson may not have sunk in completely that night, but a seed had been planted. Someday, I was to have another care for me so tenderly, kissing only my fore-head when I had too much to drink. That young man still to come would feed my soul, even more so than Art. But there was more to experience before life would gift me with what I would treasure most.

When my eyes opened, I jolted seeing Kenny sitting up in bed, staring at me.

Artist peered over his shoulder then sidestepped to block Kenny's view of me. He grumbled, "Not liking this."

I slightly leaned my head to the side to see around Art. "Kenny, lie down, okay? Get some rest." When he did and closed his eyes, I explained to Art, "He's harmless. He loves me."

"In a healthy way?"

"Isn't all love healthy?"

"*Actual* love? Yes. But some obsessions appear to be love while they truly are only control tactics."

I was suddenly feeling drained, and I was clueless why. I was unconsciously aware of the truth he was speaking. I told him, "Viola titled you well. You sound more like Oprah than a biker."

"Not so hot, huh?"

"Oh, you still have hot covered." Exhaustion from confusing emotions was overtaking me. I leaned into him again. "Since you won't kiss me, can I have a hug?"

This must've been a need he believed I truly needed. Art's arms came around me in a flash and held on, slightly rocking me. He rubbed my back while leaning his head to mine. It was nice. It calmed me. Again, I found myself being grateful. "Thank you."

He kissed my head. "It was great *meeting* you, Delilah. I mean that." There was so much behind the simple words, but again I was clueless. He hugged me again. "Get my number from V."

Releasing him, my hand rubbed over the butt of a gun tucked in his jeans. Shocked that I had yet to notice it while he stripped for our poker game, I quietly asked, "Will I get to see you again? In Daytona?"

He reached for the doorknob behind me. "Can you sneak out in the morning? I'll take you to breakfast."

My brother and Kenny were going to need sleep to take the edge off the hangover they would surely feel. "I think so. I'll call you."

After another quiet moment, staring at each other, he stared over his shoulder again, gaging Kenny. "Be careful with him, okay? If he hurts you," he faced me then leaned in and whispered in my ear, "I'll kill him."

Something in his quiet tone spooked me more than his actual statement. I was sure it was a figure of speech but his sincerity was quite unnerving. So was the gun in his jeans.

Artist disappeared down the fluorescent-lit hallway.

Shutting the hotel door, I heard Viola come out of the bathroom. I faced her to see my drunk brother with damp hair and in fresh underwear, using her body as a cane. I pointed to Kenny in a bed. "Put Tuck next to that drunky."

"Noooo," slurred my brother. "Me and V fooorrreevveerrr." He fell into her a little.

Standing between the beds, I winced at her hurt expression. I knew she wanted those words to be true. She tried to shrug, which wasn't easy with Tucker's big body practically draped over her. "He doesn't mean it. He's drunk." She stared at sleeping Kenny. "I hate to ask it of you."

Knowing how much Viola wanted my brother, I groaned, "Kenny, move over," as I pushed on his body. He rolled away. Crawling into bed with Kenny, I thought of Art, hoping he wasn't also resting his head next to someone else.

Viola pulled back blankets while maneuvering Tuck into bed. She yelped as he dragged her down with him. He laughed as they bounced. "V, time to snuggle with meeeee." After manhandling her body to where he wanted her, as if she were his pillow, he half laid his body on top of hers and passed out on her chest within seconds.

She stared at the ceiling, rubbing my brother's dark hair.

I laid on my stomach, facing her. "V, does your brother carry a gun?"

"I was wondering if you noticed Art's gun. Yes, they're packin' but have permits. They're licensed for concealed weapons, and they are highly trained."

With the room being so quiet now, and Art not presently distracting me, I could hear people still celebrating spring break outside and in the hotel hallway. "Does that scare you?"

"The reasons they may need it scares me but not the weapons themselves."

"Do you carry one?"

"No, but one is never too far."

I had assumed she meant a stored gun in a drawer next to her bed or something. Such a fool was I. "Would you date a biker?"

She blew out air while thinking. "Honestly, I'm not sure. I've never been attracted to one, so I've never put much thought into it. But I can say their view of the female race can be hostile." She held up her hand when my mouth opened to ask a question. "Hear me out. What I mean is, a woman is either a piece of ass or one they cherish. These guys don't really do in between the extremes. They either want to fuck you or die for you, and if you get a biker that wants to do both, hold on, because what an intense ride that will be."

Damn... "Art and I discussed trying to be together in a year."

"The way he looked at you? I'm shocked he left you in a room with another male."

"He made a couple of comments."

"Bikers can be a little territorial, to put it mildly."

"Do you think that's why he sometimes spoke as if already knowing me?"

She reached for her cell. "I need to turn off my alarm clock."

"That going off at six AM would've been awful."

"Right? Total rookie spring break move."

I sighed. "Do you think I'm dumb to consider anything with Art?"

"If I thought it was dumb, he would've been babysitting from a distance, not in our room."

As they say, *a lightbulb finally went off.* "You set me up, didn't you?"

"Sorry." She giggled. "Why do you think that skank gave me a dirty look?"

Viola flicking off the girl riding behind Art zoomed into my brain. "How did she know what you were up to?"

"Maybe she's not as dumb as she looks?"

After I stopped laughing, I asked, "But what you said about bikers, you think I can handle him?"

"He's exactly what you have dreamt up. Why the hell do you think you've fallen for him so fast? The only detail he is missing is the hazel eyes."

"Can't be too picky."

"With 'fuck me' blue eyes like that? That's *not* being picky or settling. Damn, he's fine."

"You sure you're not attracted to him?"

"Attracted? Yes. Want? Nah." She ran her fingers through my

brother's hair again. "Just 'cause I'm drooling over a three-layered chocolate cake doesn't mean I'm gonna eat it."

A moment of silence passed. "Art is good people?"

"He is, as you probably already know, very masculine, but he has a tender side that will love a girl hard. I'm sure of it. I pushed this meeting because he has the potential of being a great friend, wonderful protector, and hypnotic lover."

I bit my pillow. "Hypnotic?"

Her eyes closed as veins in her neck strained. "A lover that is so good he casts a spell on you as he ravishes your body."

"Have you had that yet?"

She exhaled with regret. "Nah."

"Maybe you will someday."

"If not, I'm going to be a pissed bitch in heaven, telling God he needs to send me back and try again."

In that moment, I remembered life was too short sometimes. I wasn't going to miss out on a chance of an adventure of a lifetime. "If the boys wake up earlier than expected, I need you to do some distracting so I can go to breakfast with him."

"Done. And I repeat, I'm loving this wild side, Pretty D."

"Why won't you set your wild side free, V?"

Her tone changed from light to serious, sad, heavy. "Bryce." She swallowed. "Bryce was abused as a child." She inhaled deeply then exhaled a long, torturous breath. "A distant uncle came to live with his family when Bryce was very young. His uncle hurt him, sexually, Delilah..."

Why some people hurt children bewildered me. I couldn't grasp how abuse led to more abuse. But one thing I was soon to know was how I wished the abuser knew of the everlasting damage their abuse caused. I wished violators could control their demented urges and let the innocent... stay innocent.

CHAPTER FOUR

I woke up a couple times during the night, hating being so uncomfortable in my jeans and the bra under my T-shirt, but not stripping down next to Kenny helped with the guilt I felt toward Art. I had told him I would be sleeping with Viola. I was sixteen, with my first real crush. I wanted to be loyal from the start.

Next time I opened my eyes, the sun was up. I was about to ask what time it was but giggled seeing Viola staring at me, her expression asking, "really?" She was on her stomach, my brother still sleeping—and still using her as his pillow. It appeared he hadn't let her go all night. She pointed to under her bare chest. My brother was cupping her boob like a kid with a favorite toy. Through muffled laughter, I whispered, "Why'd you take your clothes off?"

To not wake the boys, she whispered in return, "I hate sleeping in them. Too uncomfortable. I had no idea this would be the result." Her eyes suddenly popped open as Tuck started seductively kissing her bare back in his sleep, climbing on top of her. "Tuck!" she yelled.

No! Don't wake them!

Tucker jerked awake, confused, looking around. When he saw

me, he laid back down on top of V and smiled, "Good morning, my light." Bummed breakfast just went out the window, I pointed. He peered down. "What? Oh shit!" When he saw he had a juicy handful, he flew backwards like a hissing, frightened cat and rolled right off the bed that seemed small with him in it. *Thump!* He hit the floor. "Owe."

"Um, Tucky Ducky, could you please give me back the blanket?" V was now uncovered with only her G-string to cover her.

Tucker rose from the floor, distracted, all twisted in the sheet and blanket. "Can I be any more of a train wreck this morning?" He suddenly slammed his back to the wall next to the bathroom, grabbing his chest and hissing again. "Jesus, V, your ass... it's, it is spectacular!"

Not moving, possibly because that would mean showing naked breast also, she winked at me. At that moment, I knew my brother was being played by a wickedly smart vixen.

Tucker yelled, "I'm not kidding! It's, it's... *God*-like!" His fingers hungrily twitched as he stared at two mounds of tanned perfection. Then he headed to the bathroom. "Fuck. Cold shower time."

When the door slammed, Kenny groggily rolled over and hugged me from behind. "Good morning, darlin'. How'd I'd end up sleeping in bed with you?"

I sighed with him feeling like my dependable Kenny again, the funny and sturdy brother I believed him to be. "You were a bit intoxicated last night."

Viola studied me in his arms until her cell vibrated on the nightstand between us. By her expression, I knew who it was. My heart thundered, wanting to see Art.

Kenny asked, "Who was that, V?"

Her eyes widened before she gained control. "Uh, my brother." Then she said, "Kenny, no questions because no answers will be given. Close your eyes. I'm naked."

He started laughing, hiding his face in my hair. "Naked, huh? My boy had quite the night."

Laughing, I smacked his arm. "Stop. It's not what you think." Then I mouthed to V, "What do we do?"

She mouthed back, "He wants to talk to you," and tossed me her phone.

Meanwhile, Kenny was still laughing. "Hey, who am I to judge. Know what I'm sayin'? I was lucky myself."

Holding V's phone, I leaped from the bed, hoping I didn't catch what V referred to as 'skank disease'. "Ew! I forgot! You haven't showered yet!"

He laughed, reaching out for me, but missed. "Darlin', this girl was fine!"

Viola rolled her eyes, "That doesn't mean she wasn't nasty," and then rolled her body across the bed, quickly heading for the bathroom, "leaving you with a 'you won't ever forget me' gift." My brother was already under running water when V disappeared behind the shut door.

As I texted, *Hey, it's me*, Kenny kept trying to catch me with his outreached hand. I twirled away. "Not a chance in hell. And be sure the maid cleans those sheets."

Art texted: *Slept in?*

Her phone said it was noon. *Sorry. Plan has gone to shit.*

Kenny palmed his face. "My head is killing me."

Art texted. *Sucks*

I'll tell them looser at poker has to buy winner breakfast.

So u buyin?

Asshole

"V!" shouted my brother from the bathroom. "What the fuck? I'm trying to calm down in here!"

"I ain't stoppin' ya."

"The hell you're not! With that rack, you're amping me up!"

I guess she wasn't covering up her perky titties. "Settle your hormones. I just have to pee."

Thump! Thump-thump! Crash!

Viola yelled, "Jesus! Are you okay?"

Tucker's voice echoed from the tub he was now lying in. "I can*not* believe you just pulled down your drawers to pee."

"First of all, they're *panties*. Second of all, what the fuck did you want me to do, piss *through* them? And third of all, seeing my daisy is no reason to act like a buffoon and throw yourself at the tub's mercy. Not like you've never seen it before when we skinny dipped at the lake."

"Well, your daisy wasn't at the top of my to-do list when I was *ten*, so knock it off."

Kenny and I roared in a laughing fit.

There aren't many things more comical than seeing a group of burly bikers sitting at a Tiki bar sharing pitchers of Bloody Marys, but the sun was refusing to shine and the rain insisted on pouring down so I guess they figured bottoms up.

Even though the beaches were empty, Viola insisted on us wearing our bathing suits, claiming there was no better distraction— for my breakfast getaway—than a tiny piece of cloth on a girl. And she was right. I had three men to distract, and one was already going down in flames according to his shower mishap. Diesel, the second, accusingly eyed us running across the wet beach, trying to avoid getting more soaked than had to be. Only one distraction to go.

Once under shelter, Tuck and Kenny shook out their wet hair while Diesel bitched at his sister. "Why the *hell* are you wearing that?"

Tucker was very happy someone felt the same. "Right? Tell her."

V was sporting a barely-there black one-piece that left nothing to the imagination. She looked like she was entering a million-dollar contest with every intention of winning. She gestured around. "Uh, 'cause I'm at the beach?"

"It's fucking raining, dumbass *el* number two-o."

Since two out of three distractions wasn't bad, I waltzed up to

Artist, who was lazily sitting back in a chair made out of dried palm leaves, and pointed at his beverage with celery and green olives. "Can I have a sip of that?"

He handed it to me. "Sure. I know where your lips have been."

"What?" shrieked Tucker, Kenny, *and* Diesel.

Damn! I stirred the drink with the straw. "Oh, stop. He's just kidding."

"Not very funny," mumbled Kenny, now close behind me.

Artist smirked up at him. "Didn't think you would care for that much."

"Knock it off," warned Diesel, as if this behavior surprised him none.

I figured I'd ask Artist what Diesel meant while at breakfast. "Art, where's your hot date from last night?" I hoped to hell the date never took place, and hoped mentioning it would settle Kenny.

Artist gestured around. "Is it still night?"

"No."

"Then she's gone."

This wasn't the nice guy I met last night. Artist was in what I imagined to be 'biker mode' and possibly pissed that I missed our date. I told him, "That's rather cold."

Another biker chuckled. "But reality."

I peered at my surroundings and realized *all* the women were now missing. And I somewhat cared until I got a taste of the best bloody mary in the world. "Dear God, this is good."

Art winked. "Keep it." He reached for another glass and filled it from a pitcher.

Diesel caught my brother staring at Viola's bare bottom, so he flicked him in the sensitive jewels. While Tuck folded over in agony, holding his balls, Diesel motioned to V's non-existent bathing suit. "How much did this dental floss set a man back?"

"Two hundred."

"The fuck?"

Viola popped a naked hip out and rested a frustrated hand on it. "Damn, I thought you got laid last night. Why so bitchy this morning?"

Diesel avoided the question. "It's two in the afternoon."

"Is it that late already?" asked V. "Huh. I guess I got distracted watching Tucker take a shower."

"The *fuck?*"

Still holding his goods, Tucker awkwardly backed away from the hostile biker brother. "No, no. She barged in, *without* permission may I add."

Viola nonchalantly shrugged but kept feeding the fire. "You didn't seem to mind while you were checking out my daisy."

"The *fuck!*"

Tucker side maneuvered as a bloody mary soared toward his crumpled form. "Diesel! Easy, motorcycle man, she's just pokin' your buttons."

"That better be the only thing getting poked."

I asked Art, "Hey loser, ready to buy me breakfast?"

"Yep. Let's roll."

After setting down my drink, Kenny got closer to my back. "What restaurant ya goin' to, darlin'?"

Not wanting him to check on us, I thought quick on my feet. "Not sure. We'll stumble across some diner this morning."

"Afternoon," reminded Diesel.

"This afternoon," I acknowledged Diesel before telling Kenny. "May be a shocker but I earned this meal." I gestured to Art who was grinning because I'd thrown him into the loser bracket, opposite of what we agreed on. "He lost."

"The hell he did," murmured Viola.

I skipped over her remark. "So, breakfast—"

"Lunch."

I dipped my chin to Diesel then told Kenny, "So, *lunch* it is."

Trying to cover V with an unfolded napkin, my brother asked, "Will you grab me a sandwich?"

V smacked his stomach. "Would you stop? I'm not your concern. Now, buy me a drink."

Tucker followed her to the bar, busy tucking the napkin into her suit. "Not my concern? I say fuck that, but if that's the case, why do I need to buy you a drink?"

"'Cause you're my bitch, bitch. Now, pull out your wallet."

When around a motorcycle gang, it's alarming how many places don't card you. I guess the employees didn't want attitude they weren't sure they could handle.

Tucker howled laughter—pulling out his wallet, of course. "God, I love your sass."

Ignoring them, Kenny quickly took off his shirt. "At least wear this." I looked to my skimpy yellow bikini and shyly nodded, feeling a bit shameful again. Kenny chuckled at my insecurity. "Nah, girl. You look gorgeous. Just thought you would get cold in a restaurant."

I grabbed my chest, feeling relieved. "Thanks, man."

After putting the t-shirt on, I heard, "Excuse me." Art, clearly still in asshole biker mode, snuck his arm in between me and Kenny to guide me away.

Kenny stepped forward. "Don't be a dick—"

"Kenny," warned Diesel as he pointed to a chair. "Sit. Simmer. Have a drink on me. It will do your hangover right."

Pissed, Kenny sat and was pouring himself a bloody mary as Art and I started to slip away. I thought we were home free until I heard Diesel, "Stop." Artist closed his eyes and groaned, leaning his head back to face the roof of the tiki hut, I think looking for God. Diesel, so kindly, clarified, "God ain't gonna help. Ya need to face *me*." We both slowly turned. Diesel motioned between us. "This ain't happenin', comprendo?"

Artist didn't move his body but looked at me; same height put us eye to eye. "Nothing's happening here."

"Bullshit-o. We've already been over this."

Already been over what? I looked for back-up and answers from Viola, but she and Tuck were still laughing through their bickering at the bar. With a smile, a bartender watched them while they waited for their drink order. "Dear Lord, how long you two been married?"

Diesel ignored everyone. "Pretty D's underage, Artist. Last warning."

I asked, "Last warning?" but was cut off.

Art stated, "She'll be eighteen in a year."

"And how old are *you?*" asked a temper flaring Kenny.

"Not your concern," spat Art.

Kenny stood but Diesel, chuckling, pointed to his chair again. "Down, Pitbull."

Kenny plopped back in his chair, threw his straw aside, and gulped his drink.

Since this was coming out in the open, in record time, I declared, "Let's keep this in perspective. There's only a four-year difference."

Diesel held up his huge hand, ringed fingers spread. "Five."

"I'm almost seventeen."

"I'll give you that." Diesel nodded. "But this four-year difference is at a pivotal time in a young woman's life. There *is* a difference between seventeen and twenty-one versus twenty-one and twenty-five."

His point was valid. As mature as a young woman can be, there is still a veil over her eyes. One that has her easy to knock off kilter, forgetting or unable to learn about choice. One that has us unable to see the veil has already been set in place and our perception is already altered. And that is why I naively said, "Come on, Diesel, this is me you're talking to. I'm not quite as mentally young as others my age."

He blew out air. "I know that. Believe me. But losing a parent is different than trying to match smarts with a man who is far more experienced. Plus, what would your dad say?"

Two awful stings hit me with his words, my mom and dad, leaving me speechless.

Diesel glared at Art. "This is complicated. She's my dear friend's daughter, man. You know this. John is kind, but fuck over his daughter, he *will* hunt you down. So will I. You feel me, kid? I've adored this little girl since the night of my parents' funeral, when I caught this trio," he gestured to the arguing Tuck and V at the bar, "sneaking out her pop's window to rescue *my* goddamn sister. History, man. Stop acting ignorant 'bout it." He stared at me again. "Delilah, I adore the ground you walk on, understand?"

I grabbed my chest, moved and so honored.

Art softened his tone while claiming, "I feel you, Diesel. Swear it. And I'll ask for her pop's permission to date her, out of respect, but in the end, it's her choice."

"Spoken like another young selfish dumbass," Diesel said in frustration before studying me. "You really want this?"

I wasn't sure. "To be decided, but I definitely want the chance to know more about him."

Diesel almost winced. "Baby, us bikers, we're a whole different breed. Especially in the loyalty department."

Art interrupted, "Not if she's an old lady."

Kenny spat out his drink—on Diesel.

My jaw dropped as my head swung to see Art. "Y-Your w-what?"

A disturbed chuckle erupted from Diesel as he wiped off his arm. "Old lady, yeah? Then what was last night about?"

I tried to hide my internal shudder, but Art felt it and tightened his arm around me. "That was for show. To throw off suspicions."

Diesel crossed his arms, leaning back in his chair. "That was some *show*." My eyes closed. I was quickly doubting I was made of the materials needed to be a biker's girl. I shed Art's arm off me. Kenny's tense shoulders relaxed. Diesel laughed. "I see lady-lover *Artist* already has some *el* explainin' to do-o." When we all went quiet, Diesel asked me, "You still want lunch with 'm?"

"Nope," chirped Kenny.

Which was rebutted by Art, "Yes."

I slammed my hands over my face, feeling trapped.

"What's wrong?" asked my brother, who had returned, confused. I moaned. "Sweet Jesus."

"Wait," said my brother, "What the hell did I miss?"

Diesel peered over his shoulder. "The question is, what do you *not* miss?"

The bikers all laughed as if they knew my brother well, raising more questions in my mind.

Viola, who according to her expression just remembered what she was *supposed* to be doing that morning, cringed and mouthed, "Sorry."

Diesel observed us and mumbled, "I see." His quizzical and accusing glare found me again. "Two little busy bees had a plan in the works." He exhaled. "Yes, I do believe lunch and a discussion are in order." Then he sat forward again, propping his elbows on the table and pointing a firm finger toward Art. "Love ya but will *kick* your ass if you touch that forbidden fruit." That finger found me. "And you, you and V are far beyond your years mentally and physically. That can be confusing and nothing but hell on wheels for a young man desperate to get his dick wet. Don't cause his ass beatin'. You feel me?"

I looked at the ground. "I feel you."

"That's my girl. Now, go work this shit out, one way or the other. If it's the other, your dad needs to be in on this." He sat back in his chair and grabbed his drink. "Art, you nibble on any Delilah appetizers or deserts, and I'm setting lose my powerful dogs." All the surrounding bikers eyed Art to be sure he understood what powerful dogs Diesel was referring to. "And I will be keepin' that patch you been earnin'."

I wasn't sure what I wanted at that point, but Art and I had things to discuss. He knew it, too. We solemnly started walking away in the rain 'til I heard Kenny again. "Diesel! He's too fucking old for her!"

Tucker arguing with Viola caught me by surprise, "I know what you've been saying, but this guy? You trust him with my Lilah?"

Art possessively tried to lead me away by putting his arm around me again while I kept looking back. *What did Viola say to Tuck?* Artist spoke over his shoulder, "Mind your business, Kenny."

Kenny came flying around the table. "That girl *is* my business, asshole."

I quickly spun around and put my hands up, trying to stop the Lion effect; what my brother and Kenny became when they felt I was in danger. Right now, Art was being viewed as just that. "Kenny, I'm okay..."

I knew my brother was also racing around the table when he yelled, "Kenny! No!"

Art stepped in front of me in a protective gesture while telling Kenny, "The problem is you don't know where the line is, dipshit."

I knew this was a mistake. Not being able to see me would only flare Kenny's rage. As fast as I could move, I got in front of Art again. "I'm here, Kenny." He was already to us, and bikers were already to their feet, approaching to intervene. I laid my hands on his chest. "Kenny, see me..."

But the wild animal in his head had already been unleashed. "Line?" He growled to Art, "You mean like the one you are crossing with an underage girl?"

Aggressively, Artist stepped forward. "Don't be a coward. Say what this is really about."

Smashed between the two angry guys, I couldn't help but wonder if I had anything to do with the ego battle happening. They clearly weren't caring that I was trapped.

The only one helping me was Tuck. He wrapped his arm around Kenny's neck from behind and started pulling him backward. That didn't stop Kenny's mouth. "What this is about?" he sneered. "You being a sick fuck."

Art yelled, "Let him go so he can defend himself, Tuck!" In slow motion, I watched Art's fist coming over my shoulder from behind. And that fist, heading for Kenny, jolted my heart. I had seen Kenny fight many times but only with guys his age. This was a man's fist. It was bigger, fuller, angrier, and stronger. Just like the one that took

Kenny down the night he moved in with us. Kenny's mom's boyfriend beat him up so bad paramedics had to patch up his face. I promised him that night that it was over, that he wasn't alone anymore.

With my own sudden rage, and my brother giving me the room, my arms flew up and wrapped around that arm, wanting to deliver a hit to one I cared for. I put all my weight into dragging down that missile. Luckily for me, Art let me. He appeared shocked as I pushed against his chest. "No!" Bikers moved out of the way as I shoved Art again. "He's my fucking friend!"

Diesel was suddenly next to me. "Easy, girl." He grabbed my arm and Art's and pulled us out into the rain, leaving everyone else behind. "Cool off. Both of you." He released us. "Better yet, get out of here and talk this shit out like I told you to." He walked back under the covering then faced us with tattooed arms crossed over his chest.

Confused, we stared at him, both still panting.

He threw his hands in the air. "Am I speaking *el* English-o?"

Slowly, Art reached for my hand.

With a huge swing, I swatted it away.

As bikers roared laughter, Art smirked at them. A biker teased him, "Good luck with that one, kid."

Diesel turned away from us, also laughing, and headed back to the table. "She's sweet as can be until you piss her off."

Still amused, Art asked me, "Can we go for a walk?"

I stomped my sandal. "How can you be so calm suddenly?"

"Walk with me and I will tell you."

I had to know if Kenny was okay. My eyes scanned everyone 'til I found him. My brother still had a hold of him but a much more relaxed grip. Kenny was staring at me. I couldn't read his emotions. I looked back to Art who was watching me. He said, "Up to you."

I looked back to Kenny. I guess he knew my decision before I did. He pushed my brother off him and stormed off. I stepped forward to chase, but Viola shook her head. Her eyes were pleading for me to stay on course. Exhaling frustration, I walked past Art. "Let's go."

He jogged a couple steps to catch up. "I'm sorry I tried to punch him."

Turning a corner, I shouted, "What is your deal with him?"

Art tried to take hold of my arm, but I jerked it away. He said, "I can't stand by for a year while he gets to have you."

I stopped walking and glared at him. "Have me? You are completely misreading the situation."

Rainwater dripped from his dark hair. "You believing that tells me how much you need someone to look out for you. Your true brother is too wrapped around V to know he's in love with her, nor see the trouble circling you like a hungry shark."

"Er!" I starting marching down the sidewalk again. Art raced to keep up with me. People taking cover under store awnings watched us argue as we passed them. I poked his shoulder, just like he was poking my raw nerves. "I'll have you know, you're wrong. Kenny's had my back. Solidly so, Art."

"But, for what reason?"

"He's a brother to me!"

"Bullshit. He sees you as sisterly as I do. Not-at-all."

I stumbled as we walked on an uneven part of concrete in front of an alleyway. Art caught me by my arm. Once getting control of my feet again, I pulled away from his grasp. "Why are you acting as if you have a clue of our dynamics?"

"Because I do."

Abruptly, I stopped walking. "Start making sense or I'm outta here."

Art dared to mock me with a *pfft* of a laugh, so I spun back to where I came from and charged off. I wasn't surprised when Art quickly caught up to me, nor did I care that he was angry. But I did attempt to jerk free when he grabbed my left arm and guided me into the alley. He wasn't being rough, just stern. Either way, I wasn't havin' it. "Let. Me. Go."

"No."

My right hand made a fist. "Last warning."

Halfway down the alley, he let me go. "Why aren't you this stubborn with him?"

"No. No more talk of Kenny until you come clean."

Art wiped both palms down his face, only to drown in more rain. "About what?"

"The peep show I missed last night." I took a step back, needing space to breathe and think clearly. Being close to his soaking wet shirt, seeing the outline of the body I had seen last night during a strip poker game, was distracting.

But I was denied the space. Art was becoming fiery mad and took a step to follow me. "Where do ya think you're goin'?"

"Anywhere I want if you don't start talking." I took another step back.

He followed me, angrily pointing at my attire. "Fine. You want to talk? I don't like his shirt on you."

"You have no say."

"But you have say over me? For the next year?"

"Apparently not. You were just with someone else last night."

"I told you I wasn't having sex with her."

I practically spit, "Maybe you didn't fuck her, but something went down."

He gritted his teeth that were inches from mine. "I didn't think you and I were going to be open about 'us' so I kissed her."

Like a jealous fool, I immediately turned my face and closed my eyes, not wanting to see his full lips, picturing another girl kissing them.

Firm fingers grabbed my chin and pulled me back. "Like you've asked me to, I'm talkin'. You daring enough to listen?" With as much attitude as opening eyes could spill, I delivered. "If you think you're scaring me with that pissed off look, just know it's only turning me on." Even though I lacked the power to shoot flames from my eyes, I gave it a go. Fucking Artist only chuckled and stepped closer to me. Breathlessly, he moaned, "Yep. Like that." His erection pushed against my hip.

Fighting the fact his sex appeal was hormonally breaking down my walls, I growled, "Art, explain."

"You and I were on the down low. I fuck women all the time. How could I suddenly stop without raising suspicion? So, I kissed her, *only* to imply to everyone watching that more would happen later. Sex *wasn't* going to happen. I swear it. But you don't understand the pressure of being with a group like this. If you don't fuck women, they think something's wrong with your dick. If something is wrong with your dick, you're not man enough to get patched in."

Appalled, I pushed at his chest. His hand lost purchase of my chin as I yelled, "That is beyond ridiculous and sounds like nothing but shitty reasoning you're wanting me to swallow for the next year!"

"I haven't asked you to swallow nothin', yet."

My face scrunched up in disgust. "You pig!"

A smirk appeared. "You can bet my deprived imagination will only worsen as this sexless year from hell drags on."

I stared at him for a long moment, refusing to respond, because I was rapidly understanding Diesel's comments on how different men were versus the boys I was used to.

Art reached for my hand. "Come on. Try to hear what I am saying. They're important to me."

This time, I didn't pull away. No matter what my mouth was saying, I desired his touch. His jeans were sticking to his soaked strong thighs, almost having me stutter. "Which one? Bikers or girls?"

"You know the answer. Stop playin'."

"That's the thing, I *don't* know because I *don't* know you."

"Give me a chance."

"If you're going to continue kissing others, then I can do the same. Even Kenny if I—"

"You don't want to finish that sentence." I quickly regretted my last barb when his jaw locked and his fingers tightened on mine. "Threats will only get me to say yes to all the bitches throwing themselves at me nightly. That what you want?"

I tried to pull my hand away, but he held tight, so I said, "Please stop being an asshole."

"That was hardly my asshole side, *darlin'*."

After he imitated Kenny, I yanked my hand free. "Again, you fuck with my friend. I love him, Art. I need you to understand what he is to me."

His leather biker boot splattered the puddle underneath him. "I do! It's *you* who doesn't understand. Kenny doesn't want to be your friend, and he sure as hell ain't your brother. He *wants* you, Delilah!"

I crossed my arms over my chest. "You're wrong. He's just very protective. It's not what you think."

"No? A hundred bucks says you ended up in bed with him last night."

Eyes averting his, I bit my bottom lip.

Raindrops dripped from his dark eyelashes. "That's twice that you've been for a double standard. Not fair and not workin' for me."

I grumbled, "If you don't like how I operate," then pointed to the alley entrance he just dragged me through, "then move along and don't look back."

He shook his head. "Damn. That's cold."

My shoulders buckled as I blew out a labored breath. "You're right. Sorry."

He stared at the entrance. "If only not looking back was that simple."

"It was *simple* for you to kiss her—"

"How do you know? Were you there?"

"Well, no, but—"

"What else can I say, Delilah, to convince you that I didn't kiss her out of desire?"

His words were causing me pain. My foot stepped backwards as if wanting to remove me from the source.

"It was only to keep my brothers off my trail. They're on it now, so it won't happen again."

My other foot followed suit, helping to carry me backward. The fun spring break kiss was turning into so much weight I was feeling older, weighed down more and more as the seconds passed by.

With a scrutinizing glare, he watched my retreat. "What else do you want from me? I'm telling you I won't touch another girl, and I will wait to touch you."

Thinking of that touch had me longing for it right then. Waiting was going to be impossible. My eyes raced all over him, imagining what he could offer.

He growled a hungry warning, "I told you to stop looking at me like that."

Lips parted, I swallowed.

He prowled forward, licking his lips. "Is that what you want? To hear I'm willing to go to jail for you?" He stared at my mouth.

My back hit the wall. The red bricks pulled on my hair as I shook my head. "Of-Of course not." I was panting, wanting to truly say yes.

"I don't believe you." His lips barely brushed mine, but that little touch had me shaking with need. Waiting so long for any interaction like this had me dealing with a hormonal rush I had never experienced, and it surfaced as a tidal wave of lust. His eyes were closed as his lips kept brushing mine. His voice sounded breathless as he whispered, "Tell me what you want."

With his body plush to mine, I was in such an overwhelming state of want it hurt. I was literally aching all over for relief. My whole body was a minefield, ready to explode. His chest expanded against mine, his fingers gripping my hips. I was aware of his every movement. His thigh, oh God, his thigh brushed between my legs. Shamelessly, I bent my knees so that those strong, tense muscles would touch where no one had ever touched me before.

Art's face fell to my shoulder. "Goddamn." He moved closer, offering more of his leg.

Moaning, my mouth latched onto his wet shirt. "What's wrong with me?"

His hands tightened on me. "You're needin' a release like no girl I've ever known."

To my surprise, my hips moved, swiping the inner part of me down his thigh. "Art, I..." My head lulled back. "I can barely breathe."

His hands left my hips and smacked the brick wall behind me. My eyes slightly opened to see him gripping the wall with shaking hands. It was as if he was in an internal battle of his life. The gruffness of his voice sounded even more strained. "If I help you, I will be disobeying a direct order from the only man who has ever given me guidance."

His forehead now pressed to mine, our wet hair meshing together, I moved down his thigh again. "Don't help me. Don't do it."

And I meant what I said, but I didn't have the willpower to stop his hand as it left the wall, touched my stomach, and started slipping down. "This is how bad I want you. How bad I always have—"

I grabbed his wrist. "What?"

He slowly pulled back, staring at me the whole time. There was such defeat in those blue eyes, almost apologetic. My head tilted as his body left mine. "Art? What do you mean you always have?"

He didn't answer, not right away. He just kept stepping back, soaking wet.

All the little hints—what others, including him, had said—had my mind racing. "Last night is not the first time you've seen me."

He shook his head no.

"You... know me?"

Shoulders caved, he nodded yes. He sounded beaten as he spoke with a deep sadness. "I know your favorite book is *Romeo and Juliet* and that you've read it so many times the pages are worn. I know you would *die* for your brother or father. I know you're mostly quiet and always thinking. I know you visit your mother's grave once a week, something you've done since you got your pretty little red car for your sixteenth birthday." His face attempted to smile but failed, epically. "And I know I want to taste the delicious meals you cook, proud to know, for once, you cooked one for *me*."

I stopped breathing. My ears burned as I tried to comprehend how any of this was possible.

"Show yourself."

I blinked, wondering what he wanted me to show, but quickly realized he wasn't speaking to me. One of Diesel's biker brothers stepped around the corner of the alley.

Art stared at me. "We *all* know who you are, Delilah. Kenny and Tucker are not the only reasons you are without a boyfriend."

CHAPTER FIVE

An electric wave of shock shot through me as my knees threatened to give. Art paced, watching me closely as if monitoring whether or not I would recover from the news he just laid on me. "Delilah, I didn't know the harm. I thought we were just following orders, until last night, when I saw how truly lonely you are."

They've been spying on me? "Th-The bar fight. That's why you were there." I thought of Viola's words about guns, "*... but I always have one close by...*" She meant she is always being followed, guarded.

Artist exhaled as if this revelation had been a lot for him to keep hidden. "I, personally, have been watching you, from afar, since I became a prospect. That means a year."

I thought of the night prior and repeated his words, "So nice to *meet* you."

"Yes. All this time, watching you—Jesus, falling for you, yet I'd never had the chance to *talk* with you." He said 'talk' like it was painful not to share this simple act with me. "Yes, it has been so nice to *meet* you, Delilah."

My mind struggled to function as more of his words, like *falling for you*, had different meanings now. The night prior, he spoke of a past love. I tapped my chest. "Me? Last night... Me?"

He rushed to me. "You, you are the only one. Yes, I was speaking of you."

Even though he was the one telling me alarming things, I was surprised to find myself clutching the front of his wet shirt. Desperate for some stability, I quietly said, "Art... I'm, uh. Art, I—"

He took hold of my neck, his long fingers intertwining in my hair, trying to ground me, I think. "Don't be scared. We didn't watch you in a creepy way, only from a distance."

That I knew. Diesel wouldn't permit a violation of my privacy, so I wondered the why of these actions. "This is like why Diesel didn't want me on his bike?"

"Yes, a precautionary action."

Is Diesel in trouble? Is he committing illegal activities? "If—if *you* watch me, why is *he* watching *you*?" Still holding Art's shirt, I pointed to the one observing us.

The other biker explained, "We keep an eye on the whole town. Those closest to Diesel, a little more so. You and Tuck are so damn tight with Viola, only a fool couldn't figure out how to hurt Prez."

That made sense but still didn't answer my question. "Art?"

Maybe realizing I wasn't a complete fool, his fingers tightened on my neck. "He watches me because I started watching you... a little too closely."

"So, last night's kiss—"

"Is something Diesel has been trying to avoid." His thumb caressed my neck. "You are one of the most nurturing people. I've wanted to feel that from you."

Does he want me as his girlfriend or mother?

"Damn. I'm sorry to throw all this on you like this. I'm going to catch hell over it, I assure you."

I took a deep breath, staring at him. "You, one year. How long?" I shyly pointed to the other biker again.

The burly man chuckled. "I've been watching you long enough

for Tucker's nickname, dumbass, to stick because of all that happens right under his nose."

Artist told me, "As you can imagine, Diesel wanted an extra close eye on you girls during Daytona." He looked to the ground. "For some reason, V pushed for last night's watch."

I closed my eyes, feeling tired again. "She hates Kenny."

The bystander biker grumbled, "And then some."

Art asked him, "May I please just have the afternoon alone with her?"

The biker's leather boots creaked as he shifted his weight. "Art—"

"Jesus, have an ounce of faith in me. I do have *some* self-control. Damn."

Maybe some girls would find this control over men to be empowering; I found it to be unnerving. I wondered how my appearance could make someone weak or notice that their self-control was compromised. I felt flawed. My outer appearance was forcing someone to change, be something they didn't want. By the expression on Art's face, it was painful to be caught up in my snare.

He lifted a brow. "Not according to what was just happenin' here."

I cringed, completely embarrassed that this man knew Art was about to give me a very personal release, and tried to sound sturdy when I spoke to the biker. "If you truly have kept an eye on me, you know that my word stands for something. I will not do anything inappropriate with Art."

After a pause, the biker walked away.

Artist appeared mournful. "I'm so sorry."

"I need to go back to my room."

Horror crossed his face. "No, please don't shut me out."

I shook my head. "I'm cold."

He looked to Kenny's wet T-shirt sticking to me, my bikini easily seen, then wrapped his arms around me, rubbing my arms. "Shit. Sorry. Dry clothes. Got it."

· · ·

In the hot shower, my muscles finally stopped trembling. My mind was still spinning, but it was time to turn off the water and ask Art more questions. He was worried, patiently waiting for me in the hotel room, refusing to go put on dry clothes of his own.

After dressing, I exited the bathroom to see another stand-off taking place. Chest to chest with Kenny, Artist had his hands in the air. "I didn't start this one, Delilah. Reroute that pissed look."

"Kenny! Knock it off!"

The same height, Art grinned in Kenny's face. "Yeah, Kenny. Do what you're told."

Kenny growled, "I'm not going to ask you again to leave."

"What' cha going to do, big man, throw me out? Cause I ain't leaving 'til *she* asks me."

I tried to squeeze in between them, but that was more like asking two bulls to part ways after they had already begun their charge at one another. So, I tried another tactic. I touched Kenny's arm, hoping for his green eyes to look at me. Contact usually brought him back to me.

When my plan worked, I forced a smile. His shoulders softened a bit. He was ready to hear me so, in almost a whisper, I asked, "What are you doing?"

"I..." He stopped, looked to Art, turned back to me and blew out air, stepping back. "I have no fucking clue."

I quickly stepped between them now that there was room, putting my back to Art. "Because you're acting a little... peculiar—"

"Jealous," Art quickly added.

Over my shoulder, I held up two fingers. "You have two seconds before I ask you to leave."

I felt his puff of an exhale and a shift of his weight, but he shut up.

Kenny eyed Art behind me. "I don't like him."

Art's voice rang out. "It's a good thing I'm not trying to date *you* then." I held up one finger in warning. Art huffed again then went and sat in the hotel chair he was practically naked in last night.

Calmly, I asked, "Why don't you like him, Kenny?"

Kenny looked away. After a pause, he said. "He's cocky."

I actually chuckled. "Says Mr. Cocky himself?"

That got him to crack a smile. "I wouldn't say I'm cocky, just... aware."

"Aware that I may actually like a guy?"

Kenny's shoulders folded as he looked to the carpet. "This is new to me."

I whispered again, "It's new to me, too." I ducked under his view. "Can you help me through it, like you do everything else in my life?"

He gazed right into my eyes. "How can I say no to you, Delilah?"

Wrapping my arms around him, I squeezed him so tight. "I love you. Thank you for loving me, too."

When I released him, Artist was there, holding his hand out to Kenny. "I cannot express enough regret for being such a dick. I thought I saw something but clearly was wrong."

Kenny stared at his hand for a few seconds then shook it. "I'm with her every day. Fitting in someone new, uh, threw me off, I think." He pulled away and backed toward the door, appearing incredibly awkward and insecure. "Feel for me." He rolled his eyes at Art while fumbling for the doorknob behind him. "I already have one hater, Miss V, to contend with." He opened the door, bumping into it. "For all I know, she put you up to this, Art, to get me out of the picture." He gulped. "That would kill me." His eyes met mine. "Delilah, I lo—" He stopped. After recovering, he waved, entering the hallway. "See ya guys later." The door shut.

I couldn't move. I was absolutely cemented in place, staring at the closed door.

Art stood beside me, staring at the same door. "Still don't believe me?"

I grabbed my chest. "Kenny is... in love with me?"

Art was quiet for a moment then solemnly said, "Now, all you have to do is figure out if you love him more than in a brotherly way." He kissed my cheek and left the room.

I stood there, frozen in disbelief at both exits.

On the way home from Daytona, our moods had dramatically shifted. We had gone to the beach with such high expectations but were now headed home, all of us knowing a shift had taken place. I was now officially interested in having a relationship, Tucker and Viola were finding it harder and harder to deny their attraction for one another, and Kenny seemed distant yet prowling for my thoughts. This time, he was in the back seat with me. He sat behind Viola, who was staring out the passenger window, while Tucker drove, unusually quiet.

Kenny lightly shook the hand in my lap. "You talking to me yet?"

I stared at our now joined hands.

He slowly pulled away.

Watching his hand retract back to his own lap, fidgeting with his other one, I asked, "Why did you pull away?"

He rubbed his palms on his thighs. "Don't know. You just seem different."

A deep exhale was released as I looked out the window and realized... "I am." How could I not be? I learned that there was a powerful sexual drive in me, which I had doubted even existed on more than one occasion. I learned Diesel was the president of a gang that may or may not be on the criminal side of the law, possibly putting me in danger; therefore, that gang had been spying on me.

My brother's voice cut through my cloud of thoughts. "You like him, Lilah?"

"I—"

"Take your time. Put some thought into it."

So, I did, and the best I could come up with was, "I don't know him, Tuck, but I like the way he makes me feel inside."

"Example?"

"Sure you want to hear this?"

The car dramatically slowed when his foot slipped off the gas pedal. "Oh, God."

V laughed. "Dear Lord, Tucky Ducky. She's still a virgin."

The car revved up again while my brother grabbed his chest. "I think I just swallowed my tongue."

"That would be a damn shame," mumbled V.

Out of the corner of his eye, Tucker observed her. "Bryce not taking care of you, girl?"

She looked him straight on. "Sure you want to know?"

He shuddered. "So, back to you, Lilah. Talk to your bro."

"I kissed him."

"When?" shouted Kenny.

"While playing strip poker," sneered V as if none of his business.

The car slowed again with another foot slip mishap. "What? Poker?"

Viola asked, "How *drunk* were you two?" Tuck shrugged. He didn't remember shit. She said, "I showered you, Tuck."

I think his jaw hit his steering wheel when it dislocated. He rearranged between his legs while asking, "You did?"

She studied his busy hand. "Visualizing what may or may not have happened?"

Kenny asked me, "Were you clothed when you kissed him?"

"Does it matter?"

"Yes!" both he and my brother yelled in unison.

Viola laughed. "You two *do* know she is human, right? Has desires?"

Tucker winced but stopped when studying her face that, apparently, was saying much. I didn't know it then, but V's expression was begging him to be a good older brother. A patient one, and one who needed to... listen. He took a deep breath and said, "Okay, tell me more, Lilah." He watched Viola as if trying to gauge her silent response, while he slowly added, "Because... talking... is very healthy... for a young woman."

Viola proudly smiled and nodded, going back to looking out the windshield as if *job-well-done*.

Finding their communication skills comical, I was pleased with his effort and said, "I was in my jeans and bra, if it matters, but we kissed. My first, in case my babysitters thought they failed at me having the most unfulfilling love life, ever."

Tuck sank in his seat. "I never thought of that."

Viola gestured. "See? Healthy to talk."

Tuck asked her, "Diesel talks to you about this shit?"

"Who else do I have? A nun has more sexual knowledge than Delilah."

I smacked her chair. "Hey!"

She peered over her shoulder. "Am I lying?"

Crossing my arms over my chest, I mumbled, "I've read *many* books." The car windows almost exploded with the burst of *unnecessary* laughter from everyone. "They were romance novels, damn it!" I proclaimed, but bodies jolted and jerked through more laughter. "Assholes."

Viola was trying to breathe. "Read any erotica?"

I cringed. "I don't think so."

"You'd know if ya did. Talk to me after you read some of that."

"No," yelled my male jailers.

"Damn." Tuck wiped away laughter tears. "Okay. Seriously. Lilah, you were saying?"

I uncrossed my arms and readjusted in my seat. "So, he knelt between my legs—"

"*What?*" shrieked the males in the car.

"Guys!" yelled Viola. "Stop it!" Then she gave Tucker a scrutinizing glare.

He nodded and rolled his shoulders. Sweetly, he said, "Lilah, no more interruptions. Promise." Then, sternly, he said, "Kenny, shut the fuck up."

Desperate for this conversation, I gave one more try. "Okay. When his lips touched mine—" I waited for screams, but none came, causing my body to relax. "I know this sounds childish, but I felt it in my stomach." I grabbed my belly, lost in the memory. When everyone started nodding, I was in awe. "I'm not the only one?"

Tucker bobbed his head left to right. "I don't think I know *exactly* what you're talking about, but I definitely feel it in the lower territory."

Kenny pointed at him. "Bingo."

I smiled, *really* appreciating the openness I was hearing. "V?"

She sighed in thought. "No, Pretty D, not during a kiss, but I have felt it."

Tucker stared at her—as much as someone driving can—but asked me, "Then what happened?"

My eyes shut as I moaned, "His mouth opened." I exhaled, reopening my eyes. "The sensation of being so incredibly intimate was...It," I grabbed my chest, "opened me up to a whole other world, one I *so* want to be a part of." I touched my lips. "I want to be connected to someone on a level that is only mine and his. No one can take it from us. The kiss showed me why romance novels are written." The car was so quiet the purring of the engine was all I heard. Viola was staring at me in bewilderment. I bashfully smiled. "Too much?"

"No." She patted her chest. "You just made me regret—" She quickly stopped herself and sat up straight then looked out the windshield. "What have I done?"

Tucker grabbed her hand. "What's wrong?"

She clung to his offered support. "Bryce, he..." She shook her head, closing her eyes. "Too late to change—" Her blue eyes opened, engulfing my brother. "I must see it through."

He swallowed, nodding with conviction. "You're a girl to admire, V."

She pulled his hand to her cheek, looking so relieved. "Thank you." She softly rocked side to side as if silently promising my brother, *someday you and I will be.*

With an unusual maturity, Tucker cupped her cheek with deep

affection before retracting his hand, placing it firmly on the steering wheel. "Lilah?"

Affected, seeing their love for one another, I quietly answered, "Yeah?"

"If... If you felt all that, in a kiss with someone you don't even know, can you imagine one—an incredible kiss—with someone you love?"

My heart pitter-patted with such a thought. "Think I will have that someday?"

"God, I hope so. I hope we *all* do."

Viola tried to muffle an emotional reaction.

I asked my brother, "Do you think it could be with Art?"

Tucker was quiet in thought for a few moments. "When you just blew my mind with your description of your first kiss, I couldn't help but think of how beautifully innocent it was. And I don't mean that as an insult. I mean it as a sincere compliment. I never had that. My first kiss was a rushed disaster of tongues not having a clue." He started laughing. "I'm talkin' a real train wreck, and my first time having sex? That was a ten-car pile-up with no EMTs present. Know what I'm sayin'?" Viola started giggling, wiping away tears, which seemed to please him. "Anyways, my point is, whatever girl I was experimenting with, she was a part of that wreck. She was just as naïve, which was part of the disastrous magic. I say magic because that is what it was, in an innocent sense. So, I can't help but think, what if one of those girls were older? Would it still have been an experience between to innocents, or simply following someone else's lead?" He softly said, "Lilah, will you being with someone so much more advanced than you sexually rob you of the unknown? The adventure?"

Stunned. I sat there so wonderfully stunned. "Thank you."

He reached back for my hand and held it. "So much love for you, girl."

"Tucker, I don't think Diesel can call you a dumbass anymore."

That had him laughing again. "Be sure to tell him, 'kay?"

Kenny said, "Damn, Tuck. Never knew you were so deep, dude."

"I did." Viola smiled at the young man beaming for her.

CHAPTER SIX

With spring break over, we all went back to school a little wiser. Tucker walked a little taller. I walked a little braver to wait for true love. Viola walked a little happier, knowing her time would eventually come, too. And Kenny walked... a little timid. A change happened for him, too, but it wasn't for the better.

Bryce wrapped V up in his thin arms. "You are never allowed to leave me again."

Even with the weekend we just had, Viola returned affections that seemed from the heart. But, now, I could see it was in a *friend* manner more than a lover's. She probably told my brother to stop being a bitch but to Bryce, the one I was seeing so differently now as she hugged him tightly. "You don't need me as much as you think you do."

He silenced her with a kiss that made my brother pale considerably. I clutched his hand with an expression of concern. His eyes pled with mine as if wanting to go back in time and tell Viola a different answer when she asked him to claim her.

I swallowed and spoke as if not affected. "Big bro, will you walk me to class?" Staring at Viola being kissed, he solemnly nodded. "See ya'll at lunch," I announced before dragging him away. Then I whispered, "Talk to me."

He let go of my hand and wrapped the now free arm around my neck to whisper in my ear. "Light, am I a blind fool? I'm starting to think Diesel calls me a dumbass for good reasons."

I didn't have the heart to tell him he was dead on, so I asked, "Are you feeling something for V?"

His palm wiped down his face. "I... I... Sorry. I don't know what the hell is going on with me." I watched as he rubbed his chest as if needing to remove physical pain, but I knew it was not only skin deep. It was heart deep.

Wanting to talk and help him see he was mad crazy for V, I opened my mouth but shut it when Kenny ran up to us. "Darlin', you forgot your trig book."

At lunch, I couldn't help but see all our friends as younger than me. I joined them at the big round table we always sat at in the cafeteria. French fries were already soaring through the air to pelt a tablemate in the head. I smiled, somewhat enjoying the playful banter that felt harmless compared to the biker gang, and the biker I needed to make a decision about.

Cole pulled out a chair for me. "So, how was Daytona?"

Dany sat on my other side as I sat with my tray. "One party after another."

Cole opened his milk. "Damn. I knew I should've gone."

Houston laughed at him. "You weren't invited."

Cole defended himself. "Only because I don't look old enough to get into a bar."

"We got in with no issues." Kenny shoved overcooked cheesy macaroni into his mouth.

"Do you need more mac-n-cheese?" asked Bryce.

Viola smiled at him. "Wow. You did miss me, huh?"

She went to kiss him, but my brother interrupted, "I need some mac, Bryce."

Bryce moved his fingers in a walking motion. "Your legs work."

Jaz, squashed between the silent battle of the twins, Nash and Nelson, giggled. "He said get your own."

"*Hey*, Hu." All heads swiveled to a classmate named Adele.

Hu grinned. "Hey, girl. What's up?" The p had a *pop* sound as if trying to sound, well, I'm not sure. But he sure watched her walk away as she flirted with her eyes from over her shoulder.

"Dude! What are you doing with that girl?"

"Cole, she is *fine.*"

"She's a wet blanket."

Tucker spit out his juice, laughing. "What the fuck does that even mean?"

Cole Coleman shivered. "When cold and lonely, what chu want to *snuggle* with?"

Tucker wiped his smirking mouth with a napkin. "I sure the hell don't want her *dry.*"

"Gross!" I screamed as everyone busted out laughing. "I'm trying to eat!"

My brother winked. "Me too."

And up came my lunch.

Walking out through the school's doors, the sun hit my face, telling me the long school day was over. I stopped walking when I saw a motorcycle waiting for me. Artist stared at me but was smiling. It was almost as if not hearing from me since I left Daytona was answer enough of what decision I had made. He jerked his head, hinting for me to get on the back of his bike. A spare helmet was waiting for me.

"You got her keys?" my brother, observing the silent conversation between Art and me, asked Kenny.

Kenny always had my keys. Dad had offered him his own car, but driving me around was what he preferred.

Appearing irritated, Kenny held up his finger, my keyring dangling, then reached for my books. My brother walked away but was facing me. "You know my opinion. Now, it's time for you to know yours."

Feeling a little torn, I nodded, hoping what I needed to know would be clear soon. Tuck casually saluted Art as he headed toward the student parking lot.

As I approached Art, he handed me the helmet, saying, "Don't be sad. Every goodbye deserves a talk, right?"

Putting the helmet on, I apologized. "I'm so sorry."

He smirked. "You nurturing me?"

Did he know we would've never worked out? Did he know what he was asking me for—what he was truly seeking—wasn't fair of a seventeen-year-old girl? I think so. I think that is why he teased me about it. I wasn't done maturing—if that's even possible—but I definitely wasn't ready to mother him like he needed. I missed out on the same tender affections because of my own mother's death. How could I fill someone's void when I had a gaping one myself?

I slid on the back of his bike so we could ride together, toward our goodbye.

The dust of the old dirt road lifted into the air, leaving a trail that would soon disappear, a metaphor of this short-lived relationship. I held Art tight around his waist, wondering if it would be my last time. An old barn was our destination. Off his bike, he slid the barn doors open, letting the warm sun in. Artist asked, "Do you ever wonder what old walls have seen?"

"Like an old car."

He smiled at me. "Yeah. Something, somewhere, with history." I sat next to him on an old bale of hay. He said, "History... The older you get, the more stories you have to tell."

"Are we still speaking of the barn?"

He stared outside the doors, into the field where his bike was parked. "No."

Art was the type of beauty I could stare at for days. "I take it Viola talked to you?"

"Yep, and I understand."

"I wanted to be the one since I was still pondering."

"She didn't tell me it was over. I knew that today when I saw your face." He exhaled then cracked his knuckles. "Is it because of Kenny?"

"No, and for that, I feel like apologizing again."

"There's that sweet side of you, but you've done nothing wrong. You didn't lead either of us on."

I had never given Kenny the wrong impression, that I knew, but I wasn't sure with Artist. I giggled. "I thought my kiss was full of promises."

"It don't count when you don't know what you're promising."

My eyes teared with understanding.

Because I was pretty, boys always made insinuations that I owed them something, that my appearance was alluring, therefore I should pay up, even though I wasn't purposely trying to gain their interest. I was told there were girls who wished they were me, not knowing all the unwanted attention my appearance brought forth. "Art, I feel like you're my Daytona tattoo. A part of me that will always be."

His smile was full of charm. "I think I like that, Delilah."

We sat in silence for a while, rethinking all that had happened over the past few days. "Art, you spoke of Diesel's club, belonging, and him caring for you... Are you lonely?"

"Takes one to know one?"

"Sometimes."

"Yes, I have a lonely past."

"Is that why you're becoming a biker?"

He ran a hand over his face then through his dark hair. "Loneliness can be cruel."

"I wish I could change that for you."

"You saying that tells me how correct your brother is."

That statement spoke of how I was still trying, or at least wishing, to fill gaping holes and create happiness, which wasn't my responsibility. Maybe Art deserved to be lonely. Maybe he had done something and was paying a price. Maybe something had happened to him, resulting in his loneliness, still something that wasn't mine to fix.

"Then," I said, "I hope Diesel's brotherhood brings you some peace, or at least a way to find it."

He stared at me then sighed. "Delilah, you are now irrevocably a part of my soul."

I smiled. That was a compliment I hoped I had earned.

"And I will continue to... love you from a distance."

Love...

As Artist had said, love can be a control tactic when misused. I don't believe Art was doing this; I think he was being truthful. To keep speaking the truth, I believe I loved him also. It was not the kind of never-ending love written about in novels, but I viewed it to be a deep connection that would not continue to grow. That belief was yet another sign of my youth because there is no end, only continuances of beginnings that lead, in one way or another, into more growth, more connections, even if unseen.

His eyes found my lips. "Can I kiss you?"

"I would really like that, Artist."

Knowing what I had learned, what my big bro had taught me, this kiss was different. I didn't feel it in my stomach, nor did it stir my hormones into a delicious frenzy. No, I felt it in my heart. A section where good friends are treasured. Artist had been a wonderful stepping stone, preparing me for the true love of my life.

Holding my face, he said, "Damn, I will miss what we could've been."

"Art, my brother wasn't the only one to help me see what I want. You have been such a simple yet monumental part of my life. Never will I forget it."

"The guy, the one who steals your heart," he chuckled, "what a fucking lucky bastard."

I kissed him again. "I will be sure to tell him, whoever he is."

I thought of the song "I'm with You" by Avril Lavigne, and how the lyrics were so true for me. I may not have met my forever at this point in my life, but I was already *with* him. My heart... was already his.

Running my finger over Artist's lips, I joked, "Just think, now you won't go to jail."

With a sadness I appreciated, he teased, "No crime committed, right?" He smiled, the setting sun shining off his face. "It was really nice to meet you, Delilah."

A full circle moment...

Peering over my shoulder as we pulled away on his bike, I wished to see that barn again. I wished to feel as loved as Art loved me that day. Little did I know that wish would come true. A young man would take me there, hoping to romance me into sex but epically fail —practically giving me a concussion—and steal my heart even more.

The muffler of Art's bike still roared down the street as I walked into the kitchen. My brother asked, "Well, what's the verdict?" while slapping mayo onto his ham sandwich.

Kenny whined, "Dude, you stole the last piece of cheese?"

I started to pull my planned meal from the fridge. "I'm about to feed you guys. Can't you wait?"

Tucker slapped Kenny across the face with the slice of stolen goods. "Nope. I'm starving."

I pushed the casserole back into the fridge, only to hear, "What the hell are you doing?"

I answered Kenny. "If you're already eating dinner, why should I mess up the kitchen?"

Tucker balked. "This is just a snack to hold us over."

In dismay, I pointed to Kenny's triple-decker sandwich.

He shrugged. "How long 'til that's ready?" He gestured to the tin-foiled deep baking dish.

"About an hour."

He took a huge bite. "Pe'fec'. I'll b' 'eady."

I pulled the dish back out of the fridge. "I can't understand what the hell you're saying." They both started talking around all the food in their mouths, hands waving to what was in my grip and gesturing it needed to go in the oven. "Damn, you two are eating machines." I went to the stove controls and set the oven at three hundred and fifty degrees. "I'm going to take a shower."

"Bu' wha' yo' decid'?"

"Tuck, swallow."

Gulp. "How'd he take it?"

"How do you know it was bad news?"

Tuck's warm brown eyes showed sympathy. "You seem a little crabby."

"Oh." I swallowed unexpected emotions. "Whoever I'm meant to be with will find his way to me." I lingered in the kitchen doorway. "Maybe he'll move to this town."

Preparing for another bite, Kenny chuckled. "People don't move *here*. They desperately want to move *out*."

I walked away. "Let a girl dream, Kenny."

His voice echoed down the hall. "If he doesn't appear, you moving to find him?"

"Whatever it takes, I guess."

"Don't run. Stay here."

My body jolted as I recognized those words. The same ones he spoke while drunk in Daytona. I slipped into the bathroom needing some quiet.

Had I only known what such simple words could and would trigger. Within mere days, another fork in the journey of being a teenager showed its ugly face. I wished the older me could have communicated at that critical point in my life and told me to choose the other path, just like my brother warned with Art. Instead, I was alone, or so I thought, and chose the much harder of the two, creating another haunted road...

CHAPTER SEVEN

Viola stood from her chair at the restaurant. "Ladies, it's time to finish wrecking my brother's credit card." The whole gang had spent the Saturday in Atlanta, and we'd just finished dinner. V pointed to Jaz who was in another Twin sandwich. "You in?"

Nash must've grabbed her knee under the table because she looked at him and growled, "I know." She then smiled at Viola. "Rain check."

V kissed her boyfriend's cheek. "You got my bags?"

Bryce chuckled as he eyed the mound of shopping bags from the various stores we'd dragged the boys into. "I need to rent a U-Haul to get your shit home."

I went to stand from my chair, but Kenny grabbed my hand. "Where ya goin', darlin'?"

Cole argued with Hu about him texting Adele while I tried to pull free from Kenny but his hand tightened. My gut pinged at the trapped sensation, but I ignored it. "That store we saw earlier."

My brother faked a gag reflex. "More shopping. No, thank you. I'm tired of being castrated for the day."

Kenny released my hand as his expression softened. "Want me to come with you? Atlanta is not safe, especially at night."

His eyes were so sincere I was about to tell him his company would be appreciated, but Viola pulled my chair from the table. "Jesus, Kenny. Stop. She saw a sundress she liked. We'll be back, untouched and still pure."

Tuck lifted a brow. "V? Pure?"

"Go fuck a duck, Tuck." She linked arms with me and we headed for the door.

"Hey!" barked my brother.

V groaned and mumbled complaints but stopped and looked back at him, attitude soaring.

"Stop with your silent bitchin'." He held up her phone. "Need this?"

"Oops!" She rushed back to the table. "That would have gotten me an ass beating from bro." She kissed the top of his ball cap. "You da man, Tucky."

Bryce balked, "Don't you mean *I'm* the man?"

I didn't miss, nor did my brother, when she leaned right in front of him to kiss Bryce. Once done, Tucker handed the cell to her then smacked Bryce on the back of his head. "Watch out after your girl, moron."

Outside the restaurant, the street lamp sparkled off of chrome, capturing my attention. Two tires are what I saw next. In a spot on the other side of the bustling street, quietly sat a motorcycle. I couldn't help but smile at the biker watching me from afar. My hand even lifted for a tiny wave.

He didn't wave back.

Long fingers took hold of my hand and gently pulled it down. Viola met my eyes and sadly shook her head. As we started heading down the sidewalk toward the store, I asked, "Why did you stop me?"

"Anyone watching him, due to his patch—"

I grabbed her arm. "He got patched in?"

Viola proudly smiled. "Yeah, Diesel loves him." She linked arms with me again. "And he said anyone strong enough to set Delilah free is strong enough to stand by his side for life."

I quickly peered behind me, wanting to congratulate him for something I knew he wanted—to belong somewhere—but he was already gone. Over all the traffic, I never heard the loud bike leave. V's cell vibrated. She held it up for me to see. *Tell her I wanted to wave.*

I sighed, thankful for his friendship.

Viola yanked on my arm, guiding me into a clothing store. "Let's see if your ass likes this dress."

"My ass?"

"Of course. It has a say! If it likes it, hence makes you look good, we have to buy it."

"Is that why my brother's eyes are constantly locked on your ass?"

She flipped through the dresses hanging on the rack, looking for my size. "I sure the hell ain't dressing it up for my boyfriend. He hungers for something else from me."

I accepted the offered clothed hanger. "But what does Viola hunger for?"

"To be scarred." She walked to a table full of folded jeans.

"Scarred?" Following her, scenarios ran through my mind. "I can't help but picture accidentally cutting myself with a knife, so please explain."

She unfolded a pair of holey denim jeans and held them up to her, examining them along her long, solid legs. "Eww. My thigh will be exposed." Hanging them over her arm, she moved on to check out another table. "Scarred. Irrevocable marked, seared. Someone leaving such a fingerprint on my soul that I have forever been labeled his."

I grabbed my chest. "Jesus, V." I exhaled. "Is that why you don't question the decision I made with Art?"

Her fabulous blue eyes saw through me. No, not through me, *into* me. Then she spoke with such heart. I was surprised by the rare appearance of this gentle side. "You are soulful. You are courageous, and your heart is limitless. You are a true wonder, Delilah. That means you deserve the real deal. I want to witness you gazing at your man, completely and utterly enthralled. Did Art spike your interest? No doubt. But—" She stopped. I quickly motioned for her to continue. Softly, she did. "But what I saw when you stared at him was that he was not perfectly damaged." My mouth positively gaped at her. Tenderly, she took hold of my hand and held it to her cheek. Her eyes closed as she whispered, "He didn't have the perfect unseen scar to match yours."

Exiting the store, each with an arm full of more bags, courtesy of Diesel's unfortunate credit card, Viola told me, "Bryce texted that they dropped off our bags in Tuck's car and they're in an arcade this way." We walked back past the restaurant we had dinner in and passed a few more stores on the strip. I knew we were getting closer to the arcade when I saw the purple and red strobe lights shining on the sidewalk and parked cars on the street. The place was wide open with four entrances. Two on one side of the corner building, and two on the other. Kids and teenagers were entering and exiting, all lively and hungry for a good time. Viola rolled her eyes. "What, are we twelve again?"

I snarled an upper lip, not interested in video games either.

We stood on the corner studying our surroundings, hoping to find another store that hadn't closed yet. A cowgirl hat glowed in perfect showcase lighting in a store window across the street. I pointed. "Gimme."

"Yes." She started crossing the street. "It's either that or a game of Mrs. Pacman."

Once we made it to the other side, we headed for the hat calling my name, but timing was not on our side. Intoxicated men were exiting a bus titled Bachelors-n-Wheels. They were cheering and spilling open beverages all over each other, practically falling down the bus stairs. One guy was raving about a stripper still onboard the bus. Viola and I quietly tried to side-step the Man Storm we had accidently entered, but didn't slip by unnoticed.

The guy high on the lap dance he just received cooed, "Hot damn, it's my lucky night, boys." He stepped in front of V. "And *your* name is?"

"Bitch. Now, step aside."

My chuckle garnered me unwanted attention. His friend strolled up to me like I had just won the prize and should be honored. "You are," his fowl alcohol breath practically slapped me across the face, "heavenly."

I tried not to vomit but ended up unable to hide a gag.

"That bad, eh?" Viola laughed.

I gagged again.

By this point, we were gaining attention from the rest of the bachelors *off* wheels. They gathered around us as if we were an unexpected treat they were far too happy to eat. Viola and I, again, tried to see our way clear of the drunks, but the manmade circle made it somewhat challenging. So, V did what she does. Her hip popped out and she turned up the attitude. "Listen up, dipshits, my girl has her eye on a hat over there. Do you really think it's wise to get in the way of therapeutic shopping?"

A guy fingered the top of her shopping bag, trying to take a peek. "Looks like you've already met your quota."

She yanked her bag away from him. "I see I need to spell this out for the drunk and impaired. There are a few girls whom you should not fuck with because repercussion is much closer than you think. And you just happened to have, out of all of Atlanta, stumbled on two of them. I repeat, back away. You have been warned."

She stared at them.

They stared at her... then laughed.

Unaffected, V polished her fingernails against her shoulder. "Your loss. My gain. Let the countdown begin."

A guy reached for her hip. "How about we dance while you run your trap?"

Ever so evilly, V smirked as she slowly stirred her hip in his hand. "My trap won't be the only thing running. You ready for it?"

As if now his favorite dish, the dumbass eyed her up and down. "Soooo ready, sweetheart." Something behind us captured the man's attention and he froze.

I didn't even have to turn around. Observing all the guys paling by the second, I smiled and purred, "Hey, Art."

His chest vibrated against my back "Hey, baby. I see ya made some new friends?"

Then a menacing voice rumbled, "My little sister already has plenty of friends."

"Ah, shit!" Viola didn't even look behind her as she laughed at the guy now releasing her hip. "This is *really* an unlucky evening for you. He gets super crabby."

I nodded to her. "Especially if he hasn't had any."

She threw a hand through the air. "So true!" She stared at the gulping guy before her. "Big bro, been laid tonight?"

"Present company has made me late. I'm feeling... twitchy."

Art chuckled. "A biker with a twitchy trigger finger?"

"Never good." I shook my head, totally enjoying this moment.

Viola popped out another hip. "Still wanna dance, *bachelor*?"

The guy scurried off. His friends followed.

She watched their hasty departure. "I'll take that as a no."

From behind, Diesel kissed her cheek. "Where the hell is dumbass?"

"Right here." My brother jogged up with Kenny. "What the hell did I miss now?"

"Nothing now. Little Man," Diesel gestured to Art. "hand baby girl the bag she dropped."

Art smiled as if I would soon be very pleased, holding out a bag. I was about to explain it wasn't mine until I recognized the store name. Peeking inside, I gasped. "My sundress."

Art winked. "I bet it looks great on you."

Kenny mumbled, "How the hell did she have time to even try it on?"

Art backed away, smirking, "How's it going, Kenny?"

All the way home, Kenny griped, "I'm not buying the coincidence routine. Why was Artist there? I think he's stalking your sister."

Tucker turned his steering wheel. "We're talking about Diesel, bro. If that man says everything is on the up 'n up, it's true. Motorcycle Man would *never* put Lilah in danger." His whole body shuddered. "In fact, I rue the day he thinks someone's done either girl wrong." He eyed-pissed Kenny. "We think *we* got fightin' game?" His eyes went back to the road. "Shit. On that guy? That's all we got. Shit." From the back seat, next to me, Viola grinned. Tucker eyed her in his rearview mirror. "Tell me I'm wrong."

"Nah, Ducky, you is right on point."

Kenny growled, "But I ain't talkin' about Diesel. It's Artist who needs to lurk elsewhere."

"Why?" I quietly asked.

Kenny went still in his seat. My brother kept observing him. Their eyes finally met to start the silent talking they were experts at. In fact, after a moment, Tuck nodded. Kenny blew out a breath and the conversation ended.

V snarled before kicking the back of Tucker's seat.

That very night, I woke to a soft cry. Searching the dark upstairs level of my home, I found Kenny, asleep, struggling in his bed. I rushed to him, waking him from whatever terror was owning his night. At first, he seemed confused. I wasn't even sure if he recognized me sitting next to him. But then, to keep from waking my brother and dad, he whispered, "I need you safe."

I attempted a smile, even though I was fearful of what had spooked him, and whispered in return, "I *am* safe. I have you and Tuck to keep me that way."

Kenny's face literally changed right before my eyes. It contorted to an expression of pure disgust. His jaw then tightened, a stern expression taking shape. He maliciously sneered, "Yeah, Tuck and I try," he rolled away from me, "but *Art* is the one watching you best. Isn't that right, *Pretty D?*"

"Wait, what do you know about Art watching me?" *Does Kenny know about Diesel?* Kenny just lay in his bed with his back toward me, ignoring me. I was baffled to what I had done to deserve this reaction. Even if Kenny did somehow find out about Diesel's club, why was he angry with me? *I just learned about it, too!* I rushed to the other side of his bed. "Kenny, talk to me? What do you know about Art and Diesel?"

Kenny's green eyes met mine, and they looked *cold* as if belonging to an unpleasant stranger. I felt the chill from those eyes through my whole body. "K-Kenny?" Already truly scared, I was shocked into a frozen state when Kenny suddenly grabbed the nape of my neck and forcefully kissed me. I tried to escape, pushing against his bare chest, but he was shockingly strong, forcing me to stay put.

After his lips left mine, he proclaimed, "*That* is what I think of Art." His voice sounded deeper. Different. Strained. Kenny seemed to be angry like something had flipped a switch and turned-on this manic side of him.

I slowly touched my lips. A kiss had just been stolen from me. It was nothing like I experienced with Art. "Kenny, you–we–I... You're a brother to me."

Suddenly enraged, Kenny whispered, "I'm *not* your brother, Delilah." He tried to kiss me again. When I pulled back, refusing, this new Kenny gave me an expression of ultimate hatred. It felt as though a hot poker stick was attacking my heart. That stick only went deeper when Kenny rolled away from me again.

I whispered, "Please don't be mad at me." He wasn't taking the rejection like Art had. Artist had made me feel empowered by respecting my wishes, not blaming me. Kenny had me doubting my allure again. I instantly felt guilty for what I couldn't control. If I could've changed my feelings for Kenny, I believe I would have. Anything to make him as happy as his happiness made my brother and father.

Kenny's only response was pulling his blanket higher over his shoulders to shun me.

I slowly walked to the other side of his bed, hoping he would look at me, but he only stared at the draped window behind me, refusing to give me a glimmer of hope. I knelt on the floor next to his bed. Him denying me had me feeling shut out of Kenny's world, a world so intertwined with mine. That left me in a lonely, frigid place—a place I unconsciously recognized on a very deep level due to my mother's death, and I wanted nothing to do with it. My throat was bitterly tight. "Please talk to me." I hoped his words, any words, would warm me again. His refusal was isolating. I weakly choked out, "I'm sorry."

I wanted him to let me back into his universe where I used to feel safe. My real life heroes were in the shape and form of Tucker and Kenny. From this point on, I chased that feeling of safety like a meth-addict chasing their first grand high.

As a reward for my apology, Kenny raised his blanket, inviting me in. He had yet to look at me, but the invitation was a start. It was the start I needed in order to find the Kenny I adored, the Kenny who had been replaced by a cruel individual. Unbeknownst to me, walking away at that very moment would have changed all that was to come.

I looked at his bedroom door... and slipped under his blanket.

Facing Kenny, my voice shook with the fear I was experiencing. "Now, will you talk to me?"

Mean green eyes glared at me, daring me to figure out what it would take to hear him utter words. I was too stunned to think clearly on my own, so I waited. I waited for an inclination of what it would take to get his favorable attention again.

When the angered eyes glanced to my lips, my heart rate sped up with alarm. Kenny was playing a dangerous game with my emotions, and my natural kindness allowed him to succeed.

With much hesitation, I finally leaned forward and touched his lips with mine.

Afraid that I would still experience torture through more of his denial, I timidly pulled back to see his verdict. "Will you talk to me now?"

Kenny blinked his eyes as if trying to clear an unknown interference, and then sweetly answered, "Hey there, of course I'll talk to you, darlin'." His eyes had softened, his jaw relaxed, and he looked beautiful again. He looked like the young man I had set so high on a pedestal that I didn't know how not to look up to see him. Looking down to witness him was completely inconceivable at the time. Confused, he asked, "But, did you just kiss me?"

Completely baffled, I stuttered, "W-Well, yes. Y-You–we—" I was stumped. "Kenny?"

His warm, fantastic arms encircled me, cradling me as if I were his most prized possession. "Yes, darlin', what's wrong?"

Relief had me feeling like crying because I figured I had imagined this whole debacle. "I–I thought you were mad at me."

Kenny grounded me again as he tenderly touched my face, saying, "Delilah, don't cry. Baby, you can kiss me any time you want." His face beamed at the misunderstanding. "I didn't know—I thought you only saw me as a friend."

"I do."

"Oh." His arms loosened. "Sorry."

Him letting me go was the absolute last thing I wanted, so I begged, "No. Hold me."

I moaned as he immediately pulled me closer. He noticed. "You're shaking."

His arms held me so tight I literally sighed. "Thank you."

He kissed my head. "Of course." My cheek. "Always." My lips. "Whatever you want."

I should have, but I didn't fight his lips. I welcomed them. They were connected to the side of Kenny I treasured. I allowed deception while also lying to myself.

His hand spread wide, holding my cheek while the tips of his fingers reached around my neck, but he was gentle this time. It was affectionate. It was a young man finally getting what he had wanted. This kiss spoke volumes of how much Kenny loved me.

Art had been right all along.

Out of breath, Kenny gazed at me adoringly. "How could I ever be mad at that?"

Thinking I had imagined the mean Kenny, I attempted to explain my temporary insanity. "Because you rolled away from me."

He quietly chuckled. "Uh, that happens when I sleep. I roll, darlin'."

My throat tightened, sensing something was amiss with my champion. "Sleep?"

"But I loved waking to you," he said with admiration. "When did you come in here?"

"D-During your nightmare."

He chuckled, tightening his arms around me, offering comfort. "I think it was *you* who had the nightmare. You okay? You're shaking again."

As if he had been temporarily possessed by a separate entity, Kenny had not been present for all that had just transpired. And since I was sure that wasn't possible, I dismissed the signs of the grave trouble I was in and whispered, "Yeah, I'm a little shaken up."

"Do you want to stay with me?" Kenny asked. "'Til ya feel better?" His embrace and bare chest were the refuge and security this brother of mine had always offered. I was so terrified and confused that I accepted wholeheartedly, crying silently, "Yes, I would like to stay with *you*, Kenny."

If only I could...

In the middle of the night, I woke on the opposite side of his bed feeling my breasts being touched and my nipples roughly tugged on. I began to shake uncontrollably as the severity of the volatile situation unfolded. From the pillow we were sharing, I opened my eyes to see those cold green eyes had returned. I had imagined nothing, and I certainly wasn't dreaming now. Seeing that my warrior had disappeared again, I slowly retreated from his bed. As I walked backwards toward Kenny's bedroom door, those eyes never left mine until I was out of sight.

The next morning, I woke in my own bed, desperate to reach out to Tucker in hopes he could explain my newfound horror. Taking up most of his king-sized bed, Tucker was just waking up. In mid-stretch, he saw me. "Good morning, my light. Missing your big bro?"

His light... My mom's words haunted me.

I bashfully nodded, suddenly having the urge to find comfort in his bed like I had many years ago while my father would cry in the night. I wondered if that was why I so easily fell into Kenny's last night. I guess my expression was cause for worry because Tuck sat up a little. "What's wrong?"

I quietly asked, "Can I talk to you for a minute?"

"You okay?"

No! I'm so confused! I think something is desperately wrong with your best friend. I don't want you to be upset with me for not keeping him from the darkness, but I don't think the light you think I am is strong enough. Please understand.

"Hey, everyone." I jerked when Kenny hugged me from behind, saying, "Good morning." But then I noticed his arms felt familiar again. I dared myself to believe safe Kenny was back. I slowly responded and timidly turned in his arms to face him. "Kenny?"

"Yes, darlin'."

I sighed his name and hugged my dear friend. How could I turn him away? I loved him, so much, and I refused to hold a grudge since he was unaware of how much he had scared me. The heroine in my books would never give up. How could I?

Safe in Kenny's arms, he rocked me. "Babe, you have another nightmare?"

"*Babe?*" my brother asked.

Not daring to open my eyes and risk seeing the *Cruel* Kenny, I nodded, holding him tighter. He tilted my chin up. "You okay now?"

My eyes opened, and I saw the courageous young man who was willing to do anything for me. "I am now."

He softly smiled, "That is good," then gently pressed his lips to mine.

"Holy shit!" yelled my brother, causing Kenny and I to jolt. "When... What the fuck? Holy shit!"

Kenny laughed, hugging me again. "You sound as shocked as I am."

Tucker was now sitting upright, his feet on the carpet. His mouth kept opening and closing, so I asked, "This bad?"

"What?" His eyes popped wide. "No! I'm just... Well, I knew Kenny felt for you, but... But he said you didn't feel the same. So, I'm like... Wow!"

I nodded. "I know. I didn't see it coming either. Kind of... just happened." I thought of Art's warning about Kenny, but Tucker would know best, right? "But you think it's a good idea?"

"You kiddin'?" My brother practically cheered. "I trust Kenny with my life." In awe, my brother watched Kenny on cloud nine rocking me again.

Kenny squeezed me. "I'm so freaking happy right now. Best day of my life."

Pushing Art's worried eyes from my mind, I hid in Kenny's neck. Convincing myself what transpired the night prior wouldn't happen again, I held on tight. I couldn't rob Tucker of the proud sparkle in his eye, and I definitely couldn't shatter the trust he had in the one who *usually* deserved it. Kenny was the brother I believed Tucker always wanted. Tuck had lost our mom; I wouldn't have him losing Kenny, too, so I felt compelled to keep the disturbed part of Kenny a secret from everyone... including *Kenny*.

CHAPTER EIGHT

"Thank you, V." I stared at my freshly painted toes. "A little spa day was a perfect birthday gift."

Standing on the sunlit sidewalk in front of the salon, she nervously nibbled on her bottom lip. "I kind of have one more surprise for you."

"What?" I balked. "You better not have spent more money—"

From behind me, a low whisper said, "Happy birthday."

Artist.

I turned and hugged him without even looking at him. He was smelling my hair as he held me, but I didn't care. He was my secret guardian, and I was in need. Plus, I was inhaling his masculine scent. "It is so good to see you," I quietly told him.

Still holding me, he chuckled. "Ya haven't even seen me yet."

"Don't need to. Just want this hug."

"Then it is yours." He laid his head to mine. "You doing okay?"

I suddenly remembered that Art could read me like one of my books, so I pulled away, smacking his chest. "Of course! How are *you* doing?"

His eyes raced to V's. When I openly observed this, she looked away.

"Nice dress," said Art, clearly to distract me.

I let him. "Thanks. Some biker got it for me."

"Delilah, never trust a biker."

Sighing, I explained, "Not all of them are bad."

His chuckle was almost daring me to find out about his bad side.

I blushed instantly.

"I got you something else."

"Please don't. Your visit is plenty—"

"Stop. It's just a little something." When he went down to one knee, I gasped. From the ground, he peered up, smirking. "Now who's full of themselves?"

I grabbed my chest. "Asshole. You scared me."

He clipped a gold chain around my ankle. "Your gorgeous legs deserve a little pampering."

As he stood, I teased, "Not the birthday girl?"

He waved me off. "Nah, I don't care much about her."

I felt so lucky. "Thank you. It's beautiful."

He kissed my cheek. "Be seein' ya." And he walked around the corner of the building. Within seconds, I heard his bike fire up and drive away.

Frozen in place, I whispered, "See ya." I wasn't sure how to move on, to look forward, to not see what I saw when I looked back. But back is where I had to go. At home, I was surprised to see cars and trucks in the driveway and smoke spewing from the backyard. I could recognize my brother and father trying to cook—burgers on the grill— from a mile away. "Viola, was your birthday gift another distraction?"

She parked her car. "Not as handsome as Art, but yes." Before we could even get out of the car, Kenny was opening the front door. Viola started mumbling, "Jesus, can he at least properly lube before crawling up your ass?"

Recoiling against my seat, I chuckled, "Gross, V."

Heading to the porch, V continued to grumble as Kenny swept me up in a hug. "Darlin', what took you so long?" Setting me down, his eyes raced to the lower part of my leg. "Where did you get that?"

"This anklet? Uh—"

Viola practically curtsied with an intentional fake smile as she pushed past us. "That would be a gift from Artist. You're welcome." She went inside and slammed the door.

As if I had betrayed him somehow, Kenny released me. "Oh... I, uh, thought you were only going to the spa."

I took hold of his hand. "I did. Art dropped by for a couple minutes. No biggy."

Kenny swallowed and forced a smile. "Can I have a kiss before we go inside and pretend we're not together?"

His deep-set green eyes beamed as I nodded. He inhaled as his lips pressed against mine as if I was stealing his breath by a mere touch. I longed for that same desire, but it was missing.

Only Tucker knew of Kenny's and my relationship. Or, at least, I thought. Viola's actions being extra hostile quickly reminded me she was no fool.

Cheers erupted as I stepped onto the back porch. Fighting tears, I waved bashfully to Dad's construction employees, a few of Diesel's biker buddies I'd met in Daytona, and friends from school. I left Kenny's side and hugged my brother and daddy, whispering how they shouldn't have gone through the trouble but I was thankful they had. My brother and father would die for me. That made me hope to show them how well I was living, even if it was a bald-faced lie.

At one of the tables of food set up, for the second time, I was being teased by Cole. "Now what?"

I filled up a ladle with macaroni salad. "Now what, what?"

He grabbed a hamburger bun for round two. "Now that you're getting so old!"

"Asshole," I shrieked in fun while flinging the mac salad, I had yet to try, at his face.

Stretching his tongue, he licked at it. "Damn, this is good." He laughed 'til he saw horror on my face. "Delilah, what is it?"

Tiny orange specs on his skin screamed immediate danger. I spun around, searching every chair that had someone eating in it 'til I saw my Kenny. In my peripheral vision, I saw my brother already running toward me, but I had no time to explain. Charging toward Kenny, I threw my plate to the ground right before flinging his from his grasp. I yelled, "Did you eat the mac salad?"

Kenny stared at me, along with everyone else who had now gone quiet, except my brother. "What is it?"

"Carrots!" I yelled.

My brother raced to the house.

"Kenny." I quickly kneeled and shook his hand; his evening trance had already kicked in. "Please answer me. Did you eat any mac salad?"

He had such a reaction one time that my dad took him to the doctor. We learned Kenny was highly allergic to carrots. Even though his throat didn't close, the doctor said some allergies can turn deadly and for Kenny to stay away from them. Now, his neck was already turning red as if a rash was breaking out under his skin. Dad got on his cell. "I need an ambulance..."

With everyone gathering around us, I looked to Viola. "Help my brother. My bathroom medicine cabinet. Liquid Benadryl." My friend who despised Kenny asked no questions and ran as fast as she could. From my knees and between his, I grabbed Kenny's face. "Look into my eyes." He did while fisting my shirt. I knew he was scared. Red, blotchy skin was spreading to his face. "There ya go. Don't stop. They're coming, Kenny."

His mouth opened. "D."

"I won't leave you."

My dad touched his shoulder. "Son, the ambulance is coming."

Hu added, "I bet they got that shot in case he stops breathing." I peered up at him, dumbfounded by his idiocy. Houston mouthed, "Shit. Sorry."

Kenny's eyes filled with trembling tears. My shirt tightened on my back. Kenny was starting to panic. I tightened my hold on his face, trying to keep him grounded. "Listen to me right now. There is air getting into your lungs. Feel it?" My shirt loosened as he nodded. "That's right. You won't need a shot." I forced a grin. "Well, one of Benadryl." His lips were shaky but he almost smiled.

An open bottle of Benadryl was held between us by my brother. More relieved than ever before to see the pink liquid, I grabbed it and quickly tilted Kenny's head back. "Guzzle." As he started to drink, my fingers ran down his throat, over and over, wanted to rush the fluid down from the outside.

As soon as I heard sirens, I knew the experts had arrived. I pulled the bottle from his lips and observed his skin, his face, his thankful eyes. I could see his muscles slowly relaxing as if he knew he was going to be okay. I sighed. "You with me?"

He swallowed, shakenly wiping his mouth, and blew out a held breath. "Thank you, darlin'."

Jazebelle grabbed her chest. "That was the scariest shit!"

I crumbled into Kenny's lap. "You're okay."

Bryce chuckled at Kenny. "Here come the paramedics, drama queen."

Kenny rubbed my back and tried to punch Bryce. "Asshole."

The paramedics checked out Kenny and told us we did right by the liquid Benadryl, that it saves lives by giving paramedics those extra seconds needed. My brother and dad beamed with pride, saying I didn't panic. At the time, I thought they were simply thankful Kenny was okay and that I had, yet again, been the one to keep him safe. So much undeserved pressure... I kept piling it onto my shoulders as if I were as physically strong as a real-life Viking.

Expecting Kenny to require a bed due to the drug I had poured down his throat, I was surprised as he followed me around the party. It made me uneasy, and I thought of my motorcycle friend who was not present. I quietly asked Diesel, "Art couldn't come?"

My other motorcycle friend stared at me, his mind in overdrive. I say 'my friend' because that's exactly what Diesel was to all of us. I had believed he was merely ordering bikers to watch over me, clueless to how much he was overseeing everything. After a long moment, he finally admitted, "I didn't think it wise."

"Oh."

"But I permitted him to see you earlier, to give you the gift Zombie can't seem to stop staring at."

"Huh?" I peeked over my shoulder to see Kenny's eyes locked onto my ankle. Blowing out a stressed breath, I closed mine.

A whispered grumble said, "I know he almost just died and all, but need me to have a chat with him?"

I wasn't sure presidents of biker gangs had the communication skills to chat so I refused the offer and handled Kenny on my own. Another naïve move I would live to regret.

If seeing Artist in Atlanta triggered a part of Kenny to be exposed, then the gift from Art absolutely flipped a switch. That night, after my birthday BBQ had ended on a high note, I woke to Kenny on top of me. Due to the Benadryl, I didn't think it was him, so I opened my mouth to scream but it was muffled by his sweaty palm. Cruel eyes pierced into mine. His whisper was sharp, a warning to take seriously. "I. Don't. Share." His hand put more pressure on my mouth. I assumed that meant he wanted a reply. Terrified, I did my best to nod, my head sinking into the pillow. The pressure let up slightly. "You gonna scream?"

Horrified, I shook my head.

"Good." He released my mouth. "I'm tired of hearing your bitch-ing." Before I could respond to ask what *bitching* I had been doing, I was being yanked from my bed and dragged down the hallway. As we passed my brother's room, I prayed it wouldn't open. I didn't want him to see his best friend's madness first hand.

Sane? No. But what is truly sane when being led by the deranged?

My brother's door... never opened.

It may seem senseless, but the speed at which everything escalated made it impossible for me to gain any kind of control. I believe my compassion for Kenny showed humanity at its finest... and most bewildered. Completely blinded by my need to shelter Kenny, keep my promise to my mother, and please my brother and my father, I was in too deep before I realized I needed out. Then, being tragically overwhelmed, I couldn't see how to escape and soon became trapped in quicksand. If I told, how could I explain why I hadn't sooner?

Once shoved inside Kenny's room, he shut the door behind him. I gulped down fear while studying my escape route blocked by a madman. He pointed to his bed. "Lie down."

I stumbled back before I could see through the shock I was experiencing, and then raced to get on the bed, consumed with worry for what was going to happen next. I wish I could say that I was strong and wise and that by the age of seventeen I knew everything, but that would be a tragic lie and wouldn't help anyone understand how lost I found myself to truly be.

Scrambling for the covers I was hoping could shelter me, I watched as Kenny almost prowled after me. He demanded, "No. Stay on top. Get on your back."

"M-My back? W-Why—"

Veins immediately popped from his neck as he silently roared, moving his lower jaw as if making much noise. His fists were so incredibly strained my eyes flew to the door, regretting my decisions. After rolling his neck, he viciously whispered, "Do you have any idea how easy it would be to snuff out your brother's life?"

My. Whole. Body. Seized.

He grinned as he stepped forward. "That's right." He lifted his hand then slowly slid his finger across my throat. Instantly, my mind was full of visions of Tucker lying in bed, his mattress soaked with his blood. My lips moved, trying to say no, but my fear was too great to get out a sound of my own. He mouthed, "Your back. Now."

I did what was asked, believing it would keep him calmer. In trade, Tucker safer.

On his hands and knees, he crawled across the bed and over my legs. "Stop crying. Always fucking crying." I had been so petrified I had yet to shed a tear, but wetness soon dripped from my eyes and down my face. I was clueless to why he was seeing my tears before they appeared. "Every time you cry, I'm going to lick your face." I tried to control my horror as his tongue swiped up my cheek, literally drinking my pain.

As he lowered his body on top of mine, I began to tremble uncontrollably. My lungs almost hiccupped as I struggled to do the simple task of breathing. The only thing I felt I could do at the terrifying moment was pray. So I did. I closed my eyes and prayed: *Please God, bring Kenny back to me...*

"Darlin'?"

I silenced the prayers I was screaming in my head to be sure I just heard who I was begging for.

"Darlin', Jesus, breathe. What is it?"

With the sound of his kind voice returning, I busted into tears. "K-Kenny?"

Warm and oh so trusting arms engulfed me. "Shhh, I'm here. I'm here." He laid next to me and pulled me close. "Delilah, these nightmares are getting out of control." I clung to him with a desperation that rocked me to a core I didn't even know existed. "You're absolutely shaking like a leaf." My face took cover in his neck as I internally begged for this Kenny never to leave me again. "Oh, God, Delilah, talk to me." And say what? *There is a side of you that is more terrifying than the devil himself?* "Should we talk to your dad tomorrow?"

My stomach did a somersault because I didn't know how to voice the truth to Dad either. "No. No. Please." My fingers dug into Kenny's back, hoping he could hear how torn up I was.

"Shh, okay." He rocked me. "Just breathe. Just breathe." He kissed my head, he kissed my cheek. He kissed my mouth... I tasted my tears.

After a day of school, and what appeared to be a normal routine to any onlookers, I would go home and worry about who was to stalk me that night. Lying in bed, consumed with fear, I eventually would fall to sleep only to have an intimidating Kenny waking me up, dragging me to his room. He never stayed in mine. I had no idea why being in his room was important. And, before the sun would rise, I would sneak back into my room so no one would notice. But, after a few nights of terror, my body forced me into a deep sleep and I didn't wake up in time.

Tucker smacked Kenny's foot and angrily whispered, "What the fuck? My dad will kill you."

I drowsily sat up. "Tuck?"

His jaw was locked. "To your room. Now. You're gonna get us all in trouble."

My brother had never been disappointed in me before. It almost rocked me to my core as much as Kenny's night terrors.

Again, I was scrambling for safety that never appeared. I rushed into my room and shut the door, raced into my bathroom, started the shower, and cried... I was exhausted.

Kenny was, too. As the days passed, his temper intensified, and my dad was losing patience. "Boy, you get in one more fight, I will homeschool your ass. Got me? All these new porches I keep funding are becoming the laugh of the town." My dad spun on his pissed heels and pointed to my brother. "Tuck. Outside. We need to talk."

My brother followed Dad outside to the back porch.

Kenny sat on the couch in the back den, defeated. "I've never made your dad mad before."

Having recently disappointed my brother and able to completely sympathize with Kenny's regret, I sat next to him. "Getting suspended usually will do the trick."

Tiredly, he leaned against my shoulder. "What's happening to me? Since we got together, I seem to be falling apart."

Guilt. Guilt was drowning me from the inside out. I put my arm around him and cradled him to me. My whisper was as sincere as they come. "I'm so sorry." Because I was sure my allure was ruining him.

Even though my dad still didn't know about the newfound relationship happening under his roof, our friends quickly caught on. How could they not? I started to cling to Kenny as much as he clung to me. I had read once that some victims tended to stay close to their abusers. That sounded absurd when I first read it, but here I was, a prime example of the damaged. It was a mixture of trying to keep him calm so his wrath at night wouldn't be so bad, and because, when awake, he was one of the best. In truth, Kenny and I were two kids lost in a sea of abuse, neither one of us knowing how to swim back home.

From that point on, it may have been utter exhaustion, but it felt as though new personalities kept presenting themselves. It was as if one splintered into another. I was starting to recognize who I was dealing with by Kenny's eyes.

If they were wild, *Angry* Kenny was present.

On edge and highly agitated, *Angry* Kenny whispered, "Why are you running from me?"

Innocently sleeping in my bed, I had been running nowhere, but that didn't stop my arm from being practically ripped out of its socket as I was snatched out of my bed.

Quietly, at my bedroom door, I pled, "I'm not running from you. I'm here," to calm *Angry* Kenny's boiling temper to a low simmer. It was alarming how calm I stayed during *Angry's* escapades. It was alarming because this personality, the shifty one, wasn't the worst. This side of Kenny, I could handle.

Roughly guided down the hallway, I again stared at Tucker's closed bedroom door. A part of me would imagine the door opening, but the expression on my brother's face, the pain, the disgust, had me shutting my eyes. So, I was thankful he was sleeping, not witnessing my demise.

At school, I leaned my face to the cool locker as the hall lights bored down on my aching head. My tired eyes closed as I inhaled, searching for the strength to continue the masquerade. When I felt my friend join me, I slowly lifted my lids. Viola was leaning her head on a locker, facing me, concern plastered across her face. She whispered, "Talk to me."

My mouth opened...

I wanted to let her in. I wanted tough Viola to fight this battle for me because I was already too beat to do it myself, but Kenny came up behind me, his arm wrapping around my waist.

"You alright, darlin'?"

My mouth shut...

V's eyes watered, and she solemnly nodded. She whispered again, "I'm here."

I grabbed her hand while fighting my own tears. "I know."

That night, I officially met *Scared* Kenny...

Crying in the night had me opening my eyes. Kenny was on his knees, on the floor next to my bed, holding my hand as I slept. His head lay on my mattress. When I squeezed his hand, his head popped up. Kenny's green eyes were in a distraught state. I wiped at his tears. "What's wrong?"

Trying to catch his breath, he pulled my hand to his face and rubbed his cheeks against my skin. "I don't want to lose you again."

"Again?"

His exhales were incredibly labored. "Yes. It hurt so bad," he rubbed at his chest, "here." The way he pronounced hurt and here, he somehow sounded like a child.

This was the first night I led *him* to his room. This was also the night he never tried to touch me or kiss me. He only held me, tenderly—no romance or want in sight—in his bed, saying, "I'm so sorry. I didn't want to lose you."

Kenny seemed so young and innocent, so timid and afraid my heart bled for him and his unstable mind. My back to his chest, I gently caressed the arms around me attempting to soothe his broken heart. Clueless to what he was speaking about, I didn't know what else to do. "You won't lose me."

He cried, "I will fight harder this time, for you. I swear it. I will keep you safe."

My body demanded I sleep as I wondered what he needed to keep me safe from when *he* was the only one bringing me harm.

CHAPTER NINE

Mouthing off at a teacher won Kenny detention after school only a week after his suspension ended. In the hallway by our lockers, he was still so irate that my heart raced. I wasn't sure why—what my instinct of survival was reacting to—until he jerked my arm. That aggressive nature announced a game changer. Studying his eyes, I was mortified to see *Angry* Kenny present... while awake.

Still in his firm grasp, I leaned my upper body back. "K-Kenny?"

He followed my tilt and got in my face. "Did you hear me? You're to stay and wait for me."

After turning a hallway corner and reading the situation, Viola stomped toward us. "Kenny, release my girl. Not fucking kidding."

His hand let go, but his glare held me tight, paralyzing me.

Fearless, Viola stepped between us and got in my view. Her eyes flared. "You okay?"

"I-I... don't feel so good."

"Everything all right?" asked my brother as he appeared.

"No," answered V before giving him a scrutinized stare. "But you don't want to hear about it."

My brother rolled his eyes. "Not true! I just think you've been one-sided about Kenny and Lilah since you learned they're together."

Her face turned beet red. "Are you mental?"

Tuck's jaw dropped in dismay. "Like you?"

Viola was about to explode all over my brother, so I intervened. "Everything is fine. I just don't feel good."

Tucker put his arm around my shoulders. "You do look pale. Go home."

Kenny stepped forward. "I have detention. She's waitin' for me."

My brother playfully slapped his face. "Well then, it's your lucky day, whiny bastard. I'm staying after school to work with the counselor on my college submissions." He opened his palm. "Give me her keys." With a locked jaw, Kenny reached in his jean pocket and handed them over. I trembled as they were placed in my hand, against *Angry's* orders. Tuck then turned my body toward the office and gave a gentle shove. "Go get a pass. Get your ass home and into bed." I didn't dare look back. I didn't want to see the rage on Kenny's face, the worry on Viola's, or the smile on Tucker's. It was all too much. And I had just learned, daytime no longer meant I was safe from Kenny's deranged behavior. No, his personalities were finding their way... to the *light*, to me.

With a yellow slip from the office in hand, I frantically ran to my car. As soon as the engine was on, I threw my car into reverse and high tailed it out of the parking lot. When an alarm on my dashboard *dinged* that I was running low on fuel, I hit the steering wheel. "Nooooo...." I just wanted to escape, to anywhere.

After squealing my tires into the gas station, I jumped out of the car, rushing to the pump with my credit card. That's when I heard a bike's muffler roaring toward me. Artist pulled up right behind my car. His eyes were seriously reading me. So, my sleep-deprived mind reacted accordingly. I immediately scanned my surroundings, expecting to see Kenny catching me in the vicinity of Artist—his imagined Achilles Heel—and slipped back inside my car.

I tore out of the gas station and headed for the interstate. My state of mind was not able to comprehend that the open free road was too far, and with no fuel, I was screwed. Nope, with a motorcycle riding my ass, I pushed the pedal to the floor and raced down a country road to nowhere.

As my engine began to sputter, I started to cry and experienced more than one breakdown.

On the side of the road, with my car no longer running, Art knocked on my window. Trying to wipe away tears, I peered up at him. "Please go away. *Please*."

"Ain't happenin'. Unlock your door, baby."

I crumbled against my steering wheel, refusing.

Knock. Knock.

Not lifting my head, I shook my head. "No."

Crash!

I jumped with a yelp only to see Art's hand reaching into my car from the now open rear window. I screamed, "What are you doing?" His finger unlocked the driver's door. My hand flew to relock it but was outmatched with speed. The driver's door flew open.

Art squatted in the opening and smiled. "Hey, baby."

My jaw hung. "I need sane people."

"Then stop acting nuts."

"Fuck you."

"That chance has passed."

I shoved him.

As he plopped back on his ass, I slammed my door shut and locked it.

A tattooed hand reached back in and unlocked it.

And repeat.

Art squatted in front of me, grinning. "Hey, baby."

I couldn't help it. I laughed. "Hi."

He gestured around. "Off your medication, pretty girl?"

Sighing, because that laughter felt so good, I replied, "Something like that. Can ya hook me up with a refill?"

He stood and offered me a hand. "Why else would I be here?"

I blew out a breath and accepted the offer of friendship.

As we leaned back against my car, he didn't say anything. It was nice. I needed a moment of quiet to collect my unraveling sanity. After a bit, I chuckled. "Artist, I ran out of gas."

His arms were crossed over his chest. "Yeah, that tends to happen when you leave a gas station, minus the fuel."

On its own accord, my head found his shoulder. "I seem to have lost my back window, too."

His head leaned to mine. "I will get you another one."

After a moment of silence, he quietly said, "Tell me I was wrong."

Kenny.

I exhaled heavily. "You are literally the last person I can talk to about this."

He jolted. After another quiet moment, he asked, "Why?"

Pushing off the car, I faced him. My expression was deadpan as I told him, "Because you have a gun."

All color faded from his face. "Delilah, what's going on?"

My expression changed none. "Nothing. Not a damn thing."

By the time my brother and Kenny pulled into our driveway, Diesel and a couple biker buddies had my door in pieces and were replacing the glass. Kenny rushed to me. "You okay?"

Relieved sweet Kenny had returned, I hugged him. "Yes. Just ran out of gas."

Tucker smirked. "I usually need a window replacement, also, when that happens."

Diesel studied Kenny as he said, "My friend here," he pointed to a biker, "was lucky to have rolled up on her. She was so relieved she got out of the car and accidentally locked herself out." He shrugged. "Shit happens." Then his dark deep-set stare held me.

I looked away, ashamed he had to lie for me and ashamed I couldn't tell him why.

Not being able to comprehend what was happening, I sunk

deeper and deeper with Kenny. We both plummeted into his delu-sional states of mind. It wasn't hard to do since I had rapidly become so deprived of sleep that reaching out for help quickly seemed ludi-crous. I was so preoccupied being on a razor's edge because *Angry* Kenny, now present during the daytime hours, wanted to attack any male within a ten-mile radius of me, that confusion effortlessly consumed me even more.

That confusion was compounded with guilt when Kenny would have a good day and stay sweet, openhearted, a soul I adored. Those sincere days were what gave my heart the courage to forge ahead. They gave me the courage to hope this insanity would all soon end and pass undetected by others. The need to escape didn't return until my nights became pitifully tortuous.

"Did you hear that?" *Protective* Kenny loudly whispered.

"Hear what?" I nervously asked, listening for any unusual sounds. Kenny had me squatted in the corner of his dark bedroom, shielding me with his body, saying, "Jenny, don't move."

"J-Jenny?" I cautiously asked, realizing I was witnessing another paranoid version of Kenny.

"Shh, he will hear you."

Wondering who "he" was, I was oddly detached from my own reality and thankful for the rain pounding on our roof so my father and brother wouldn't wake to Kenny's hallucinations. Tears fell as I sunk even further, trying to understand Kenny's torture. "Who, Kenny? Who will hear us?"

I thought my run-in with Artist was merely a memory, but small towns talk...

In the kitchen, I fed my men—Dad, Tuck, and Kenny—ground chicken sandwiches. They sat around the island while I stood on the other side, loving the garlic bun wrapping my specialty patty covered in gouda cheese.

Wiping his mouth with a cloth napkin, my dad innocently asked, "Hey, Lilah. Bert at Gas n Chic said he saw you hauling ass out of there last week, with a bike hot on your tail. What was that about?"

I choked on my chicken burger. "Huh? That old coot is mistaken. Wasn't me." But the damage was done. Somehow, Kenny read between the lines and knew, beyond a shadow of a doubt, it had been Art chasing me.

That is how I met the *cruelest* side of Kenny. And he was staking his claim.

My fear of him would literally paralyze me. In my disabled state of mind, I found myself lying underneath Kenny, and I would stare at the ceiling, wondering how this was happening to me. Even though my body refused to move, my mind was still thankful to be clothed. Because of the way Kenny aggressively rubbed his body against mine, I knew he desired to be inside me, where no one had ever been.

His low voice rumbled against my neck, "You're so gorgeous, every part of you. I need you so fucking bad," as he sloppily licked me while his clothed erection gyrated against my pelvis.

This was when I truly understood what my brother had tried to protect me from. It was heartbreaking to hate my beauty in the same moment as I unwilling stirred Kenny into a frenzy. My outside appearance was the curse that I would detest...

Cruel Kenny's fingers dug into my hips as if barely controlling his urges. Swallowing my whimpers of pain, I was positive I would see bruises in the morning. But those markings wouldn't be permanent, not like Kenny yanking on me, wanting me to get on my hands and knees. The idea of him soon at my back made me feel even more vulnerable; possibly a victim of something I believed I would never overcome.

Desperately whispering as I was pulled up from the mattress, I begged, "Kenny, please. Stop. I don't want this."

He pulled my back up against his chest, his hands roughly groping my breasts. "Bend over and do what you're told." A nasty pinch on my nipple had me trying to swallow a yelp.

Pure self-preservation had me quickly pulling the nipple abusing hand to my mouth. My lips trembled to the point I barely had any control, but I managed to give that aggressive fist a kiss. I held his warm skin to my mouth as pleading tears rushed from my eyes. I whispered, "Please hear me, my Kenny."

Kenny stopped moving...

"Darlin'? You came to see me again?"

Sobbing, as quietly as possible, I peered over my shoulder.

A now tender hand grasped my cheek. "Baby? You come to see me again?"

So thankful that my *sweet* Kenny had returned to me, I found myself tilting my head back and kissing him frantically. "Yes, I came to see *you*, Kenny." I opened my mouth, begging for his kind affections. I was becoming desperate for a fear-free moment.

As concerned as he appeared, the young hormonally driven man in him couldn't find the strength to deny me. So, we had a beautiful, heartfelt, only the two of us, kiss.

Slowly, and so gently, he laid my body down, our lips still attached.

Breathless, he finally pulled his wet mouth from mine and whispered, "You're shaking."

Shaking from the trauma he had just caused me, I nodded. "For you."

It wasn't a lie.

How could I explain his insanity without crushing his heart? I couldn't, so I continued my unbalanced trend and said nothing more.

Sweet Kenny lay on his side and held me to him. My body would begin to relax as his torturous embrace once again became the warm safe place I craved. His voice was once again soothing to my broken heart... "I love you, Delilah."

A single tear sliding down my cheek was the only show of my inner battle scars.

I forced my voice not to tremble as I said, "I love you, too, Kenny.

Sleep. I wanted sleep. And that's what I was finally getting before

I felt heat at my core. My eyes quickly opened to see Kenny's face between my thighs, licking my panties, while staring at me. His eyes were full of evil lust.

Surprised I was allowed to move, I cautiously moved up the bed then crawled off the mattress, our eyes locked the whole time. My lungs panted as I backed toward the door. He watched me, licking his lips, and whispering, "I love little girl honey on my tongue."

I ran into my bathroom and threw up.

"Lilah?"

I flew back from the toilet, my back slamming against the wall.

My brother ran forward. "Jesus. You okay?"

Wiping my mouth, I exhaled a labored breath. "Yes. Sorry. I didn't know I had been followed."

He smirked. "Followed?"

"I mean, you know."

He wet a washcloth. "Got the flu?"

So exhausted, I shrugged.

"I'll stay with you tonight."

I gasped. "No. Umm, you may catch whatever I have."

My brother rolled his eyes. "You kidding? I've got the strongest immune system in Georgia."

Once he fell asleep in my bed, a garbage can and water bottles next to us, I slid out from under the pile of blankets he figured I needed and snuck to my closed door. As quietly as possible, I locked it, terrified Kenny would try to hurt Tuck. My brother was much larger and stronger than my abuser, but my abuser had me so mentally warped, I believed he was superhuman.

Backing away from the door, I muffled a whimper as my door-knob twisted then slightly rattled. Praying he wouldn't knock down the door, I kept retreating 'til I felt my safe bed at the back of my legs. My brother didn't even stir as I quietly slid back under the pile of covers.

That night of lunacy progressively rocketed to the deranged night

Cruel Kenny wanted revenge for allowing my brother to care for me, and demanded his own needs be met. "Touch it, Delilah."

My every panicked exhale rang in my ears. I had never seen a penis in the flesh, and I certainly didn't want to touch one without it being in the amorous settings I had envisioned because of my books. "Please, don't make me do this," I whispered in his bed, grabbing my nauseous stomach.

Lying on his back, Kenny appeared enamored as he continued watching his hand while stroking himself. "I visited your brother's room last night. It will be so easy to hide and slit his throat—"

My sudden crying stopped him. So, I begged, "Kenny. Don't say such things."

Ignoring my pleas, he moaned. "Like this. Delilah, touch me like this."

Watching beads of sweat gather on his bare chest, I was mortified when he suddenly grabbed my hand, demanding I take over his masturbation. Forcefully, he wrapped my palm around his enlarged erection, making my hand move in an upward and downward motion. I gasped and frantically attempted to be set free, but his hand, secure around mine, kept me trapped. The soft skin of his penis stretched and gave to the awful pressure he was enforcing. I feared he would be angry at the pain I was causing him, but then his eyelids slid shut. "Harder."

My mouth gaped open as I hissed my refusal.

Kenny's stomach muscles suddenly flexed, incredibly taut, as his upper body lurched, putting us face to face. He growled, "Want me to use your teeth?"

I could feel my face wince with dread. "No."

His fingers tightened on mine. The duress was so intense I expected to hear my bones crack, but the up and down motion started again, and Kenny slowly lay back, his eyes seductively rolling into his head. "So. Fucking. Good."

Unfamiliar white wetness spewed from the little opening on the head of his penis.

Every day and night, I was unknowingly losing another part of me...

Especially, one night in particular.

I was in my room, blow-drying my hair to get ready for a party that *Angry* Kenny insisted we attend. I wanted to stay home due to being depleted both emotionally and physically. No one else was home when Kenny came stampeding into my room in the midst of an uncontrollable rage. Immediately turning the blow dryer off to deal with the upcoming explosion, I gasped when hearing a Harley muffler fading away. Before I got to ask if someone had been there, Kenny pointed at my bookcase and screamed, "You always choose these books over me!"

There was no reasoning with the unreasonable, so I didn't even try and watched in horror as Kenny grabbed one of my most treasured books, *Romeo and Juliette*, from my richly stocked bookshelf and ripped pages from its binding. My fingers floated in the air, not daring to reach out, as I watched the innocent pages flutter to the ground.

He growled hatred and jealousy, "I'm not taking you fucking anywhere. You need to learn a lesson. You make me sick!" Kenny snatched my keys from my dresser and left me sitting with a blow dryer in my hand, completely dumbfounded to what I had done to deserve such cruelty.

Not knowing if Kenny would return before anyone got home, as soon as I heard my engine roar down our street, I quickly hid any other treasured books of mine as if Kenny had superpowers and could return without a sound and catch this defiant act. I did my best not to leave any detectable empty spots on my bookshelves to inform Kenny of my deceit. It's sad to say that I felt those wonderful books were worthy of protection but never imagined the same value in myself.

Crying, I sat on knees on my bedroom floor and woefully tried to piece my ripped *Romeo and Juliet* back together. But there wasn't enough tape in the world to glue me or my novel back to what we once were. Holding the broken pieces to my broken heart, I rocked myself for many minutes, searching for inner relief.

None came.

With my tattered mess clung to my chest, I ran down the stairs and out the door, only to remember my car was gone. Another stolen slice...

Knowing no one would hear me because my dad built our home on an isolated road with no neighbors, I was about to scream my frustrations 'til I heard that damn Harley muffler again. When I saw Art's headlight in the night, zooming down my road, I backtracked and ran inside the house.

A fist pounding on the front door, and his voice, "Delilah. I'm not playing with you!" had me running through the house and out the back door, into the yard for a quick exit.

To where? Only God knew.

A dark figure leaped over the fence, landing in front of me. "Where ya headed, babe?"

"Far away from you." I turned away, rushing back to my porch.

Heavy Harley boots stomped on the earth as he cut me off from my goal. "I see we're off our meds again?" He froze when he saw the tears dripping from my chin. His eyes widened as he stepped to me. Not asking what was wrong, his finger slowly touched the rim of the shredded book tightly in my arms. "This, uh, book has seen better days?"

Staring into electric blue eyes, the moon shining down on this beautiful man, I nodded, causing more drips from my chin.

The fingers left my book and gently rose and wiped more forming tears. As he smeared them against his other fingers, his jaw ticked, but he sounded kind. "Can I... hold you, baby?"

As if my last mental stitch had come undone, my mouth parted. I panted. I fought for my breath, my shoulders caving around *Romeo and Juliet*. My voice was full of the deepest desperation I'd ever known at that point in my life. "*Please.*"

I didn't let go of my book, and he didn't let go of me.

The silence was as comforting as the movement Art was creating. Ever so cautiously, ever so tenderly, he rocked me. Finally, I was finding a moment of solace. I melted to his offered friendship. I melted to the innocent affections I desperately needed, until his lips touched mine.

He whispered, "I'm sorry. You're just so beautiful, I needed to feel you."

My lips didn't respond, but my body did. It hardened, as did a piece of my soul.

Anger began to storm inside my heart. I was exhausted with my outer beauty. I was absolutely tired of my appearance causing changes in those around me. My voice was not gentle as I demanded, "Please leave. And please don't return."

I didn't physically smack him, but I sure did mentally. His hurt expression was evidence. He swallowed. "No. Delilah. Wait. I'm sorry."

Pulling from his embrace, I explained the honest truth. "I am too. For it all."

My brother found me sitting in the dark on our back porch swing, still clutching my damaged goods. He laid a blanket over my bare legs then sat in a chair. "Talk to your big brother... please?"

With emotional injuries dazing me, I was unaware of my brother's willingness to help me. I didn't know he sensed something was drastically wrong with me and that I could have successfully reached out to him and been protected from whatever else the *Kennys* had in store for me.

Now, as a grown woman, I still find it hard to speak of past terrors.

As an emotionally injured teenager? It felt impossible.

Sometimes 'telling' feels more humiliating than the actual crime committed against you. And that was only one layer of my issues. Unexplainable guilt and responsibility for failing Kenny and Art, for my brother's wellbeing, because of how he had sacrificed for me and my mother's dying plea, had me asking Tucker, "Are *you* happy? I make you happy, right?"

My brother answered wholeheartedly. "Very. You are my light, Lilah. You are my sun."

That means God is reaching you... I stared into the dark night. "I love you, Tucker."

"I love you, too."

"She would be proud, you know?"

Tucker's eyes immediately misted. "You think so?"

"Yes, my brother. You have grown to be a wise young man, and you're my best friend. I'm thankful for how you take such good care of me. I know our mother sees, Tuck. I know she sees. I hope she sees me, too."

Later that night, the house was dark and quiet, and we were all asleep when Kenny returned home. *Cruel* Kenny was drunk when he abducted me from my bedroom, and my situation elevated yet again. Standing in his dark bedroom, Kenny was belligerently kissing me and grinding into me. My lips and lower body felt bruised when he groaned, "I need to come, and you're gonna make it happen."

I only got to look to his locked bedroom door for a mere second before I suddenly found myself on my knees, facing his crotch. In horror, I watched as he unbuckled his jeans then yanked them down, along with his boxers. I quickly retreated, now being eye level with an erect naked penis, but *Cruel* Kenny grabbed a fistful of my hair and barbarically yanked my head back to him while bending over, bringing us face to face. He angrily whispered, "Now, I'm going to kiss you one more time before you put your mouth on my dick like I've taught you."

"T-Taught me?" I had never had oral sex with Kenny. I was clueless to his meaning.

And I never received an answer. He cruelly smashed his alcohol smelling lips to mine.

Before I could recover from the intrusion, two fingers invaded my mouth. "Have you let anyone else in this mouth I own?" They were forceful and salty, making my tongue want to hide, but that natural reaction was denied. "Suck." So, I sat back on my feet in effort of a retreat. Attempting to shake my head no, stars raced across my sight, stopping me. My hair was fisted so tightly, I was sure there would be blood soon. Fingers left my mouth while I gasped at the onslaught of pain.

I hadn't had the chance to even exhale before Kenny shoved his penis into my mouth. It was so skillfully fast I was sure he had done this before or had at least witnessed the mastery. My natural reaction was to close my mouth, but more stars threatened to blind me as my head was yanked back so far it rested on my own spine.

As if he knew this terribly uncomfortable position aligned me perfectly for him, Kenny stepped closer and forced his erection down my throat. I involuntarily gagged, and my stomach tried to purge, but there was no room for either. Shockingly, my jaw and throat opened wider as if trying to make room for air and vomit, in turn only giving more access to the abuser.

He sunk deeper 'til pubic hairs were against my mouth and nose, hot sweaty testicles against my chin. My watering eyes nor convulsions were of any concern as his eyes slowly slid shut. "*Yeeees.*"

As much as it hurt my head, I squirmed to break free of his hold because, not only was I being totally violated against my will, but I was seeing stars for another reason. I was out of air.

With me smacking and pushing against his thighs, Kenny opened his eyes and cheaply smiled down at me. "You keep beggin' for air and it's going to make me come..." He kept talking, but the ringing in my ears was becoming so intense, a true fight for survival had commenced.

Knowing I was seconds from passing out, I shoved against his muscular thighs as hard as I could. It only bought me a slight movement, just enough to cause the friction Kenny needed.

Condescendingly, he teased, "Fight me. That's right." His eyes rolled to the back of his head. "That's it," he sneered, right before warm jets of semen started to pulse down my throat. As if routine, he quickly pulled out, sure to leave a trail of his orgasm in my mouth. Not releasing my hair or allowing me to move, he continued to come on my face as I coughed and gasped for air.

My fingers gripped his jeans for so many reasons:

Silent pleas to set me free.

Silent please to come back to me and never let go.

And silent wishes to not walk away... before I killed him.

But I was too tired to voice anything, murder him, or hold on to him.

As if it was all just a joke, Kenny let go of my tender scalp then playfully pushed against my cheek. "Whiny bastard." My brother's words echoed in my mind as leftover adrenaline danced through my shaken body.

I realized the gruesome act was over when this wretched Kenny left me as if I were used goods not worth acknowledging. He fell back onto his bed and slipped into alcohol-induced unconsciousness. With the horrid night coming to an end, my body gave way and I fell to my side, disorientated and... lost.

I lay on his bedroom floor, white fluid dripping from my tainted, shocked lips.

Sadly, I thought of Bryce. I wondered if this was like what he went through with his uncle. And I wondered how he recovered. Viola had told me that, when memories were overtaking him, she had advised him to go back to the basics; just breathe. I had yet to have time to form a memory of the onslaught but was desperate for a cleansing breath.

Inhale... Exhale...

That's when I noticed my new rhythm wasn't my own at all. Kenny was breathing heavily and slowly in his sleep, and him being unconscious and calm lulled me into a motionless state and the moments needed to recollect my scattered thoughts. And the thoughts I found?

Inhale... Exhale...

I somehow, beyond all reason and all that had just transpired, believed it to be my fault. Listening to Kenny breathe so freely and peacefully reminded me of the sweet soul he usually was. Only when with me did he become unhinged and erratic beyond measure. So, my damaged thought process had me believing I had epically failed with keeping Kenny sane, that I had now created a monster. Those thoughts brought on an abundance of shame that diminished whatever chance I may have had left to speak out loud.

Even though I had no courage to ask for help, I still knew I could not handle one more terrorizing night. So, drowning in my own growing insanity, I decided I would find a way to prevent my own consciousness from holding me hostage. I had to find a way to break free... without ever telling a soul.

CHAPTER TEN

Every school has 'that kid' who can get you whatever you need in the drug industry, even in poor, country schools such as the one I was attending. I had texted my drug dealing acquaintance with a request, and they had responded: No prob

Now, I was sitting in class, staring at the clock, barely hearing Viola talking. "... Yep, Diesel and his buddies will be back tonight. Miss the boog Baboon."

Diesel and his buddies coming back tonight was code for: My brother, the president of a motorcycle gang, and his outlaw brothers are returning tonight from illegal activities.

I didn't care. I didn't care if Artist rode off the edge of the earth.

The clock's minute hand had just announced it was time for a change.

"I have to go to the bathroom."

Kenny stopped writing on his sheet of paper. "But class is almost over."

I didn't care about that either.

Kenny observed me as I stood. "Why do you need your purse?"

My jaw locked with the question. "On my period."

Viola peered up from her desk when overhearing my lie. She would know. Our cycles had aligned years ago.

I met up with the dealer by the girls' bathroom. Alone in the hallway, my connection said, "You're the last person I expected to hear from Sunday."

I sneered, "Life's full of surprises." I was shocked at my own tone.

He was, too. "Wow, you sound a bit like a scorned female."

Losing patience, I asked, "Got what I want or not?"

"Chill, pretty girl, I got what you need."

I wanted to punch him in the face for mentioning my beauty. Those looks had entranced and took possession of a friend I now perceived to be mostly evil and heinous.

A bottle of prescription pills was discretely dropped into my palm after I handed over a roll of hundred-dollar bills that I had stolen from my dad's safe. As I stuck the bottle in my purse, he inquired, "These are for recreational purposes, right?"

I suppose I appeared out of sorts, and that was a very appropriate question, but I had just been mouth-raped over the weekend and was in a foul mood, to say the least. With menace, I retorted, "You a dealer or a counselor?"

He took a step back, raising his hands as if he expected me to strike. "Whoa, easy. Just don't wanna be a part of your obituary."

Obituary... I walked away thinking about the carnage I would soon be leaving behind. Breaking my father and brother's hearts had me nervous, jumpy, completely on the verge of a hysterical breakdown, and the guilt was violent to my body, but the thought of facing *Cruel* Kenny again was even worse. Mentally overpowered by fear, my plan was, at that moment, concreted.

The bell rang out and kids started filling the halls. Approaching my circle of friends, Kenny's eyes changed in an instant as he stared over my shoulder. *Angry* Kenny growled to someone behind me, "What are you looking at?"

The drug-dealing teenager I'd just made my purchase from shrugged his shoulders and walked past us, foolishly grinning. I needed my secret to stay just that, a secret, so I stepped into Kenny's view and distracted his ever-changing temper with my lips.

He responded in an instant, his mouth opening, but his eyes stayed focused elsewhere. As he deepened the kiss, his fingers tangled in my hair. I winced, having no choice but to pull away for air. The pain on my tender scalp had stolen it.

Cole stepped toward us while reaching out for me. "Delilah, you okay?"

Kenny released me and was in Cole's face so fast I squeaked my reaction. Then I dove between them. "Kenny! No!" Cole was a life-long friend. I couldn't bear the thought of him being mistreated by a side of Kenny that I had provoked. "Please." I grabbed my boyfriend's face, crying. "Please, Kenny. I need you to see me."

His eyes blinked. "Darlin'?"

I sighed, collapsing into his chest. I gripped his T-shirt in my fists that were so tired of clinging to the insane roller coaster I had a permanent ticket to. "Kenny. Stay with me."

Again, those warm, familiar, safe arms blanketed me with uncon- ditional love. "I'm here. You're shaking again. Shh, baby. I'm here. Goin' nowhere."

I snuggled into his heat, trying to dismiss the chill in the air. "Walk me to class?"

During second period, I finally had my body's shakes to a minimum when Kenny walked into my classroom, *glaring* at me while handing my teacher a pass announcing the office had requested me. So unsure of what Kenny was up to, I watched him march out the door. My teacher called me up, handed me the yellow slip of paper, and sent me on my way.

Sensing impending danger, I collected my belongings and took a deep breath. After walking out the door, Kenny suddenly appeared and shoved me up against the wall. *Angry* Kenny was present and accounted for. In a heavy whisper, he growled, "Where are they?"

"W–what?"

He practically spat in my face as he shook me. "You think I wouldn't find out about the pills?" He showed me his bloody knuckles. "You think I wouldn't beat the truth out of him?"

I covered my gasp with my books and folders, hoping they could shield me. The dealer was bleeding somewhere, wishing I had never involved him.

Suddenly, Kenny's eyes softened and watered, and he sounded lost. "Delilah? You want to leave me?"

My books lowered, and my frazzled mind screamed more blame at me for hurting this fragile side of Kenny. I went to touch his face and comfort him, but before I could, Kenny tightly latched onto my wrist and growled, "Shit is changing, right now." Books and folders slipped from my grasp as he dragged me down a hallway. More pages fluttered to the ground.

With incredible rage brewing inside Kenny, I scoured the hallways but knew it was pointless. Not only were the hallways mostly empty, but what could I have said if I found someone willing to help? If I drew attention to myself, and someone was to stop Kenny, he would either hurt them or tell them about the illegal pills in my purse. It wasn't the chance of being suspended that kept me quiet; it was the awful thought of someone taking away my only escape. At that point, I had truly preferred to face Kenny's wrath one more time than live a lifetime remembering how tragic my life had become.

I suddenly spotted a little freshman that had a crush on Viola, gathering my belongings, and he looked as if he was contemplating interfering. As did he, I knew he was no match for Kenny on a normal day, so I shook my head no to him, knowing this outraged Kenny would devour him and possibly kill him.

I stayed quiet as Kenny shoved me into the passenger seat of my car, trying mentally to prepare myself for whatever was to come. It's beyond surprising how far I had fallen and how easily my self-preservation had faltered, allowing myself to be whisked away for an afternoon of hell. But, the knowledge that the next act of abuse would be my last gave me the strength to surrender.

Kenny punched my dashboard the entire drive home, shattering my radio and other knobs with his fist, while screaming, "Who do you think you are, leaving me?"

I tried to talk softly to calm him, while lying, "Kenny, I'm not."

"Never! Fucking never!" Kenny was unraveling.

I whispered another lie, "Never."

Racing down the road to my house at an incredible speed, Kenny grabbed the nape of my neck and slammed his lips to mine. He growled, "You are mine. Do you understand me?"

"Kenny! The road!"

He swerved back onto the pavement, not releasing my neck while moaning, "All of you. All of you is mine."

Knowing exactly what he was referring to jolted me out of the shock I had been willingly lingering in. Even though I had planned to take my life, I had somehow thought my body would be laid to rest... intact. It probably doesn't sound relevant, but somehow, it was to me. Every part of me had been abused by Kenny; my breasts, my body, my heart... even as deep as my soul. I wanted my virginity to be the one part of me that I could claim as my own.

Without another thought, I opened the door of the moving vehicle and tried to jump, but my fucking hair was tangled in his fucking hand. While pulling into my driveway, he violently shook that handful, shouting, "Where the fuck you think you're going?" forcing a scream from me.

Needing his hand to put the car in park gave me a momentary reprieve, freeing my hair. The door, still opened, was my moment to run. So, I did. I tore across my yard as fast as my trembling legs would carry me, but I was only a baby gazelle being hunted by a lion.

I was tackled to the ground in no time. Kenny's hips surged forward as a menacing voice reminded me of his desires. "All. Fucking. Mine." When he rolled me over to my back, I feared he was going to rape me right there, so I kicked at him wildly. Being completely outweighed and overpowered, he captured my wrists and overcame my legs with barely any effort. "Keep struggling. I like a little fight."

The last fight I delivered had him ejaculating down my throat. I couldn't go through that again. Hence the pills in my purse. So, when I managed to break one hand free, I smacked him across his face. I had never done such a thing before, to anyone, and feeling the sting of my skin slapping his felt unnatural, but he was terrifying me. I wanted to hit him into the awareness of how he was scaring and hurting me. I wanted a *human* reaction and an acknowledgment for the torment he was causing me. I searched his eyes, his expression, for any sign of compassion, but all I received was a... smile.

Complete. Horror.

Yes, that is all I felt as I realized I was utterly alone. There would be no Art to rescue me because I had sent him away. Viola had just reminded me her brother's club wouldn't be back until that evening.

Lost in thought, I was pulled from the ground and hoisted over Kenny's shoulder so easily that it was just another inclination of how outmatched I was. Before I knew what was happening, the madman was forcing me inside my own home.

As he ran me up the stairs, I attacked his back with all I had, punching and clawing. I didn't sense one ounce of the Kenny I loved being present, so I wasn't going down without a fight this time. I begged and pleaded for his humanity to hear me and stop the horror underway. "No! Kenny! Please, don't do this!"

On the second floor, he marched down the hallway, demanding, "And I want to fuck you on your bed. I'm to be the *only* one in your bed."

After being thrown onto my bed, I tried to control my bouncing to find my footing while watching Kenny kick off his sneakers and reach for his belt, but ended up falling off the mattress instead. Once on the floor, I scrambled to my hands and knees and frantically crawled toward my bedroom door. Kenny laughed, undressing while stalking me. In the corner of my eye, I saw his belt hit my carpet.

I scrambled faster, only to have my feet yanked out from under me. Kenny pulled. My stomach burned against the carpet as I was dragged backwards. As soon as my boots and socks were ripped from my feet, he let me go to continue undressing himself. I pulled my knees under me and race-crawled for an escape.

His jeans hit the floor.

No! From my knees, I gripped my doorknob and pulled myself up, but it was too late.

Naked arms that were connected to a naked body wrapped around my waist, and I was heading back to my bed. That warm, safe, familiar bed now resembled every woman's worst nightmare or worst fear. The closer I got, the more panic seared every part of my being.

Struggling and pleading, I was thrown to the mattress. Landing on my stomach, I immediately tried to push up to run, but Kenny's weight came crashing down, overpowering me. I screamed into my fluffy pillows that threatened to suffocate me as he used his left forearm to restrain my upper body while his free hand ripped down my jeans and panties. "Kenny! Noooo..."

My heart was thundering. I was sweating through my fight, but it was to no avail. I was eventually stripped. From the waist down. Against my will.

Kenny shifted his weight, one leg firmly over my thighs.

"Oww!" Teeth viciously sunk into my naked behind. Heated breaths left a trail down as his mouth traveled to the crack of my butt. To my horror, his tongue snuck in between my cheeks. I jerked. "Stop!" My other cheek was bitten. "Oww!" The awful burning had me suddenly remembering years ago, when Tuck and I saw teeth marks on Kenny's butt cheek at the lake. Kenny had been in the eighth grade then, but I could tell the scar had healed a long time before.

My body went eerily still as my mind raced, finally making connections to Kenny's horrendous actions. Was Kenny like Bryce? Abused? Was I now a slave of his past? Part of a hellacious cycle neither of us was to blame for?

Kenny having ghastly ghosts to hide was confirmed as his free hand began to pull my butt cheeks apart. He groaned, "Oh, little boy, I'm getting' in this ass today."

Little boy? No. No.

His elbow dug further into my upper back as his hand investigated; two fingers of his large hand held me open while his middle finger touched my hole.

With all I had, I tried to break free from under his weight but, again, was completely confined. My legs could barely move under his thick ones trapping me into submission. I could feel his erection against my thigh.

I begged, "Oh my God. Kenny, don't." The finger pressed harder into the tightness. "Please, stop!"

A forced finger slipped into my anus.

I seized, clenching my buttocks, but it was no use. The foreign sensation of discomfort, someone searching my tunnel, continued and even intensified into pain as he pushed deeper.

"Please, stop!" I cried.

His erection pushed against my leg. "I'm so ready to crawl in there." He pulled his finger out slightly only to add another one. They both drove back in. It stung and throbbed, compelling a grunt at the intrusion and more tears to escape me. That day, I cried out for two souls as this stranger at my backside happily sneered, "And don't bother tellin' your mama." His fingers were ruthless, diving in and retreating just enough to be able to penetrate me over and over. "She already knows this is what I truly want and said I could have it if I stayed with her."

As I was being impaled, so was my heart.

Kenny started gyrating his nakedness against my thigh more aggressively, at the same time forcing his fingers impossibly deeper, his knuckles digging into my skin. I attempted to arch my back, desperate to run from the pain, but was only punished more for my efforts. A third finger threatened entry, along with a warning that spooked me into silence. "It's either you or Jenny."

How, at that moment, I could even care for Kenny or the girl's wellbeing, whose name I had heard a few times, I can't explain, but I did. The love I had for *my* Kenny was true, so pure, that to know he had been violated in such a raw form, at such a young age, to protect another being, and that his mother had given permission for her own selfish reasons, made me lose faith. I did. At that very moment, I didn't believe in a god or *the* God, or any religion claiming a magical being oversaw our pain or answered our prayers. Nor was my mother somewhere bearing witness to all my unneeded sacrifices. That is when I knew, for sure, that I didn't want to be a part of this world any longer. It was simply too cruel of a place to coexist when no happily ever after I had read about would someday make this all worthwhile.

Once my final decision had been made, everything stopped for me. Time ceased to exist. I stopped struggling and thinking about how little Kenny's pleas must have been ignored, like how mine were being ignored. I stopped thinking about how his mother deserved to die for such a heinous crime. I stopped thinking about how Kenny and I both became victims because of her unforgivable decisions. I can't explain my thoughts or tragic actions. All I can say is that my hope and faith drifted away as if lost in the wind.

As if sensing all my fight was gone, Kenny slowly eased the pressure of his elbow in my back, removed his fingers, spread my legs, and knelt there.

There was no escaping the rape to come, nor was there pity for my succumbing to his desires. Completely aroused, he moaned, "Mmm, I need to get this little, dirty hole ready for me." I imagined the male voice that once said these words to my sweet Kenny. And, I now understood it hadn't been Kenny talking all the nights I was forced to hear him.

Kenny spitting is what pulled me from my thoughts. Wet fingers shoved saliva inside me before slipping out. Then two sets of fingers pulled my cheeks apart right before the wet tip of his penis began to prod my rear.

Traumatized into a numb sensation, I softly said, "Not there."

The cruel bastard chuckled. "It's a little late for modesty."

"No," I weakly told him. "Please, not there. I'll stop fighting."

He rubbed the full length of his penis at the entrance, eerily saying, "You already have."

My eyes closed in shame. I had. I had lost all my will. I had lost everything but the desire for it all to be over with... *permanently*.

Not gently, a dirty finger slid inside my vagina. The first time ever to be touched...

"Here?" he hungrily groaned.

The female part of me was made for sex, unlike my behind, so I figured it was the best place to be assaulted. It was the lesser of the two evils during my last hour on this earth. I slowly nodded and surrendered to the conditions I felt I could not change, the conditions I no longer had the energy to alter.

This may make sense to some hearing my story, but I felt as though life had sucked the *life* out of me.

Lost. I was utterly, hopelessly lost.

Kenny rolled my lifeless body, licking my leg as it passed in front of him.

Once on my back, with him again between my thighs, I was in the missionary position I had asked for. Taking his time, Kenny finished undressing me, removing my shirt and bra. My arms were like rubber, landing where he dropped them. My exposed breasts were his to touch, grope, and pinch. Every tainted caress was with intentional malice.

He grinned as he spread my uncaring legs apart, his eyes locked onto my invaded privacy. I let my head fall to the side so I didn't have to witness the spit dripping from his lips onto my opening. And I did my best to ignore the inspecting he did at my entrance, pulling my lips apart as if coldly studying the origin of my pubic area.

Unlike how he attempted to prepare my rear, I lay on my back and stared at the ceiling while Kenny tried to force his penis inside my virginal territory. He poked and prodded with much frustration. "Damn it, Kenny, stop crying!"

Kenny was now his own rapist.

I wasn't crying, so I knew he was no longer seeing me but the scared, little child that had been forced to endure the desires of an extremely demented man. My battered body was only mirroring the little boy his abuser was sickly craving.

Between my legs, Kenny's hips forged forward over and over until my opening finally gave. I audibly gasped as tissue ripped with the violence.

Suddenly, sweaty lips were on mine. "Shh, every time will get easier, Kenny."

As my body rocked with his every punishing thrust, I wondered how many times *Sweet* Kenny had to experience such horror.

The only peace I had, aside from my numb state of mind I was in, was the fact that there would never be another time for me, or for Kenny. Kenny was no longer a little child or easy prey, and I was to swallow every pill in the bottle in my purse. I was going to help say goodbye for me and the traumatized little boy who had no one to protect him.

Knowing I was heading into the unknown when given the opportunity, I hoped to someday see the real Kenny again, wherever broken souls went to rest.

As Kenny grunted and sexually abused my body, I hoped I was to be his only victim.

Wet warmth filled my channel that I was sure would never experience semen again.

Kenny rolled off my sore, tender body. "You need a shower." His voice was cold, unattached to the event we'd just experienced, not accountable to the fact that he was the one who had made me dirty.

I don't even remember starting the water or getting into the shower, only standing in the steam as I tried to clear the traumatic fog of shock circling my mind, my shaking body. The hot water trickling down my back was trying to soothe me, or maybe I was hoping it could so I could find the strength to scrub away the shame, the guilt, and the confusion.

When I pulled my hand from soaping between my legs because the bubbles were stinging me, I was shocked to see blood. My virginity was dripping from my fingers, washing down the drain... *I've been raped. I tried to protect him and paid tremendously for it.*

Without warning, my legs gave out from underneath me, and I crumbled to the shower's floor. Treacherous tears began to fall at a thunderous rate. Shock was violently being ripped away as reality repeatedly smacked me across my face. It was like trying to breathe while a hose was being sprayed directly into my mouth. Only drowning gasps escaped me.

A knock on my bathroom door startled me. "Darlin'?"

My Kenny had finally returned. He was far too late to save me, but he had returned nonetheless. A part of me, clothed or not, wanted to run to him and be held as I cried about the tragedy he had just inflicted, scarred me with. The other part of me wanted him to bear witness to every pill I swallowed and watch me slowly pass away, knowing he'd indirectly caused my death.

"Kenny?" I timidly called out.

"Yeah, baby. You need me to come in there?"

His caring words reminded me that the true part of him was innocent of all this, and I wished that part of Kenny no harm. I somehow mustered up courage, inhaled, and continued to keep my secret of his insanity so that he would never connect my suicide with his actions.

I told him, "No. No." I didn't want him to see the aftermath he'd unknowingly caused. "I'm fine. *You* okay?"

"Uh, yeah, I'm good, but... I–I don't remember..." He stopped talking.

I knew he didn't understand his lapse of lost memory, so I lied and gave him a false memory to use. "Thank you for bringing me home when I asked you to, Kenny." I shook violently in the tub as I explained, "I, uh, got cramps, ya know?"

After a pause, he answered, "Uh, anytime, darlin'. I'll be downstairs."

I whispered to myself, "I can't help you any longer, my dear friend. I must go." But, the thought of how the sweet Kenny would react to my death had me wanting to do whatever I could for him, one last time. So, once dressed, I rushed to my laptop and frantically searched the internet for *split personalities*. This led me to *multiple personality disorder*, now referred to as *dissociative identity disorder*. An article explained how this disorder was thought to be the result of a severe trauma during childhood and, or repetitive, extreme abuse. I knew firsthand how horrific his past had been.

I knew I was finding answers when the article revealed that *dissociative identity disorder* was characterized by the presence of two or more distinct or split personalities. As the article further explained that there was more than one kind of dissociative disorder, I came across *dissociative amnesia*. It was as if they were speaking directly about Kenny.

So far, the disorders were described to have disruptions or breakdowns of memory, consciousness, and awareness. But *dissociative amnesia* was described to have a degree of memory loss that went beyond normal forgetfulness. Someone with this disorder could have a loss of time and show distinct personalities or split identities that he or she developed to cope with whatever traumatic event or events they are or were experiencing.

The article said that when the one with the disorder came across a 'trigger' and showed their spilt-personality, that it was called *switching*. I thought of how so many of our events happened at night. Storms definitely triggered a memory and caused Kenny to want to hide me.

These dissociated states were described to be not fully mature personalities but disjointed senses of identities. If Kenny had this, his personalities would all identify with one name, yet not know each other existed. Other symptoms were night terrors, hallucinations... all of which described Kenny.

Still sitting at my desk when Kenny came back into my bedroom, I jolted and had to figure out whom I was dealing with. As soon as he smiled, I knew *my* Kenny was present. His eyes were clear, green, coherent, and kind.

It was beyond baffling to be terrified by one I truly treasured.

My survival instincts screamed to run while my heartstrings, which were irrevocably attached to Kenny, demanded I stay and love, unconditionally.

One side of my internal war won. I patted a chair, gesturing for him.

His smile grew. "Watcha doing, darlin'?"

My heart truly broke with what I was about to do, but I tried to ease my guilt with assisting him to find help. I told him, "I'm doing some research. Wanna join me?"

"Sure." He sat next to me. "Cramps better?"

I tenderly touched his face, understanding him so much more now. I slowly kissed his lips that had just been so cruel to me, silently telling him goodbye, and realized how much I would miss this beautiful Kenny.

He patted his chest. "You're right here, Delilah."

My eyes welled. "I know."

Innocently, his head tilted. "Why are you cryin'?"

"I need to talk to you."

Kenny's brows crunched together but he nodded.

"You know how sometimes you experience, uh, time loss?"

He suddenly became reserved, and I prayed Kenny wouldn't change or *switch*. He asked, "How do you know about that?"

I tried to stay calm and non-threatening, to not trigger him. It wasn't hard because I actually did feel calm. Knowing it was all almost over made every moment seem surreal. I later learned that suicide victims sometimes have the happiest moments right before their death because the anguish is almost over. Even though I was still on earth, I was already feeling free.

Softly shrugging my shoulders, I said, "You sometimes don't remember us doing things. You sometimes claim to have been sleeping."

He paled. "What do you mean?"

"Well, I wasn't sure, but," I pointed to the screen on my laptop, "I think I'm understanding more now." I faced him again, taking his hands into mine to show support. "See, when you think you are sleeping or simply forgetting—" I struggled with how to word it, then finally explained, "There's another side of Kenny that comes forward."

Kenny shook his head in denial.

"It's happened to others, too."

"Others? What are you trying to say?"

"It's okay, Kenny. Look at me and remember who I am to you. How much I love and adore you." He softened, inhaled deeply, then nodded. "Thank you," I told him sincerely.

"I love you, Delilah."

My eyes welled even more because I believed him and because I was throbbing between my thighs. "I know you do."

Just then, I heard my front door open. "Delilah! Where are you?" Viola was screaming for me so loud that Kenny and I ran to the hallway as she came running up the stairs. She took one look at me and froze. I don't know what I looked like, but she looked to Kenny and said, "What did you do to my friend, you bastard?"

Kenny looked appalled and turned to me. "Did I hurt you?"

V was baffled. "What? Wait, why wouldn't you know?"

Kenny pointed to me. "She thinks... she says... I don't remember. Oh, Jesus." Then he asked, "Delilah? Tell me I haven't hurt you."

I grabbed his hand. "Shh, I'm okay. Look into my eyes again, Kenny. Remember who I am." He looked at me like a scared puppy but nodded.

Viola went pale. "Pretty D, why do I feel every little hair on my arms standing?"

Calmly, I asked them both to follow me to my desk. I sat down and explained to V about Kenny's memory lapses. Then I said, "Kenny, you've been having what seems to me as *split personalities*. I looked it up online, and think I may have found what we're experiencing."

"We?" Kenny, standing next to me, asked as if feeling ill.

"Yes. I say *we* because I'm with you all the time. Do you understand?"

Standing behind my chair, Viola covered her mouth to muffle her gasp as her witty brain started putting puzzle pieces together. Kenny looked somewhat horrified but, again, nodded. I explained what I had read and then pointed back to my laptop. "Kenny, it reads here that a switch can happen within seconds, and it explains your hallucinations."

Kenny looked to be struggling to swallow. "I hallucinate?"

"Yes, especially during storms."

Viola read the article from over my shoulder. "While there's no cure for dissociative identity disorder, long-term treatment can be helpful if the patient stays committed. Effective treatment includes talk therapy or psychotherapy, hypnotherapy." Viola surprised me when she gazed to Kenny and said, "We can get you help." She sounded warm and caring, sincerely worried for his wellbeing. My eyes watered, knowing how much I was going to miss her, too.

As Kenny nervously paced in my room, I swiveled my chair to study him. He appeared on edge and agitated, confused and completely overwhelmed. Holding the sides of his head as if it were about to explode into thousands of pieces, Kenny rested his back up against my bedroom wall. He stared at me, deep in thought. I knew *my* Kenny was still present; his tortured eyes told me so.

Eventually, he slowly slid to the floor, watching me the whole time. After a few moments of Kenny sitting motionless—I believe in shock—he asked, "How many do I have?"

"How many what?" I gently asked.

Sounding beaten and defeated, Kenny asked, "How many personalities do I have?"

I prayed to find the gentlest way to deliver his truth. "Well, you have this one." I timidly smiled. "I call you my *sweet* Kenny. Uh, then you have a very *scared* one. He cries and is usually extremely confused with who he is." Viola stared at me with such an expression, as if she knew this story was only going to get worse. I inhaled a shaky breath. "Then there is a *protective* one. He–He hides me, shelters me, and... calls me Jenny."

Kenny went positively ghost white...

Then his eyes went cold. His voice became the one I hated most. "Why are you talking about her, you bitch?"

My shoulders slumped. I had planned to be far from this world before *Cruel* Kenny ever arrived again. But since I was putting someone else's needs before my own, I now faced the possibility of more relentless torture.

Viola cautiously stepped to my side, looking horrified and completely aware that she was witnessing a switch. "Who's this one, Delilah?"

"My nightmare," I whispered, feeling as if he was stealing my voice all over again.

V's shaky hand rested on my shoulder. I had never had anyone with me when Kenny's switches would happen, or at least never anyone comprehending what they were witnessing. It was nice to not be alone for a change. That moment deposited a seed that would eventually take root like Viola did. She took root by my side....

I raised my shaky hands to try to show no protest to the rapist before me, trying not to aggravate him, and explained, "I have nothing bad to say about her. I don't even know who she is. It's just a name you have called me."

He demanded, "Whores are not in the same league as my Jenny, so you must be wrong." Then he grinned at Viola while lazily gesturing to me. "Did she tell you? How I stuck it to her? I didn't even mind the blood she got all over my dick."

Viola slowly began shaking, muttering, "*No*," as his words spoke of the secret I had no intention of ever sharing.

As if my body no longer contained bones, I slithered out of my chair and crumbled to a heaping mess on the floor. All of it, everything that had happened to me slammed into my chest and robbed me of air. I curled up on my carpet in a fetal position, completely shattered from all the abuse I had endured for so many nights, leading up to this epically, miserable day.

Viola fell to her knees, pulled me into her lap, and held me while screaming to Kenny, "You fucking bastard! I will fucking kill you with my bare hands!"

"Darlin'? Jesus, Delilah." *My* Kenny had already returned and was scrambling toward me on his hands and knees. "What's wrong?"

"Get away from her!"

Viola's bloodcurdling demand had Kenny freezing on his knees. His mouth gaped. "Viola. What happened? Did I hurt her?"

"You fucking raped her!"

Kenny fell back onto his rear, totally stunned. He mumbled and stuttered, "No... N–No... no..."

Sobbing harder than I ever had before, I reached my hand out for my *sweet* Kenny. He was innocent. *He* wasn't guilty of this crime. I needed him to know that I loved him and would never blame him for his erratic, out of control, split personalities, but he looked into my eyes... and saw his truth. He had raped me.

Kenny tilted his head back and *screamed* to my bedroom ceiling, "Nooooooo!"

Viola, hysterically crying, held my fractured soul in her arms as Kenny wailed to the heavens I no longer believed in.

Refusing to let me go, V pulled her cell from her pocket. Snot running from her nose, she cried out, "I need you, Tucker," as she attempted to dial.

I knew, just knew, the mere mention of my brother's name would trigger more horror.

Cruel Kenny shot forward and was in Viola's face in an instant. "Don't you mean *Art,* you bitch?" She stopped working her fingers, and all color left Viola's face as more dots were connected. He laughed, an inch for her gaping mouth. "That fucker being near my girl made for interesting nights. I'd get *real* pissed. And guess who caused them?"

Viola's head kept jerking, as if trying to shake her head no, but too paralyzed with guilt.

Kenny's lips made a mocking "oh" shape before he laughed even louder. "But don't you worry. Your bitchy ways were *all* worth it when Pretty D stroked my dick. She even got to choke on it." His chuckle echoed in my pounding ears. "Should've seen it, *V*, her watering doe brown and golden eyes, pleading for air," his voice lowered with hunger, "as I came down her throat."

V's cell slipped from unmoving fingers.

Kenny picked it up. "Wanna call your biker buddy now?" His evil smile vanished. "Didn't think so, but just in case you get any wild hairs up your snotty ass—" Kenny, with full strength, threw her cell against the wall behind him.

Viola and I watched it shatter, along with our hopes of ever having a normal life again.

Then we both watched as Kenny gawked at me as if finally noticing I was there. "Darlin'?" He reached out to touch me, but V hovered her body over mine as we both cowered away. Kenny stopped, observing us. "Oh, God. What did I do now?" He shrunk away from us and started to cry, his voice changing once again. "Is my mommy here?"

Viola busted into tears and started rocking me in her lap. "This is not fucking happening."

I guess it was all too much for Kenny. This poor young man kept switching between personalities, trying to cope with whatever was eating him alive inside his treacherous madness. Suddenly, *another* switch was brought about. "*Delilah?*" Tears fell from those green eyes, and I knew who was now with me. "Who am I, Delilah? I'm so confused."

Tears streamed from my exhausted eyes, and with a broken heart, I weakly cried, "You are Kenny. You are my dear, dear friend, Kenny."

Viola squeezed me tighter. "Oh, Jesus. Oh, Jesus. Please, help us."

When *Scared* Kenny got up and started leaving my room, I tried to get up and follow. That lost Kenny needed guidance and structure to properly function. He needed me. But Viola refused to release me, crying, "What have I done? Delilah, I'm so sorry..."

"Kenny?" my brother's voice echoed from downstairs.

That had her going absolutely motionless. She whispered, "This will kill your brother."

As I heard my brother follow Kenny outside, I knew *Scared* Kenny wouldn't even remember anything; he wouldn't tell Tucker about the rape. So, I raced to sit up and face Viola. "Then don't tell. Ever."

Her eyes slammed shut. "I can't lie to him."

Shaking her shoulders to wake her from the delusion, I asked, "Do you want to visit the man you love in prison."

"W-What? N-No!"

Snot was leaking from my nose. "You probably know my brother better than I do, so tell me this. What will he do when he finds out what Kenny has done?"

Her mouth opened. It closed. It opened again. "Jesus, Delilah. You—You have been violated. How can I say nothing?"

"Kenny is sick. You saw it firsthand. I don't want him in prison either. We can get him help. Please, *please*, V. I am *begging* you to save my family from a horrible future. You know how hard it is to lose a mom. Don't make me lose my brother, too. V, please."

It was unbelievably unfair to ask her to carry this burden, but my dear friend finally started rocking me again, wiping her uncontrollable tears. "Okay, baby. Okay. To the grave. I'll take it to the grave."

In her lap, I cried, "I need you, V." Viola was taking pressure from my shoulders, and because of that, I melted to her. She was a wonderful relief. The rescuer of my lonely prison.

Viola kept rocking me, trying to soothe me. "I will protect you.

I'm here, Delilah, you beautiful, naïve creature. Oh, God, I'm partly to blame."

Just as I was ready to explain that none of this was her fault, my front door opened, and I froze. V suddenly sat me up and grabbed my chin. "I need to buy you time. Wash your face while I distract your brother." Viola got up from the floor then helped me to my feet. Our weak, shocked legs stumbled a little, but she kept her promise and went to buy me some time. I heard her whisper to my brother, "I'm sorry I yelled at you."

I splashed water on my face, trying to pull myself together. After I dried the water with a hand towel, I looked in the mirror and took a deep breath.

When I walked back into my room, I saw Viola was sitting at my laptop. She looked so pale that I asked, "What is it?"

Haunted, terrified eyes met mine. "I just found... Jenny."

CHAPTER ELEVEN

The streetlamp was the only light on this dark night, and it shined through my motorcycle figurine that Diesel had given me for my Sweet Sixteenth birthday. When Kenny left my house, he had taken it from my rearview mirror and handed it to my brother who was trying to convince him to stay home.

But Kenny left.

Kenny epically altered my world several times that day.

Viola, Tucker, and I stared at the glass motorcycle as if needing our hero to hear our silent plea. Diesel saved our worlds once by not taking Viola from us. I think we were praying he could save us once again.

As I heard a real-life motorcycle race down my road, I knew Diesel's gang was back in town and searching for his sister who wasn't answering her broken cell phone. And, I knew it wouldn't be long before her brother was notified.

Tucker didn't notice, nor did V and I tell him of the shadow in the hallway, gun drawn. We knew we were acting far from our norm. But I didn't want to speak to the *biker* brother in the gang. We wanted *V*'s brother. I think that was understood. The shadow tapped onto his cell.

Diesel's crew cab truck roared up my driveway.

None of us moved, including the shadow guarding us.

Diesel stormed up the stairs.

We still didn't move.

After I heard a pat on the back, releasing our silent guard, Diesel cautiously walked into my dark room. When we didn't acknowledge him, he flicked on the light and inquired, "What the fuck is going on?"

As if a zombie, Viola stared at her brother. "We don't know where he went."

"Does it matter?"

She nodded as her eyes closed. "It does. I'll explain later. But it does."

"Shit," he grumbled before texting someone.

Diesel drove his truck with three silent, lost kids staring out the windows, looking for our missing friend. It wasn't 'til I heard him on the phone, sounding highly agitated while giving out instructions to leave, and that he was calling 911, that I finally started coming out of my daze.

His engine picked up speed.

My body tensed.

And the fire shining through the night and against his windshield burned a hole through my soul.

The huge oak tree was now irreversibly a part of the car wrapped around its core; my car.

Diesel's truck doors opened...

My vision swam with flames as I set my feet on the ground that now trembled like my heart. The earth felt unsteady, as did every step while my mind raced to catch up to what I was seeing. Burnt leaves fluttered to the ground after the searing heat damaged them beyond repair. Reaching out to the ravished vehicle, one of those leaves fell into my palm. Numb, so incredibly numb, my other finger tried to caress it, but... it disintegrated against my skin.

It was like a symbol of what my touch could do...

Burn you alive.

Slowly, my sight rose back to the flames...

The awareness that Kenny was now a ball of fire crashed into my reality with a violence that not even the devil himself would dare challenge.

As screams sliced my throat and sanity, Diesel caught my melting body.

His mother wanted his ashes.

Kenny was beyond recognizable after the fire, so my father had what was left of the young man he considered a son cremated. Due to the apparent speed with which Kenny had hit the tree, no skid marks, there was an autopsy to see if alcohol was the cause.

It wasn't.

It was an overdose of sleeping pills.

I killed Kenny.

My pills were in my purse. My purse was in my car. My car was...

I killed Kenny.

The guilt that my weakness brought on Kenny's death made living excruciating and positively unbearable. I now wanted death *even more,* but my father and brother were so mortified by the news that Kenny had possibly taken his own life, that I knew my own escape, my own serenity, had just been ripped away from me. If I followed suit with Kenny, my death would altogether destroy my brother and father.

I knew I had to stay and face life. And. That. Pissed. Me. Off.

We had a service that Kenny's mother was too high to attend, and I numbly shuffled through it myself. After what I had learned about her decisions, and what we learned about Jenny, I didn't think Kenny's mother deserved to grieve or have what was left of him.

Still in black clothes, I sat on Diesel's couch, huddling over Kenny's urn in my lap. Viola sat at my side, rubbing my back. Cole and Hu, being so supportive, had taken Tucker home. I had just upset my brother because I wouldn't let him into my world. But, how could I? I was no longer able to keep my head above water. I was drowning in my own storm. And, like a tidal wave, everything in my path was destroyed into smithereens. Yet, the massive amount of water was helpless against the fire in our hearts. Hence the burnt young man in my arms.

Moans escaped me as I rocked harder, pain overtaking me from the inside out.

Viola laid her upper body over my back and cried with me.

From her den's arched opening that led into the kitchen, a very similar layout as my own home, Diesel stood, flanked by bikers. As angry as my own brother, he growled, "Sis, I'm done with this silence. What the fuck happened?"

Her head lifted from my back. "Leave it be."

"Leave it be? Did you just fucking say that to me?"

"Diesel, please—"

"Look at her!" roared her brother, causing me to flinch. "I know you've said Kenny was with this-this *disorder* or some shit, but you won't tell me fuck about what he did!"

"Diesel! Let it rest."

"I need revenge, V. I need to know who to go after."

"It's over now."

"It's over only when I say."

Her weight thickened on my back. "I don't need you in Prez mode right now."

"Too late. You called—"

Viola never gave him a chance to finish a sentence that would've changed everything. Instead, she *screamed*, "I gave my word! I gave my fucking word!"

At the time, I didn't know how monumental those four words were in the biker world, but they are huge. They are as deep as you can go when material things hold no value, but your promise is embedded into your essence.

Diesel's leather boots creaked as his weight shifted. He finally said, "Never would I ask for you to betray such a trust, but don't ask me not to fight for this baby girl." His voice lowered as he quietly told someone, "Bring him in."

When Viola stilled, I knew something was wrong. She leaned to me and whispered, "Breathe for me. Keeping breathing."

Diesel's door opened and more leather boots shuffled.

Someone knelt in front of me. I stilled, knowing exactly who it was.

After moments of silence, I whispered, "Everything hurts."

He exhaled. "Life can be shitty like that."

My head rested on the urn as I quietly asked, "More artistic words?"

"Art doesn't have to be beautiful to be meaningful."

Tears slid down the side of the urn. "Art?"

"Yeah, babe."

My throat felt raw. "She wants his ashes."

"What do *you* want?"

"For the funeral home to not make me hand him over." My dad paid for the funeral but, legally, Kenny's mom still had rights over his remains. She never fought my dad when he asked to have him move in with us, so my dad never legally adopted him. I swallowed. "For Ke —" I couldn't voice his name. "For him to have freedom."

Artist sounded so timid, as if afraid of the answer. "Does he deserve freedom, baby?"

My eyes finally lifted to see the man in front of me. My whisper was full of pain... and truth. "More than I do."

Art's eyes widened as he leaned back slightly. His mouth opened but no words formed.

Diesel wiped his palm down his face. "You sound like you believe that."

I finally looked at him. "I'm ashamed. Diesel, I should have asked for help long ago." I tried to get air in my lungs. "It could have prevented—" My eyes closed. "It doesn't matter now." I reopened my eyes and said, "But, I am reaching out to you now."

Diesel grabbed his chest as his shoulders sunk. "Name it."

I wiped tears, but more kept falling, and my voice broke. "Don't let her have him."

His mouth gaped.

I begged. "Let me give him some peace, Diesel. Let me do anything I can... to help him, one last time. He deserves it. I swear he deserves it."

Diesel swallowed. "Okay, baby. I'll help you, help him." He walked to his den's extensive bookshelf and grabbed a lidded vase. "That high bitch won't know ashes from a donkey's ass." He handed Art the vase. "Transfer the ashes into this and replace them with other ashes." Diesel gently touched my chin. "Give her the urn, while you give freedom to Kenny."

It was two a.m. by the time Viola and I had changed our clothes and made our way to my backyard. I was surprised when my brother approached. Our friends were gone; I thought he would be sleeping like my dad. Dad was drained. I think he was blaming himself, too.

Solemnly, Tucker asked, "What are you two doing?"

Viola and I stood before my dad's fire pit, burning papers. I watched the flames sparkling in the night, feeling numb, and answered accordingly. "Nothing."

Growing even more frustrated with V and myself, Tucker went back inside.

Art stepped out from the shadows. "He's trying."

Viola covered her mouth, nodding in a pain I couldn't understand at the time. To leave your other half out of life-altering events in your life is torture. I asked so much of her, when what she wanted most was the young man who was begging her to let him in.

Staring into the flames that mimicked my life, being burned alive, I answered, "Sometimes, the lie is better than the truth."

"So, shutting him out is not what you want?"

My hand crawled up my body and clutched my chest. "I would literally do anything for him." A cry escaped Viola before she gained control again. Artist stared at me with a haunted expression as he slowly backed away into the shadows again. At the time, I believed he wasn't strong enough for the truth either.

No more words were spoken as we filled Kenny's urn with fake ashes; Kenny's true ashes were in Diesel's vase in my room. The next day, I gave Kenny's mother what she believed to be the remains of her son. Had I had a weapon in my hand, I most likely would have used it against her. I was becoming bitter, cold...

On the back of Art's bike, V on the back of her brother's, they drove us to the river. The open land at the water's edge was where many teenage parties took place, but tonight it was quiet. Art and Diesel stayed back to give us the time for a much-needed goodbye.

Tears rolled down Viola's cheeks as she watched me pour Kenny's true ashes into the beautiful, flowing water. My face was dry as my fingers skimmed the cool water that was carrying him away. I whispered, "Be free, my friend. My dear, dear friend Kenny."

She choked on her tears. "You were never attracted to him. You never saw him as a boyfriend, did you?"

"No," I sadly admitted.

Viola fell to her knees. "Sweet Jesus, help me."

Diesel and Art rushed forward.

I knew what she was thinking. I was raped... by a man I loved like a brother.

Viola accepted the comfort offered by her brother. I denied Art's. The next time I was to return to that river, I would cling to the only young man who could reach me. And I would beg him to steal me from the ungodly agony still robbing my life.

He would. He did. With a kiss.

After witnessing Kenny's ashes float away, I cried myself to sleep that night, jealous that Kenny was set free while I was stuck with what remained: reality and recovery. None of what I wanted. I felt cheated that he got the outcome I had planned for myself. I guess a part of his insanity had fused with the fibers that made me who I had become and refused to let me go.

Confusion and heartache had time blurring for us all. Our whole group of friends had been dragged into the darkness with Tuck, V, and I. Even though they weren't present for the abuse I'd endured, or aware of it like Viola was, they all seemed to sense something had transpired. School as a whole recovered, but not Kenny's closest. We were all tainted with ghosts. Laughter ceased and reminders remained. Our lunch table was silent, every day. Even the sight of something as simple as carrots was complicated and a burden.

Before I knew it, the school year ended, and the time had come where my brother was to leave us behind for college. I still wasn't letting Tuck in on my secrets, but I didn't want him absent either. But the chance to build new memories called at his soul like a Siren offering pleasures to distract his broken heart. He followed that song... while the rest of us were trapped, now feeling abandoned. What I hadn't realized at the time was, I had already abandoned him. He suffered deeply for me shutting him out. The same with his love, Viola. We two girls were his world, and we let him drift in our orbit, confused why he wanted to feel grounded again.

The sight of Tuck's packed suitcases being loaded into his car was throwing Viola and I off the cliff we had been dangling on. Losing two sons within months was too much for Dad. He was at work while Viola and I begged Tucker to not leave early for college. But our pleas weren't enough to keep him from running.

Even after an hour of Tuck being gone, I still sat in the yard, staring at the haunted road that swallowed my brother's car. With dried tears staining her face, V sat on the steps, appearing numb and in shock. Neither of us moved as Cole pulled up in his old white dually. Assessing the wreckage my brother had left behind, he slowly got out of his truck.

With his thick country accent, he quietly told Viola, "Take an afternoon off. You look beat."

Needing no convincing, V wearily nodded then got into her car without a word.

Cole crossed my yard and stood in front of me, purposely blocking my view. A cowboy hat shadow blanketed me from the sun. His voice didn't have an ounce of the life it usually sung. "Wanna go for a ride?"

Thinking of the place he was standing, where Kenny had tackled me his last day on this earth, I muttered, "I'm already on a ride, Cole."

One that won't end...

Cole grabbed my hand, "Let's get you the fuck out of here," and put me in his truck.

We ended up down a dirt road that led us to a secluded spring with a huge fallen tree crossing it. I hadn't said a word the whole drive. Once parked, Cole blew out an exasperated breath. "He loves you, girl."

On the verge of losing my last shred of humanity, my eyes finally found Cole's. In a monotone, I asked, "Do you?"

The saying "reaching for straws" is exactly what I was doing. I knew I was falling, so I clung to any sign of stability. That was presently in the form of a sweet young man named Cole Coleman.

Green eyes, full of suspicion, glared at me. "Do I what?"

I swallowed the lump in my throat. "Love me."

He ran his warm palm over his mouth, staring at me the whole time. "I'm startin' to wonder if you know what that word means."

He was preaching the truth. "Then teach me, Cole."

Cole stared out the driver's window. I was making him incredibly uncomfortable. "Didn't Kenny?"

I grabbed his hat and threw it to the floorboard.

Tiredly, he leaned his head back against the headrest. "What did he do to you, Delilah?"

I scooted closer to Cole. "I don't want to talk about him."

His head still resting back, he stared at me for a minute. As if already regretting his inquiry, Cole timidly asked, "What *do* you want?"

Trying to be flirty, I smirked. "Whatever you brought me into the woods for."

Cole could barely speak. "Tell me you know that's not why we're here."

I exhaled a shaky breath, then admitted, "But... I think it's what I need."

Already shaking his head no, he said, "This is not a good idea, and you know it."

Pain was threatening me, so I leaned closer, putting us face to face. "That's the thing, I don't. Not anymore. But what I *do* know is..." I grabbed my chest and whispered, "I hurt."

This kind country boy, his eyes misted. "I see that, my friend."

I laid my palm to his chest. "No. No friends. Not right now."

His jaw shifted as he stared at me in thought. "This is not who we," he gestured between us, "are."

Ashamed, I nodded but didn't stop. "Cole, I need to feel something other than this mutilated heart that wants to stop beating."

I was suddenly yanked into his arms. "Delilah, fight that urge to shut down, girl. Please, don't give up."

I clung to him, feeling disabled. "Make me feel something else, Cole."

"Jesus, Delilah. I came because I need to talk to you."

My lips brushed his neck. "I don't want to talk."

His breathing began to quicken, so I dared a kiss against his skin. Cole groaned, struggling with desire and morals. "Delilah—" His hands grabbed my shoulders and started to push me away.

"I'm dying inside."

I was. Dying for someone to cement me to this world I detested so that I wouldn't vanish into the jaded young woman I was rapidly becoming. I was pleading for Cole to undo the destruction that had left me feeling vandalized. An impossible task had been bestowed upon Cole Coleman, and he would fail.

His lips finally met mine. They were unsure. They lacked the commitment needed to shelter me from my own demise and caused another laceration to mark to my soul. Cole was a good person and did not want me in that fashion. My erratic, insensible thoughts had me believing I was a menace who would only entice evil.

I started crying with my pitiful truth.

Cole leaned his forehead to mine. "I'm so sorry."

Frustrated and embarrassed, I pushed him away and opened his door, then ran from his truck. I ran from shame. I ran from grief. I ran straight into the vexed storm that would consume me until one would dare and enter my hurricane... and prove that my self-destructive thoughts were all misconstrued.

Cole chased me across the log balanced over the spring. "Wait! Delilah!"

His command meant nothing to me, and always would. It would take far greater strength to pull me from my ruthless endeavor of torturing myself.

Once across the spring, I started to run into the woods. I had no intention of stopping until I heard, "I know about the pills!"

I froze.

Out of breath, Cole added, "Yes, Delilah. I saw you buy them. Why? Why did you buy them?"

I couldn't face him, afraid he might know I killed Kenny. "I–I was having problems... sleeping."

"'Cause of the nightmares?"

I cautiously asked, "My nightmares?"

"Yes, Kenny said you were having nightmares."

I slowly turned around. "What else did he say?"

Cole adamantly told me, "I'd like to leave the past in the past."

The 'new' me took shape and formed right before Cole's eyes. With hatred, I stalked toward him. "The past? Then why are you bringing up the pills *from the past*? Huh, Cole?"

Appearing appalled, Cole said, "Delilah—"

Wanting the discussion about the pills to end, because it was maiming my conscience, I rerouted and became the accuser. "You didn't come to take me for a ride, did you, Cole? You're a liar. You just wanted to know about some *fucking* pills."

"I want to help you! How'd I know you would want sex?"

Infuriated, I yelled, "Sex? You think *that* is what I was searching for? You. Don't. Know. Fucking. Shit."

Cole grimaced. "What the hell happened between you and Kenny?"

I got in his face and growled, "Don't *ever* ask me that again," and then began my long walk home.

Cole drove next to me down the dirt road, leaving the spring behind. "Please, Delilah, get in the truck."

Again, a demand I had no desire to follow. Flipping Cole Coleman off was my only reply. I would've kept on walking home but about an hour later, a damn motorcycle joined the parade. I threw my hands in the air. "Of course." I marched forward.

Cole slowed the truck to investigate the newcomer.

On the driver's side of the truck, Art pulled up and his feet walked his bike. "Hey, Cole. I'm a friend of Diesel's. Want some help with this, uh, situation?" He gestured to me ignoring them both.

My friend's accent rang out. "I trust Diesel, but I don't know you, so I will be staying with her, thank you."

I kept peering over my shoulder.

"Completely understand," said Art as he tapped on the screen of his cell phone. "And I respect that. Here."

Cole got on Art's cell. "Hello?... Hey, Diesel... You-da-man, so if you say so, but I don't think *anyone* can handle her right now." He handed the cell phone back to Art. "You'll watch over her?"

Art dipped his chin as if pleased with Cole's concern. "She'll make it home safely. I swear it."

Cole shyly waved to me as he drove off.

The damn loud Harley rumbled as he caught up to me. Then he walked it next to me. "Babe, get your ass on this bike."

"Not a chance."

"I'm not as sweet as that kid, Delilah. Get your ass on this bike." He held out a helmet.

I took it, knowing if I didn't, he would cause a scene. "Fine, but you're an asshole."

"Tell me somthin' I don't know, babe."

Instead of showing an ounce of gratitude for the ride, my ill-natured, newfound self only muttered, "Thank you for seeing me home," and stormed into my house.

As the door—I had just locked—opened, I didn't turn to face him but I made fists. "You have a fucking key to my house?"

"Diesel says it's cheaper than repairing broken locks. All Pretty D watchers have one."

I started up the stairs. "Isn't that comforting."

"Hey, my brothers would never hurt you."

Brother... My body seized as flashbacks of my adoptive brother terrorized my nights. Being yanked from my bed had me jolting as if it was happening all over again. The present time and memories bleeding together, causing pure panic in my veins. As my mind replayed being shoved to my knees, I whispered, "No," as if it that night was one I couldn't escape.

Feeling my bed touch my back, I spasmed, trying to crawl away as fast as I could. When I realized I was climbing up Art's body in attempts to avoid my bed, I froze.

He was breathing hard, his arms not sure whether to hold me or keep me from falling. "You okay?"

"What happened?"

"You fainted. I caught you on the stairs. Tried to put you in bed so I could call Diesel, but it didn't go so well."

"Please, don't call Diesel. Just leave."

He ignored me and stared at my bed as if it was alive. "I'm sorry. I wasn't thinkin', bringin' you in here."

I pulled away from him. "What do you mean?"

He pointed to the bed at the back of my legs. "Is that where it happened?"

Blood rushed through my body. "V told you?"

His jaw locked. "She won't tell me shit. I assumed. Now, I know I'm right."

Any energy I had left slipped away, completely. I crawled into bed. "Keep assuming and you will never even be close to what happened. Where's my dad?"

"Trying to mend a broken heart."

I didn't even want to know what that meant because then I would've had to think of how it broke. I already knew that answer. *I killed Kenny.*

My eyes slid shut right after I saw Art sit in my chair. I was already falling asleep as I complained, "You're still here."

"Yeah, babe. By your side is where I have to stay for a little bit."

He did. He tried to get past my well-built ice walls that formed the Maze of Delilah's Madness, but no map existed. Only natural instincts and destiny would see someone through the intertwining paths in my mind.

On the back of Art's bike, we pulled into Diesel's club. At least, he claimed it was a club, but the razor and barbwire fences surrounding this compound screamed "secrets" and "stay the fuck out." I had enough of my own secrets to shelter; adding more was nauseating.

I didn't even know this block two-story building existed on the outskirts of town. Many bikes lined up along another wall of another building as the massive gate rolled shut behind us. Artist was bringing me to a bonfire, trying to make me feel better, but it wasn't helping. This was all another part of my life that I wasn't ready for. I was seventeen and wishing I felt like it. I was craving anything that was the opposite of complicated. Gazing around to a bunch of faces I didn't recognize was anything but. They all did chin lifts to Art and studied me. Art put his arm around my shoulders in such a manner the claim he was stating was undeniable. Chuckles roared out from the bystanders.

Art whispered, "We have visiting chapters. They don't know you, nor the rules that pertain to you."

"Which are?"

"You're off limits." Art guided me around the building. In the field behind it, there was a blazing pile of rubble. Old rock-n-roll was blaring, and people were dancing and standing around drinking beer. Some teenagers' dream party, but I wanted to go home. I had no desire to socialize when I could crawl into bed and read a book.

"JB!" Rung out.

I looked closer to a group of bikers. I smiled when I recognized them from Daytona. "Hey." I forced a smile. "Since I apparently have a 'road name' can I ask what JB stands for?"

They laughed and one man with a long red beard teased, "Jailbait."

I rolled my eyes, surprisingly entertained because I was quickly reminded of the good moments in Daytona. "Long time ago, boys."

"Not that long ago. You're still jailbait."

I sighed. "Can't be jailbait if you're not with anyone."

They went quiet as Art grumbled and backed away from me.

Confused, I opened my mouth to ask what was wrong, but a barely dressed individual with huge breasts waltzed up to Artist. Stunned, I stood there and watched her seductively rub her hand down his arm and purr, "Can I see you tonight?" Her body did a frontal swipe to his while she waited for the answer.

Art stared at me coldly, but replied, "It's lookin' like it."

My jaw dropped.

A water bottle was held up for me to see. Viola gave me a

knowing eyebrow lift. "For the record, Pretty D, I informed everyone this was a shitty idea."

Not sure where my friend came from, I was relieved to see her and accepted the offering, holding it to my flushed cheek. "Can you take me home, V?"

"Sure. I'll get my keys—"

Art sidestepped his biker babe and said, "I'll take you home."

An evil chuckle escaped me. "Before or after your planned *activities?*"

"Before."

I winced. I couldn't help it. His cruelty stung.

Once back at home and sliding off his bike, Art asked, "What do you want from me?"

I handed him his helmet. "What have I asked you for?" The answer was friendship. That is all I needed, but he kept pushing for more. "What kind of reaction did you think that skank would get you?" I turned away from him and rushed to my house.

"Wait." He chased.

Always fucking chasing me when I need space. I spun on my heels. "Were you hoping for this?" I slammed my mouth to his, so hard my lip busted against his teeth.

Art was dumbfounded, staring at me, both of us bleeding. "Why did you do that?"

Wiping blood from my mouth, I replied, "You asking confirms how unaware you are of my misery." I angrily backed away. "I'm broken, Art, and mostly will never be well again."

Baffled, he stared at me. No words were shared, but something happened between us. A silent shift transpired. Maybe it was a much-needed assessment of sorts. The tip of his finger smeared the blood on his lips. He gazed at it as if reading a sign, a message he was to follow. Maybe the instructions told him to leave me alone, because he did. It would be months before I saw him again.

I entered my home with a rage that pressure-cooked into total numbness.

CHAPTER TWELVE

Being numb can be a beautiful thing. Peacefully numb was how I stayed until my brother visited from college the weekend before school was to start back up. Curled up on the couch in my den, I was annoyed as my brother announced, "Get together at Bryce's. Put clothes on." My brother sounded... older, wiser.

I wasn't interested in wisdom. "Reading. No thanks."

Viola sat next to me, staring at my brother with a silent message I didn't bother to decipher. Next thing I knew, my book was yanked from my hands and soaring through the air. "Clothes. Now."

Even though it wasn't happening, all I could see was pages of *Romeo and Juliet*, fluttering to the ground. I gasped, "No," and rushed to the ground to pick up the book. With it clutched to my chest, I sat there, rocking.

"I'm ready!" June, my brother's girlfriend, bounced in.

June was a tiny girl who my brother met at some restaurant by his college. I didn't know much more than that, nor did I ask questions. My brother didn't do the girlfriend thing, ever, so I was annoyed he left his girls behind and replaced us. Apparently, Viola didn't agree. She was holding my brother's hand who had nothing but horror on his face. Viola kissed his arm after giving his hand a shake, then went to June, asking, "Are you excited?"

Her auburn hair bounced as she squealed, "Yes! I've never gone to a friend's house to hang out."

Swallowed whole in my tragic memories, I missed what she was actually meaning; her history was even more horrific than mine. I just sat there watching my brother stare at me as if just now getting a grasp of all that was hidden from him.

Getting up from the floor, I tried to act normal. I patted my brother's chest. "I'm good. Let's go to Bryce's."

Tucker reached for me as I walked from him. "Light?"

To barely be heard, I softly said, "Snuffed out, brother."

June grabbed his offered hand as if meant for her. "Can we go now?"

"Uh," he said, sounding as if his brain was now muddled. "Yeah, let's travel."

In the car, Viola and I sat in the back while June sat up front, talking excessively about every adventure Tuck had her experiencing. "And then, he took me to Dunk—Dunk... Tucker? What is that place again where you can get donuts at a window?"

He smiled at her as if she was sprouting wings before his eyes. "Dunkin Donuts, baby."

My eyes involuntarily rolled. I almost gagged when V acted impressed. "No! I love that place!"

"Yes!" June's green eyes almost popped from her skull. "And, Tucker bought me the most delicious coffee I've ever tasted. They stuck in caramel. Oh, Viola, it was heavenly."

"Let's go there now," voted V.

My mouth opened to protest to this idiocy—being excited over an everyday morning stop—but when I saw my brother smile over his shoulder at Viola, as if she, too, were growing wings, I crossed my arms over my chest and went back to staring out the window.

Bitter. So very bitter was I.

Being in that state of mind can make you... blind.

My brother was letting go of his rage and maturing at a rapid rate. That was evident when, smiling at V, he noticed something past her. "Hey, is that one of Diesel's friends following us?"

Entering Bryce's home, Cole balked, "Coffee? What the fuck?" I took a big swig of my iced brew, delivering a glare. Cole nodded, looking to the floor from under his cowboy hat. We hadn't talked since our kiss in his truck.

Houston hugged Tuck. "Dude! You're home!"

"Hi!" June practically bounced on her toes. "I'm June!"

Hu grinned. "Big guy find him a girl?"

As I walked past everyone, I waved to Jazebelle who was sitting at the kitchenette table, still in her twin sandwich, then found the comfy chair I was to own for the night. In the den, my body was present to keep my brother off my ass, but I was going to set my mind free in someone else's world.

A card game, which I refused to take part in, had only just begun when Adelle decided she needed sweets. *Your love handles are telling me something different, sister.* But off Cole and Hu went to Gas-n-Chic for snacks.

"Sure you don't want to come play this hand with your bro?" asked Tucker a while later.

My answer was flipping a page in the novel that had yet to grab my full attention, and I flung a leg over the arm of the chair. To my surprise, my brother's chuckle at my sass had me fighting a smile. That was quickly soured by complaining Adelle, yelling over her cell phone. "Hu! I didn't ask for a Jesus awakening. What the hell is taking so long?"

I had no idea that, at that very moment, the young man I had just been so rude to, Cole, was about to right his every mistake I wrongly accused him of.

What a wonderful world.

A little girl, with a handful of licorice and wearing Scooby Doo slippers, was being safely buckled into her car seat and driven to me as I sat there, stewing in ugly thoughts.

Law of attraction? Not even close. My mom's intervention?
Maybe so.

Was intervention needed much sooner? Possibly before my body
was caught up in a battle of mental illness? As the victim, I would say
absolutely, but I can't pretend to be of higher power and claim to
understand the ways of the magical. So, as a human on earth, it was
my sole responsibility to keep walking my journey, hoping to find the
beauty amongst all the frightful elements of life.

I didn't peer up from my book as the little beauty was carried into
Bryce's home, but I watched her as she shuffled past me with Jaz's
little sister, Hailey. The two were instant friends and unbearably
adorable. I sighed at the site of them and their innocence. As a spark
of jealousy crossed my heart, shame quickly followed so I sunk back
into my boring book. They had a right to be free. At that age, what
could have already rocked your world? Just because I had lost my
mom at their age, I knew that was rare, and that little girl was safe.

"Earth to pretty D," sung out Viola, demanding my attention.

Oh, and what she wanted me to see immediately had my iced
walls vibrating as if the earth under my feet was violently shaking. I
hoped no one could see instant hunger, nor hear the gasp that wanted
to be heard. My eyes scanned the magnificent young man standing
there. He was perfection for this country girl from Georgia. A smol-
dering ruggedness that demanded attention, if not pure respect. He
was almost as tall as my brother and had shoulders that—oh, God—
said, "You can rest your little head here—" *I've said that before. Did I
just read it in this book?*

Now, my eyes were scanning past pages, trying to find the
familiar words. The only thing to stop my concentration was words
spoken, not on the paper my fingers were flinging through.

"... my dad passed away." I peered up at the young man speaking.
"...and my mom is not taking it well." I looked to the little girl who I
had assumed was innocent, but she was nothing of the sort. It's
amazing how we think we can read someone, know their backstory,

yet be truly clueless about what is being hidden beneath an adorable smile.

My throat tightened, but I had to know when his world had been shattered. Was he like me? "When?"

The stranger who had found his way into my life spoke solemnly. Pain laced simple words. "Last year."

The same for me, yet here he was... trying. I had not. Swallowing down my lost sense of pride, I looked back to my book. For a couple of hours, I did my best to ignore the stranger's deep voice that made me tingle. And I desperately tried to ignore my friends welcoming him, V already giving him a nickname. In fact, I didn't move until I needed the restroom. Sneaking past Maverick, perched on a stool as if a sex god, I was undetected.

Returning, wanting to pass the muscular back I wanted to run my hands along, I was stunned to see tiny hazel eyes staring at me. Bailey was resting her cheek on the shoulders I felt I had described before. Envy raced through me again. Safe arms holding her from an earth she might have wanted to leave to follow her daddy. My eyes almost bled for her as they said, *I understand. But don't let go. Your brother seems to love you very much*—I covered my mouth. *Tucker.*

My brother's back was to me, but I studied his shoulders. The ones I used to lean on, just like little Bailey. But she was smart, still accepting the offered comfort. I had turned mine away like a damn fool.

Timidly, I gazed back at the wise little girl.

Her eyes were locked on to mine, and I swear she was speaking, too. *Trust is key. He won't let you fall.*

I slowly exhaled. *But I've already fallen.*

While everyone was talking, unaware of our silent communication, Bailey reached out to me. As I took her into my arms, she melted to me as our souls communicated. And what I heard her soul tell mine was, *Then get back up.*

Needing to feel the peacefulness a rocking child enjoys

immensely, I started rocking Bailey. It was soothing. So much so, one of my ice walls began to melt.

When I noticed Maverick staring at me, I asked, "What?" Not even my present state of ruin could save me when his gorgeous hazel eyes sparkled.

He shook his head, his longer hair looking as if in a shampoo commercial. "Uh, nothing, I guess. It's just that Peanut doesn't go to anyone she doesn't know."

I rubbed Bailey's head, which rested against my chest. *She knows me. And I know her.*

Then, with a dimpled smile I couldn't ignore, he said, "Peanut must like you."

Bailey was so incredibly tiny, I wanted to gobble her up. "Peanut. How appropriate for her." Maverick's nickname for his little sister had me thinking of Tucker's for me. Light.

Light. I exhaled as I quickly remembered how my light had been deprived of oxygen. A tiny glimpse that it could come back to life sparked something I hadn't felt in so long it now seemed foreign. Hope. And with that hope came pain, a natural order of balance I was ready to face.

Emotions erupting to the surface, one I believed I had buried under the strongest line of defense— self-misery—I began to unravel, right in front of everyone. Needing air and space to lose my shit, I handed Bailey back to her brother. "I—I can't do this." And I ran from every set of loving eyes that begged me to let this stranger into my world.

I had locked tight every entrance into my world. I didn't want anyone else to have the power to ever rock it again. It was the only way I knew how to survive at the time. Because of my unfortunate and unwise wisdom, I attempted to shut my body back down to death mode. Standing in Bryce's yard, I was furious because I didn't have a car to escape in. Just another thing Kenny had stolen from me. It sounds heartless, but it's how I felt. I had morphed into a bitch, appreciating how everyone gave me a wide girth. Hence barely controlling my temper when my brother hunted me down.

I growled, "Tuck. I need space."

"I don't think so, baby."

"I'm mad as hell. Stay away from me." I was so angry that someone found a way to tug at heartstrings I thought had been permanently severed.

"Can't do that."

I hated myself, severely, with no chance for parole. That's why, deep down, in one of the caverns I'd created inside my wickedly cold heart, I was thankful my brother was fighting for me. I tried to explain my insanity. "It's not your fault I'm mad at you."

"It is. I should've stayed here for you. I ran like a pussy."

My brother admitting what I didn't even know I needed to hear had my shoulders sagging in some sort of inner relief. A part of me even desired to be held. I needed a set of shoulders to rest my tired head on. But the reason I was so tired suddenly entered my thoughts again. "He got to run first." Envy for Kenny's escape scorched me, setting my entire body ablaze.

My brother watched me, then said, "Lilah, you're scaring the shit out of me."

I needed Tucker. I needed him so much but had been too damaged and stubborn to let anyone in but Viola. And that was a volatile relationship no one could envy. So, when my brother wrapped his arms around me, I melted to him. That night, I actually hoped, twice, that I had a chance at mentally surviving Kenny.

The next day, floating in the lake, I stared at the trail where Kenny and my brother once saved me from a hungry Bobcat. It's also the path to where I saw the bite marks on Kenny's behind. Thinking of how much things had changed from that day had me closing my eyes in agony. I begged for the release of his grasp from the grave. I begged not to remember...

Splash! "I'm a growing boy and *always* hungry."

My eyes opened to see Maverick sitting on the lake embankment with Bailey sitting between his legs. She looked absolutely tiny being sheltered by her big brother while munching on a sandwich. She looked... safe. My eyes welled as I thought about how feeling safe used to be so gratifying, and how horrid it feels when you fuck it all up.

"Where're your thoughts, Pretty D?" Viola treaded water next to my Dollar Store yellow raft.

I whispered through my torture, "Where they stay."

She grabbed onto my raft and floated with me while eyeing Maverick. "You need new blood."

"What?"

She turned and looked away from our friends to gander across the lake. My eyes followed. "Delilah, Kenny is stamped all over your friends. You see any one of us, you see him."

I lay my head down as tears fell. "I'm sorry."

She grabbed my hand. "I'm not. Someone had to have this role in your life, and I'm honored it's me."

"But it's awful! I make you lie. I'm always depressed."

She whispered, "Because you're stuck, baby! Muck all around you. Reach out! Dare to find something else. *New* blood!" She spun my raft so I'd be facing Maverick. "I'm not asking you to have a relationship with him, but I *am* asking you to accept that maybe, just maybe, you could have a new friend in your life. One that won't be overshadowed by Kenny."

I sighed. "That's what Tuck said. Well, the friend part."

"I do believe he's a smart man."

I giggled. "No, you think he's a hot man."

She looked to my brother in the water, with June clinging to his back like she didn't own her own set of legs, and growled, "Boy do I."

. . .

Hazel eyes shined as Maverick watched Bailey play. Being in blue swimming trunks only, he was breathtaking, which surprised me because I usually looked at a male and felt nauseated. It was like he somehow triggered hormones that had been asleep. Maverick wasn't completely chiseled, but his muscles were well pronounced, rounded around his unseen bones as if perfectly formed to create a delicious man.

"Hi."

He seemed surprised to see me, and said, "Hey." One syllable from his gravelly voice had me wanting to hear his next word, spurring another touch of hunger I hadn't expected.

"Sorry I made you uncomfortable last night." The way I rushed out of Bryce's had me embarrassed now.

"No, no worries. I'm good." His big hands were twisting around each other as if I made him nervous.

I'm nervous, too. I'm stepping out of my box of hell... "Well, I wanted to explain why I reacted that way—"

"Delilah, I don't think your *ex* would appreciate us talking."

Shock. I was in complete shock that he already knew, he'd already been tainted, seeing nothing but Kenny when he saw me. *Viola was wrong.*

As if my past with Kenny was nothing but an inconvenience, Maverick rambled, "I'm sorry. I think you're hot as hell, but I don't want any part of the drama with you and your ex."

Drama? My life has been inconceivably altered, and you wrap it to be titled 'drama'? "You. Are. An. Asshole."

"Look, I'm just trying to be honest—"

I stood up, ready to run from even more fucking pain. "You've succeeded in being an *honest* asshole." I marched off, leaving behind the coldest bastard I'd ever met.

I was about to turn and swing on Maverick when I heard someone running up behind me. Viola quickly said, "Just me. Breathe and tell me what the *fuck* just happened?"

I was at my brother's car, away from everyone. "It's hopeless! I'm doomed to be Kenny's!"

"Explain."

After I did, V looked dumbfounded. So, I snapped at her, "What?"

"It's just... It's just—"

"Just fucking what?"

"The way he looked at you!"

I froze. "What do you mean?"

Viola appeared regretful for yelling at me, nervously rocking on her feet. "Maverick looked at you in such a, uh, healthy way. Not like —" she stopped.

Fucking Kenny. "How did Kenny look at me, Viola?"

Her eyes were so pitiful I felt guilty for yelling at her. She hadn't deserved such disrespect. Viola started crying. "A way that I should have done more to help you."

I hugged her. "No. What happened was my fault, not yours."

We stood there, holding each other for a while, trying to find the strength to keep my secret buried. Complications were distractions to my mission, so I told her, "No more talk of Maverick, 'kay?"

She wouldn't let me go. "'Kay."

Sitting on Tuck's trunk when he approached, I knew he had much to say. "Tuck, I don't want to hear it."

He didn't listen and proceeded to tell me that Maverick believed my brother and I had been boyfriend and girlfriend. It was confirmed; Maverick was a *dumbass.*

CHAPTER THIRTEEN

Since Jazebelle lived closest to me, she volunteered to be my ride to school and back. Jaz was always so giving and kind. The twins clung to that kindness as if a lifeline. In her car, I asked, "Where're your shadows?"

From her car seat in the back, Hailey asked, "What are shadows?"

I covered my mouth while wincing and mouthing, "Sorry."

Jaz sighed in thought but answered her little sister. "Bailey, you know that dark reflection on the ground, always following you?"

"Oooh! Like when I ride my bicycle?"

"Yes! Exactly. That's a shadow." Then she told me, with a touch of tiredness, "They can be a bit much at times but they are harmless."

"What *are* they to you, Jaz?"

"Do you mean, am I in a relationship with two guys?"

"What is a relationship, Jazy?" asked her little sister.

Jaz turned into Hailey's daycare parking lot. "Something to be discussed later. We're here!"

Waiting for Jaz to return from walking Hailey to her classroom, I stared out her windshield, dreading *my* first day back to school. I wasn't looking forward to more memories plaguing me. Just then, an old truck pulled up next to Jaz's car. After a jolt, I immediately slouched down in the seat, to not be seen, until I remembered Jaz's windows were heavily tinted.

"Do you think I will make friends, Mavowick?"

He held Bailey in his arms and looked right into sweet, inquisitive eyes. He wasn't even walking toward the door of her school. He was giving this little girl his full attention. "I *know* you're going to make friends."

Tiny hands grasped his face, and her forehead rested on his. "Will you make friends, Mavowick? I don't want you to be wonely."

My. Heart. Melted. And my palm pressed to the window, wanting to assure her that her brother would survive. How could he fail? Girls were going to flock to the specimen. I had no intention of being snared. Even with an ass that was so incredible I couldn't stop gawking as he carried Bailey into the building. No joke. Levi's were designed for that man. *Fucker!* When the door shut behind him, I blinked my eyes and dabbed at my sweating upper lip. "Get a grip, girl!" I demanded.

Jaz got back into the car and buckled up. Turning on the engine, she groaned, "That Maverick is gorgeous. Damn, Pretty D, you have *got* to see him in jeans. Sweet baby Jesus kind of good lookin' because only God can make something look so good."

My hand gripped the door. "Maybe you should go for it."

"He's a marvel, but not my type. Plus, I saw the throwdown yesterday at the lake. I'm not touching that heat."

"Heat? Not even close. The new guy is a baboon."

She grinned. "Name is Maverick."

I flung my free hand through the air. "Goat Boy. Whatever."

"Uh, I don't think he's into that nickname."

"And I'm not into him."

"Hmmm."

"Here we go."

"Well, you're lying."

"Jaz, that brute 'look at me' handsome thing he's got kickin' isn't my type."

She laughed. "Tell that to my door you're killing over there."

My hand was red and strained, so I loosened it. "How about we chat about *your* type? Like, double types?"

Her car turned a corner. "Do you really want to know?"

My chest tightened. "I guess I should already know, huh?"

"It's okay. Losing Kenny changed us all."

"I'm sorry I haven't been a good friend to you, Jaz."

Her little shoulders shrugged up to her pixie black hair. "Ya just had things to deal with. Still do, I reckon."

A deep exhale released. It felt good, someone to not be angry with me for behavior I could have avoided. I wanted to return the favor. "Okay, talk to me about the quiet dark-haired men in your life."

She stopped at a red light, her hands wringing the steering wheel. "Not sure how to explain it. Not sure if anyone in this small town can understand." She rested her forehead against her nervous hands. "I don't even think *we* understand."

I laid my hand on her back. "You care for both of them."

Without lifting her head, her eyes found mine. "In their individual ways, yes, I do." A horn beeped, making us both jump in our seats. Jaz rushed to press on the gas. As the car moved forward again, she explained, "They're twins, yes, but very different. Both have qualities I adore. I do prefer one over the other, but I won't speak the name out loud. They don't know how to separate themselves yet. I must be patient."

"Jaz, that sounds so... complicated."

"Do any teenagers truly get to be young and free?"

My fingers fiddled in my lap. "No. I guess not."

"The same for them. Something happened to Nash and Nelson. I don't know what, but I'm positive it was bad. I'm not sure, however, if they even remember whatever it is that haunts them." She shook her head to clear it. "I must sound nuts."

"No." I stared out her window. "I actually totally understand."

A bond, in an unexpected place.

After stopping for Dunkin for some java, Jaz parked in our high school parking lot. Opening her door, she teased, "Maybe Mav will be in a class of yours?"

"Jaz, you sound like my brother. He wouldn't shut his trap all last night. Drop it."

My plan to ignore the gorgeous creature Jaz was referring to went down in flames. In the hallway, standing with my friends, was who my brother referred to as Goat Boy. I think Tuck sensed V's admiration for Mr. Mav, and even though wanting me to be friends with him, was a tad jealous. I rolled my eyes, said, "See ya later, Jaz," and walked into class.

And let the reminders begin...

The little freshman—now a sophomore—that had a crush on Viola, the one who witnessed Kenny dragging me from school the day he raped me and died, was sitting in a desk toward the back of the room. The little guy had untamed blond hair with sunken blue eyes that were stricken with guilt. I think he still felt guilty for not helping me. The blame was all mine, so I sat in the back with him, leaving a small desk between us. "Hi." Not sure how to start a conversation I sensed was needed, I shyly asked, "You, uh, in the wrong class?"

He timidly smiled. "No. Just a little advanced."

Feeling unbelievably awkward, I nodded before pulling out a novel from my backpack. I was surprised when my mind raced back to Maverick's expression when I refused to acknowledge him and came straight to class. I shook my head, telling myself, *No. Delilah, keep your plan "Ignore Gorgeous" on track.* And I did. Until the bastard walked into the classroom. *You have got to be kidding me. And he's headed this way. His thighs fill out those jeans like—No! Don't mind Dumbass boy and read, Lilah. Read—and stop thinking about his muscular ass!*

"Will you smack me if I sit here?" Maverick pointed to the desk between me and the sophomore.

I glanced at the advanced student, then replied, "I'm against violence."

Unaware of my meaning, Maverick was chipper. "Very good to hear, for *some,* that is." He proceeded to *shove* his country strong and delicious body into the impossibly small desk. "Jesus! This thing made for a toddler?" Not able to move without moving the whole desk, he asked, "Hey, have you met the 'new' guy?"

His approach was completely unexpected, so I had to ask, "Excuse me?"

"Yeah, I hear he's a real... What was the word? Oh yeah, real *honest* asshole."

No, Delilah, don't fall for this crap, nor that smile. No, damn it! He saw me looking at those 'kiss me' dimples. "Oh, *that* guy. Yeah. I met him."

Maverick did a horrible impression of a shocked female, gasping and covering his mouth, not giving two shits he looked like a fool. "You should stay away from him."

The sophomore forced down his laugh, probably not wanting to have his ass beat by the beast of deliciousness. Observing Maverick's godly body again, I moaned, "Oh, I'm trying. *Believe* me." Heat flushed through my whole body like an underground river searching for the light of day.

Heat? Shit. Jaz was right.

Maverick was shockingly witty and adorably comical, rambling on about the Mayor shutting the gates of the town. He even made me chuckle, having no idea it was the first time in months. And I kept smiling. I had no choice. I didn't know it then, but I had just fallen in love with the bastard. But life has cycles, and so did the beginning of our rocky relationship. By the time the bell rang, and Maverick was trying to free himself from the man-eating desk, I laughed freely. When I caught myself having a moment outside the misery I was committed to, my body froze. It was as if it had forgotten what the free sensation felt like.

The sophomore looked to the ground and left the classroom.

I don't deserve to be... happy. Not after what I have done to Kenny.

"Are you okay?"

I stared into the kindest hazel eyes, wishing things could be different, as I said, "I can't do this," and left the classroom to rush to a bathroom and cry.

As if being guided by an angel, Maverick didn't give up and stayed persistent. Underneath his big demanding persona—and mystifying appearance—there was a young man with nothing but good intentions. His father's death had his mother in a very concerning depression, which took him time to admit. He had Bailey, a five-year-old sister who needed stability. Maverick offered that and so much more. The openhearted soul stuffed into a tiny desk, sitting next to me every morning, had hit his knees with circumstances out of his control, yet rose to every occasion. Including me.

Even when he tried to touch my hand in class once, and I retreated with some sort of post-traumatic syndrome due to Kenny, Maverick showed nothing but understanding. He actually apologized and told me he should have asked permission to touch me. I sat there staring at him in disbelief. It had only been a week, but a sense of trust was building. It was a tough road, but he stayed loyal and gently fierce to the process.

I say fierce because the intensity of how he would stare at me as if I was the only person he saw, told me he was never giving up. I say gently because of his undying patience.

One morning, the sophomore gestured to the desk Maverick would soon be tormenting and stretching. "It will never be the same."

I chuckled. "Maybe I should take pity on the poor thing?"

"Most definitely."

Maverick was late dropping off Bailey that morning—I would know because my eyes were scanning for Levi Event—so I had a few more minutes before he would waltz into class on his quest to annoy me. "Help me?"

Sophomore smirked. "I'll find the biggest one." He jumped out of his seat.

We both scanned the mostly empty classroom because Sophomore and I were apparently the only students to rush to class first thing in the morning.

My young friend started dragging a slightly larger desk from the front row. "The big guy might fit into this one."

"May I inquire why you two are rearranging my classroom?" asked our teacher, Mr. Bristol.

I shrugged. "Sophomore is advanced and told me to do it."

Sophomore chuckled. "What will my name be next year?"

Nibbling on my bottom lip, I thought. "Junior?"

He smiled as if pleased we had an understanding.

Once all desks were in their new and proper place, we both slid back into our own. Sophomore leaned a little closer and whispered, "You know he's right, right?"

"Er... What?"

"That he should always ask permission."

A shaky exhale left me. I slowly nodded. Then I quietly told him, "You did nothing wrong."

His lower lip slightly trembled. He had been feeling shameful for so long. "Doing nothing *was* wrong."

I stared at his hand. "May I?"

His eyes welled as he nodded.

Squeezing tight, I assured him, "That day," I swallowed, "was set in motion, long before you saw anything." I grabbed my chest as I begged myself not to cry. "Yes, you and Maverick are correct; you should always ask permission. K—He didn't. And he certainly wouldn't have when it came to harming *you* for getting in his way."

Students started rushing in, so I let go and we both went silent. Mr. Bristol was writing on the chalkboard when Maverick and his work boots came strolling in. As he pushed his desk closer to mine, he was beaming. Before I could comment, Mr. Bristol complained, "Must all the furniture be rearranged this morning?"

Before sliding in his new desk, witty Maverick rambled on about me having poor eyesight, not knowing he was speaking to my dad's good friend and my Godfather.

"I fit!" Maverick was finally in his desk and able to breathe at the same time. Once I informed him of my intervention for his lungs' sake, of course he teased me. "Look who is showing her sweet side."

"Don't get carried away, Maverick. I just felt guilty for causing your daily discomfort."

"Who says *you* were the distraction? Maybe it was this student." He thumbed at Sophomore, who was cracking me up by batting his eyes at Maverick, who was recoiling in horror. The entertainment continued as Maverick did some sort of manly chin lift, his voice dropping an octave, "Hey, dude, how's it going?" totally turning me on.

As this yummy brute kept knocking down my defenses, climbing his way further into my heart, I realized how closed off my heart had been. If Sophomore had guilt, how did the rest of my friends feel?

After the bell rang, I decided to face them. When Maverick and I approached our high school friends, their expressions told me this young man wasn't only giving me hope. It shined from their eyes. They had yet to move on, too. Kenny was still present in their hearts because I wouldn't let him go.

Maverick wasn't replacing Kenny. I wasn't rebounding—running into another relationship to mend a broken heart. It was a trust factor. Maverick showing me a glimpse of the ability to have faith in someone again was giving me the space to dare to rejoin the world that I felt had abandoned me; abusing Kenny, and in turn, harming me. A cycle no one was able to break before the damage was done. Kenny had truly been a victim of the system, being lost in paperwork and overworked and loaded counselors.

Yes, there was no denying the attraction between Maverick and myself, but I needed more time. "We are just friends."

Viola, Houston, Jaz, the twins... they all nodded but still appeared to have a sense of relief. Shoulders softened as they agreed, "Just friends."

Cole stared at the ground with sad eyes.

What have I done?

A childhood friend had been mistreated, by me. I wrapped my arms around his neck and squeezed him with every ounce of sorrow I was experiencing. "I'm so sorry."

As if slowly allowing me to take the blame off his shoulders, he held me tight, his arms trembling. "Me too, D."

It felt so good to have some healing... I kissed my friend's cheek. "I love you." Then I whispered, "Thank you for being a true friend."

Cole couldn't speak. He finally let me go, his Adam's apple working overtime.

My friends had waited so long for me to be present again. It wasn't a done deal, but they also showed patience. Like, while in the cafeteria, when I found myself physically too close to Maverick after he stole a French fry. I backed away from the table, bewildered how it felt to have such contact again while wanting more. And my heart literally sighed when Maverick stood but didn't chase. Instead, he gave space. Room for me to make my own decisions.

"Can I come with you?"

He wasn't dragging me from my room, *or hunting me down with his motorcycle—*

That thought caught me off guard. *Is Art borderline abusive?*

With Maverick watching me as if my next words held value, a memory of the rear window of my car exploding—due to Art's antics —blew through me. I wanted to ask Maverick if he would ever force himself into my car, but I already knew the answer.

More trust grew in my heart. I could literally feel it, making me clutch my chest. "I know what everyone is hoping to take place here... and I think there might be a part in me that is hoping, too, but... I need... slow."

A promise was made that day. One Maverick kept. "I can do slow."

Having just waved at Maverick, I slid into Jaz's car, sighing an exhale that was wondrous. Yes, that is what he did for me. His forbearance gave me the courage to breathe, suspecting there was a chance that the strength would continue to flourish.

Jaz slid into her car and behind her steering wheel, giggling. "Need some water to put out that fire?"

"I can't stop smiling."

Her eyes welled. "We know, and it is beautiful."

At Gas-N-Chic—to put out my fire—I walked out the door with a cold water bottle in hand. Jaz was in her parked car waiting for me. My feet stopped when I saw Art also waiting for me in front of the store. He was smiling, directly at me, but I still couldn't stop my body from seizing. His shoulders caved at the sight of my change. He exhaled a labored breath as he closed the short distance between us. "I didn't mean to startle you. That smile you were sportin' was... Wow."

And now that smile was gone. I already missed it. That meant I was already missing Maverick. It's wild, but I had thought Artist was entrancing, that there was a chance I would never meet someone like him again. It was a lesson to never doubt what could be right around the corner of life. Diesel had been so right. I was young and so naïve. At this point, I still was, but I was also opening up to learn more. Growth can be marvelous in its own right.

There was no more healthy growth in the relationship with Art. I nervously gripped the water bottle in my hand. "Haven't seen you in a while."

He rubbed the back of his neck. "Had, uh, some club business to tend to."

"Not in Georgia." I didn't mean to sound harsh, but experiencing fresh breaths, I was now concerned they would be stolen. If Art had been in town, he would've bulldozed his way into my business, something I hadn't realized 'til now.

The biker winced. "No. I was in Austin. Just got back."

"And needed gas?"

He shook his head. The movement was laced with sorrow. "No. Have gas. Came lookin' for you. I didn't know it would be such a bad thing."

Now my shoulders sunk. "God. I didn't mean to be so rude."

"Yeah?" He smirked, then reached out and took hold of my hand.

I stared at the connection as more growth took root. "You didn't ask."

His brows scrunched. "To hold your hand? I didn't think I had to."

My eyes searched. I saw biker boots, black jeans, a blue T-shirt, a leather vest, and piercing blue eyes. I didn't want to be pierced anymore. I suddenly didn't want 'protection' anymore. I wanted the ability to think for myself.

"You're gorgeous, babe. Just wanted to touch you."

"And you did."

"I'm not following you."

My eyes closed. "In the hotel room, you watched Kenny with me and said you'd never witnessed stolen freedom before."

His hand fell from mine.

Getting into Jaz's car, her eyes were silently asking questions. I shook my head. To explain who Art was would be telling her about Diesel's position. I had a promise, too, and kept it. So, she put her car in reverse and started backing up. "I want that smile back." She raced us off to Hailey's daycare, where I would learn several things:

Hailey's teacher, Pepper, wanted Maverick.

Maverick wanted me, so the bitch, Pepper, could live.

I also learned that Maverick had much restraint. He admitted to wanting to kiss me but didn't. He just held me, after asking for permission.

But most of all, a fear had been uncovered. And, it was a scary one. Misconstrued, because of some of Kenny's words and actions, words spewed by young boys throughout school, and from Art for that matter, I believed that my appearance may change Maverick. I knew, beyond a shadow of a doubt, if he changed—became like the rest—I would be doomed to miserable relationships for the rest of my life.

CHAPTER FOURTEEN

Friday night, on the way home from the local pizza parlor we always ate at, my brother teased, "So, what's up with the Lady and The Tramp moment with you and Goat Boy? Even little Bailey called you two *friends* out."

I could feel my cheeks blush. "Oh my God. I had Bailey in one arm, her spilling applesauce, all the while cheese was dripping from my mouth, so—" I couldn't finish and tell my brother Maverick's lips on mine, to catch the cheese, was beyond divine.

"I think I saw tongue."

"Viola!" my brother and I both yelled to the back seat.

I evil-eyed her. "Don't you have a boyfriend to take you home?"

She glanced at the back of Tucker's head then kicked his chair. "Yes, but this fucker lives closer to me." She shrugged. "Why make Bryce waste gas?"

My brother chuckled. "Or brain cells Bryce will lose trying to handle your vixen ass."

She cheered, "Mavy Wavy!" because he's the one who nick-named her Vixen.

Tuck grumbled, "*Mavy-Wavy?*"

"You like him, right? Why else would you have invited him for a tat tomorrow night?

"Yum," growled V. "My bestie in my *house.*"

Tucker reached behind his seat and madly tried to find and smack the girl pushing his buttons. Laughing, Viola grabbed his hand and bit it. "Great," said my brother as he retracted his injured hand. "Now I need shots."

Whack!

He laughed as his head flew forward.

Watching them play, I knew they had a relationship where permission was no longer needed. Their constant contact was the results of an open invitation... of love. I smiled, hoping someday they would admit the deep feelings they had for each other.

"Hey." My brother smirked at me. "Dad said your blue '69 Chevy will be delivered in a week."

"Maverick says I'll look *smokin' hot* driving that car."

Tucker grumbled, "Fucking Goat Boy." But he was smiling. All was good.

Alcohol had taken complete charge of the evening once Diesel set down his tattoo gun. By three in the morning, Diesel was slurring, "Wha' you mean it'sss empty?"

V held up the Tequila bottle—that she had just emptied in the kitchen sink—and acted as shocked as the three drunks. "I know! Can't believe it! Guess you guys drank it all."

A bandaged Tucker stood. "We should get more!" Then he fell back into a recliner that perfectly unfolded with the pressure of his sudden weight. His eyes slid shut.

Viola mumbled, "That couldn't have worked out any better."

In one last fight to save the night, my brother lifted his hand. "To da liquor sto'!"

Chuckling, V kept up with her non-award winning performance. "Yes! Wait, damnit, all liquor stores are closed."

"Whaaaat?" squeak-slurred a freshly tattooed Maverick.

Viola shrugged. "I know. I'm heartbroken, too."

One of his eyes no longer opened as wide as the other. "You lik' Teeequila, too?"

"I do, Mavy Wavy."

He tried to lean his hand on his knee but missed and fell forward into his own lap. It was a sign that he didn't drink often and the night needed to be over, but he slurred, "Beer?"

Viola laughed, observing him trying to sit back up. "More bad news. All gone."

"Whaaaat?" he squawked.

I felt the many spinning tires as I was thrown under the bus. V thumbed my direction. "Pretty D drank the last one."

I went to gasp because it wasn't true but froze at the smile that stopped me in my tracks. Maverick's. "Pretty D iiiiis pretty." It was a crooked smile, tainted with a serious drunken state, but it stole my heart. Maverick's glossy eyes shined as he stared at me. "You can aaaalways have my last beer, 'Kay, Pretty D? Anyyyythin' you want." He hiccupped. "Yours."

My heart gushed affection for the hot mess. Even unaware of his words—because he totally wasn't going to remember any of this in the morning—he was still *kind* and *sincere*. No fear had me worrying about how the night would turn out, or his temper may flare. So, I asked, "Anything?"

He fell to his side on the couch. "Youuuu betcha."

"Lie down?"

He pointed to the couch cushion his face was smashed against. "Here?"

Diesel stood. "Alre'dy puuuussy whipped." He then fell into a wall. *Slam!* "The fuck? Who put dis God'amn wall in'meh way?" I could hear him bounce off more walls and furniture as he made his way to the stairs.

Viola, smiling, rolled her eyes. "I better make sure he makes it to his room without breaking his neck."

Maverick suddenly did a sharp inhale while sitting up straight. "Pe'nut!"

I quickly knelt in front of him and grabbed his hand. "Shh. Look." I pointed to the loveseat. "Snuggled in all those blankets."

He fell to the couch while rolling over. His back and shoulders melted into the cushions. "Dat baby, Deliiiilah."

Smoothing his dark hair from his face, I quietly said, "I took care of her."

"Yu're gonna be a gerrrr-ate mom someday, Del-Delilah." His eyes drooped then shut. "Da way you look afterrrr m' Peeeanut? Geeer-ate mama you will b'." He never finished the sentence. His mouth stopped working and went completely lax as he passed out.

Maverick wasn't asking me to mother *him*. He wasn't admiring or noticing me mothering grown men. He was seeing my potential of mothering a child. An ease took place in my chest that night. I felt more normal, or at least saw the possibility of being a normal person.

Grateful for the tender moment, my finger slowly stretched out. As the tip of my index felt the warmth of his neck, I thought of Art and how I had caressed him the same way once. As much as Artist had enthralled me with excitement, Maverick did the opposite. He calmed me. Lovingly rubbing my skin along his was like touching a miracle; a cloud of hope wrapped in a masculinity I had been unaware I was craving.

"Lilah," he uttered in his sleep.

The only two permitted to use that nickname were my brother and father, but when Maverick spoke it, I felt like one more person was meant to use it.

I sat back, wondering if I dared to possibly have even more faith in this young man when Viola came around the corner. "One down. How's it going in here?" She quickly peered over her shoulder then rushed to the entertainment center and pulled a handgun from a decorative basket.

I jumped to my feet and whispered, "What's wrong?"

Obviously well trained, she aimed the gun toward her living room, while whispering, "The door opened." Just then, the door to the kitchen made a tiny squeak. Viola redirected her aim as I placed myself between Maverick and the intruder. Maverick was too intoxicated to protect himself. And Bailey, who was farther behind me, was hidden under so many blankets she couldn't be seen at first glance.

When Art came around the corner, also with an aimed gun, I squealed.

Viola pointed the gun to the floor. "Fuck. Art. Jesus."

Art kept moving in a circle, scanning our surrounding area, gun still leading his searching eyes. "You guys good?"

Viola's raised her gun up as she quickly put her back to his. It was like a dance. Art didn't flinch. They just moved together.

I could barely breathe. My gut was screaming we were under threat.

Another biker entered the den to be confronted with two guns before Art and V recognized him.

The biker also dropped his aim. He claimed, "Prez is passed out drunk, why he wasn't answering, but now under surveillance." The man caught something behind me and tilted his head.

Before I knew it, Maverick was stepping directly in front of me and took a stance that blew us all away. As unsteady on his feet as his drunk body was, there was no denying the technique. Fist raised, his upper body tight and slightly hunched... Maverick was a professional boxer.

"Holy. Shit," uttered Viola. "This fucker keeps getting hotter."

Slowly, I circled him, admiration and awe combined. He had never bragged of such an accomplishment, nor wore his evident strength on his sleeve in a constant combative measure. Discipline from his craft made him look like an extremely focused machine, and his eyes were locked on the two bikers he clearly viewed as strangers.

If I thought Kenny was powerful, then Maverick was downright mighty.

Ignoring my trepidation, I touched his shoulder. He didn't jolt or react with an unsteady mind. He kept staring at who he was deciding whether or not was his enemy. "You squeaked."

A disturbed chuckle escaped me. "Yes. They accidentally scared me."

His glossy drunk eyes blinked. "You scared now?"

Astonished, I smiled. "No. Not of you."

His eyes met mine. Then dimples shined.

Feeling euphoric, I quietly asked, "Will you lie back down for me?"

Maverick stared at me as his knees bent and he lay down on the couch. "Anything."

His eyes closed.

And mine watered. A joyful cry escaped me.

"He's a lucky bastard."

I gazed at Art, covering my gaping mouth as my chest panted through more tears that felt cleansing.

"The one who wins your heart?"

With no point in denying the obvious, I nodded through more tears. "Yes." I looked at the drunk on the couch. "Irrevocably, yes."

I didn't bother to check who had left when the kitchen door closed. I knew who was gone. Kneeling next to Maverick, I clutched his hand and pulled it to my cheek. Holding it there, I peered up to my friend. She had tears as thick as mine streaming down her face as she studied her cell phone. So, I whispered, "You okay?" That young woman closed her eyes and shook her head in some sort of awe. "Sometimes, I'm reminded there *is* a God."

"V, I've never heard you speak of a God."

Her crying eyes opened. "When your parents fall from the sky to become a ball of fire, you tend to believe in only the devil." Her hand shook as she faced her phone so I could see the revelation.

I stopped breathing altogether as I understood what I was seeing.

At a bar in Daytona, Viola had taken a quick picture of a young man dancing with a stranger, claiming he was a perfect example of my dreamt up novel boyfriend.

That *dream* had yet to grow his goatee, but now, there he was lying on the couch, right in front of me.

So many past moments echoed through present moments and made me start to understand where I belonged. My mother had told me to trust my brother, so I did when he was happy about Kenny and I getting together, but that wasn't fair to him. Tucker never knew all the facts. With Maverick, my brother seemed to be investigating the poor guy as if Tuck were an undercover agent with unknown narks feeding him information. This time, I chose to trust my brother again. At a field party one night, he gently shoved me into Maverick's arms, and I became the girlfriend of a boy I had yet to kiss, but madly loved.

I wanted a kiss, but Maverick treated me with respect and only kissed my forehead, reminding me of the time Art told me, "Wanna know when someone really cares for you? They only give you what you need." Maverick, deep down, sensed I was in no shape for my first kiss since Kenny. He was right. The next morning, I woke in my bathroom, up against Maverick's chest, with my brother and my pissed dad. "Hi, Daddy."

My head was pounding, but I could still hear Maverick sick with worry when talking to Bailey on the phone. It was our true first inclination that something was very wrong at his home front. The second one was, later that day at his home for a Bailey 'cookout', Maverick's shocked reaction after hearing his mom laugh. Because I was the one making her do so, Maverick kissed me, on the lips, right in front of my brother and dad.

With Kenny, everything was a secret.

With Maverick, there seemed to be no secrets except mine.

The touch of his lips on mine made me hungry for more. On Monday, I asked to be alone with Maverick, so we left school together. When I realized Maverick was taking me to the spring where Cole and I shared raw emotions with no outlets, and no knowledge of how to plow through excruciating pain, anticipation ended and anxiety replaced it.

Holding on to Maverick's arm while he drove his dad's old truck, I begged myself to believe my kiss would not change him, and I begged myself to believe he wanted this moment as much as I did. I found myself touching Maverick's lips with the tips of my fingers, hoping he could pull me from my internal distress.

As if he knew what I was asking, Maverick took my hand that was touching him and kissed it. Hope. I felt more hope...

When Maverick's truck stopped, I found myself quickly unbuckled and on my knees, beseeching for unanswered prayers, hoping this spring wouldn't witness another failure.

"You don't have to do this," Maverick whispered. "It's okay." Those words spoke of him knowing who I was thinking of.

"I'm sorry," I almost cried out, not wanting him to feel as if he were competing with a ghost, even though, in some ways, he was.

"I'm not."

"Why not?"

"Because this is not forever."

We were very new as a couple, so I understood him not thinking of us as 'forever', but his words still stung because I felt he was my fate. Viola's picture had me believing that Mav was so much more than a teenage boy I had a crush on. The sting in my chest had me pulling away from him.

Maverick moved so fast, unbuckling and gently grabbing my arm to stop me. "Will you hear me out?"

I stared at him, not sure how he could change what had been said.

"I didn't mean you and I are not forever. I meant, what you're going through is not forever. A day is going to come when Kenny is not in your every thought. Look, I never knew him, but I'm guessing he was a huge part of your world."

I nodded, thinking, *In a way that will never be denied.*
"I won't try and compete with that. I won't try to be him. I'm my own man, baby, so know that's all I'll be for you. I will be me, and I will leave your past behind you. And, if that past is something you want to talk about, or if it's sneaking up on you, I'll stand by your side 'til that shadow of a memory fades again, because... it *won't* be *forever.*" His strong hand touched my face with a gentleness I didn't know he possessed. "Someday, Lilah, you're gonna be free of what's trying to keep a strong hold on your future."

I was lost somewhere between emotions and appreciation for this man in front of me. I know I once believed feeling numb was a beautiful thing, but this echoing moment was when I learned a valuable lesson. To feel *hope* was beyond beautiful... it was glorious.

After a moment, he asked, "Now, where are you?"

Are you real?

He cautiously asked, "Do you want to talk about him?"

Terrified I was dreaming up this perfection talking to me, I looked away, pleading for God to stop being so cruel to me, but then I heard magic. "Or, maybe you're in the mood to create a *new* memory?"

My eyes snapped back to his, and I took the chance offered. "New."

"Okay. One more question. Have you been here with Kenny?"

And let the roller-coaster of healing begin.

I thought of Cole. "I've been here, but not with him."

As if that was all Maverick needed to know, he busted out with, "Let's play!" pulling me from another round of mournful thoughts and embarrassing memories. I watched Maverick in wonder as he walked in front of his truck—my rollercoaster beginning its uphill high of excitement, only to be released into the unknown.

The passenger door swung open, and I was playfully yanked from my seat. I was speechless, even more so when, face to face, chest to chest, he told me, "I'm crazy about you."

The forming new memories had me gleaming. "How crazy?"

Walking backwards, he pulled me toward the spring. "The craziest kind."

The log laying over the water, one I had crossed with Cole, was singing out to me, daring me to take advantage of this do-over. I asked him, "Coming?"

"Oh, I'm coming for you, girl."

To be chased in such a healthy, flirty way had me feeling so fearless.

"Do it again."

I was confused. "Do what again?"

"Laugh. Laugh for me, Lilah."

His words felt like the permission I needed to live... and love.

As I stepped onto the huge log, Maverick yelled, "No!"

Nothing will stop me now. I feel so good! "You worried for me?"

I kept backing away from him, luring him into my world, until his deep voice went gravelly, "Wait for me," sending heat through me with such a force, my body took over. It stopped and I stood there marveling in the sensation of arousal.

It wasn't his command that had me in such a state. It was the knowledge and trust that he could handle me. I had been a loose cannon, believing *no one* had the strength to blow out my lit fuse. But here he was, full of energy and grit. The allure to surrender to him was rapturous, seductive, and so full of promising tranquility that I willing became submissive.

Consolation for succumbing, emotions had their final burst from their captivity. Through all the tears I had locked way since Kenny's death, since the rape and torture of my heart, my body finally experienced the exhaustion of going through the motions of survival.

I had been on auto-pilot for so long, I no longer knew how to operate my body on my own. "Help me." I could feel Maverick's intense eyes watching me, but I needed more. He was the one I would allow to enter my hurricane. He was the one that would be strong enough to withstand my mental storm. That knowledge had tears exploding from my hurt soul. "Help me."

As he raced across the log, his voice was full of compassion. "I'm coming, baby."

Reaching out to him, I begged, "Steal Me." Steal me from Kenny's grip from the grave, but mostly, from me. At that moment, I realized I had been my own worst enemy.

Maverick had me in his fierce embrace, causing me to sigh in relief as he soothed my soul.

Still acting on its own accord, my body, my tongue licked my lips as if knowing a much-needed barrier was about to be crossed.

Engulfed by his masculinity—his raw power and dominance—Maverick slammed his mouth to mine and stole me from every single past kiss I had ever known. Once we tasted each other, a sensational wildness took control, the force so intense we both plummeted from the log and into the water as if nature was baptizing us.

Maverick wanted to devour me that day, and in his own way, he did. He scarred me with his passion, and being marked, branded, and owned had never felt so liberating.

I felt... *alive*.

Most of all, I wanted to... *live*.

CHAPTER FIFTEEN

To truly appreciate beauty, maybe you have to witness or endure the ugly side of life. Maybe that is why Maverick's fresh energy became a beam of light we all clung to. Maybe it was as simple as his scars matching ours, creating a bond amongst best friends.

I certainly know a bond was formed between Maverick, Dad, Tuck, and Diesel while they restored my '69 SS Camaro. In the garage, so much laughter boomed I thought the walls were going to implode. Cooking in the kitchen with Bailey, she would giggle. "You're right, they are so loud." I had told her that was the reason she needed to hang with me in the kitchen, but the truth was the colorful additions to her vocabulary. The garage innuendo talk was a bit concerning, also. Hence the title they gave themselves *Team 69*. They claimed it was due to my car, but the way they chuckled and mumbled under their breaths, it was clearly a play on words.

One night, after Bailey and I set the table to feed the garage grease monkeys, I placed her on my hip. "Want to help me with something else?" She squealed, clasped her hands with glee, and nodded with bright dreamy hazel eyes so perfectly matched to her brother's.

All four men stood quietly when I came into the garage, clutching a symbol of growth in my hand. Bailey proudly pointed to what every man was already staring at—the crystal motorcycle figurine that didn't perish with Kenny. "Can you bewieve it, Mavowick? I get to hang it on Del-liah's wearview mirro." It was as if her speech impediment was a sign that she could sense the lingering tragedy.

Maverick, the only man able to speak, swallowed. "Can't believe it, Peanut. Be careful not to break it."

"I will be weel careful, Mavowick." Bailey, ever so gently, took the glass bike hanging from my finger and stared at it in awe.

Maverick forced a smile. "Peanut, do you know what a rearview mirror is?"

"No, but I pwomise to hang this there as soon as I find it."

The sweet baby broke the moment of tension and everyone started laughing. I kissed her cheek, unaware of how she instinctively knew her brother was in the same boat as me; needing to heal from the loss of a parent and from what was slowly killing his mother.

Depression is an ugly beast that deserves attention and respect. The ones trapped in its vicious cycle suffer immensely. The one snared by depression this time was Maverick's mama.

Maverick had become the man who could handle me best. Subconsciously, I trusted him beyond all others. It was unfair to my brother and father, but I unknowingly viewed them as failures at keeping me safe. So far, Maverick had yet to lead me astray. So, I held no grudge when Maverick unexpectedly became distant and began canceling plans. That trust stood strong.

Over my cell, I would hear his deep voice sounding solemn. "I'm sorry, Lilah, I can't go to the movies tonight."

Bailey would cry in the background. "Mavowick, pwease? Wif Dewiwah?"

My eyes closed, not hearing him correct her pronunciation. It was as if he was too worn down to put forth the effort. I sighed. "You okay?"

He cleared his throat. "Yeah, of course."

But he wasn't.

His silent scream for help was heard when my brother spotted Maverick in the McDonald's drive-thru, with Bailey. My boyfriend had been adamant about his sister's eating habits, always feeding her the most nutritional food, including fruit shakes with lots of spinach. She loved them! When she smiled after sucking one down, her teeth would be discolored and adorable.

Still in his car, Tuck called me right away and told me he would meet me at Maverick's home after picking up Jaz to help with Bailey. I hung up, grasping my chest. "I'm coming, baby."

Arriving in my "Team '69" car, Bailey was in the front yard on her swing set, her little legs in the air. Maverick was in a lawn chair, hunched over with the heaviest set of shoulders I had ever seen. My hand shook as I reached for the door handle. What was I going to find out? I had no idea, but I got out of my car anyway. When my door shut, he looked up to see me. Recognition crossed his haunted eyes that were surrounded by dark circles.

To see the man you love in such duress slices you, scars you, and has you launching into action. Artist had once commented on me being too nurturing to the men in my life, but this was different. Maverick was sinking. He needed help, and I knew how to begin. I'd care for who he loved most—Bailey. If I could successfully eliminate that worry, maybe Maverick would take the time to care for himself.

When Bailey jumped into my arms, she whispered, "Mommy is making my bwothor sad."

Digging deep for the compelling strength to not break myself, I held that baby girl tight, offering stability while her brother's body shook through his cries. He had heard Bailey and was reacting as if he had epically failed her.

He hadn't. His mother had failed them both.

"Wi-Will you hwlep my bothor?"

I dug even deeper and swallowed tears that shouldn't be shed in front of her. "Yes, baby." *You incredible little girl.* "I promise."

After Bailey ran inside to pack for her first sleepover ever, I cautiously approached Maverick. Tears rushed down his tan face as he tried to keep me away from him. Again, the trust held strong, and so did my arms when he finally surrendered and melted to me. Me standing between his legs, his thick arms wrapped around my hips and held me with a tragic desperation.

He was on the brink of ruin.

Exiting Maverick's home and heading to his car where Jaz was buckling in Bailey's car seat, my brother whispered to me, "I think we have a pill issue. Feel me?" I had asked him to check on Jessica. "Depression, anxiety, sleeping... same shit docs have June on."

Maverick's mom had become so debilitating with an addiction, she was able to pull her son down with her.

With a delighted baby girl driving off with my brother and Jaz, I handled Maverick with special care. I held his upper body to my stomach, running my fingers through his thick beautiful hair, and whispered reassurance. "I'm here. I'm here, Maverick."

The first thing he needed was rest.

I led him through his front door and tried to not pay attention to his unconscious mom on the couch, or to the Christmas decorations that were on the floor—not the bare tree, or to all the evidence Maverick was losing the battle of his mother's depression because he was fighting it alone. Jessica had given up, absolutely checked out of her life, leaving Maverick to plow forward on his own.

The weight I was pulling behind me spoke of his exhaustion as we traveled up the stairs. In his room, it appeared as if he had gathered all the supplies to keep Bailey occupied while he hid from the destruction downstairs.

I dug deeper and forced a smile on my face. "Looks like I missed a party."

Maverick could barely move but numbly followed me with his last ounce of strength. "So tired but can't sleep."

After clearing his bed of Bailey's stuffed animals, and getting comfortable by removing my bra and jeans because I knew we were going down for hours, I lay back on his mattress, asking him to rest with me.

Maverick is a big man, but I accepted every pound of his upper body that rested on my chest. As if being close to me was bringing him instant relief, his weight thickened and he exhaled. His body was demanding sleep, and was winning, but he managed a slur, "Lilah."

I ran my fingers through his hair, trying to soothe him even more. "Yeah?"

"I love you."

Have you ever had the air sucked from your lungs yet you don't feel starved for oxygen? That's what those three words did to me. The stir, the feeling of being in love, was magical. I could feel his truth, his honesty, and kissed his forehead with an abundance of bliss. "I love you, too."

With Maverick avoiding me, I had missed him dearly. So, laying there with him, so thankful he finally let me in, I caressed his back, his rounded shoulders... until my eyes closed and I drifted into a deep sleep myself.

I didn't wake until a warm mouth touched my breast. Only one person had ever touched me while I slept, so my mind reverted to what it knew; I was in danger because Kenny had returned. Not a rational thought, Kenny was in Heaven, but after being severely abused, your mind sometimes has a difficult time differentiating between past and present when in a sudden Fight or Flight situation.

Fight or Flight: a physiological response to a threat, preparing one to battle or run for safety.

I'm not exactly sure which action my body was choosing. But when I jolted, I heard the deep voice that always brought me the immediate sensation of being safe. Maverick's tired vocal cords graveled, "I'm so sorry—"

"Maverick?" My eyes flew open, needing to be sure it wasn't Kenny half on top of me.

His bedroom was dark now, but I could still see alarm then sorrow race across his face. "It's me. You're okay."

So relieved to have been pulled from a nightmare before it had a chance to begin, I yanked on Maverick's arms and neck to force him closer to me. Answering my silent and desperate plea, he was on top of me in no time, letting me kiss him with my fury of gratitude. With every touch of his lips, my madness slipped further and further away, allowing room for sanity once again. Deep sighs were released as a relaxed state resumed over my body. "Maverick, you can touch me anytime."

I guided his hand to my breast.

Instead of being aroused, his eyes studied me. "Lilah, what is it? You sounded scared."

Not wanting to speak of Kenny or the past, I whispered, "And you can kiss me here," I put a little pressure on his hand touching my breast, "any time you want to."

The trap had been set, and my victim, willingly, crawled in to taste the bait.

Another exhale escaped me as safe lips wrapped around my nipple covered with only a T-shirt. Apparently, the cloth was an unwanted interference because Maverick went to lift the hem but then stopped, his eyes asking for permission.

I thought of my brother and Viola, and their playful actions in the car, no need for permission pertaining to any hungry touch. I was hungry, too. I was starving for the young man on top of me, for his every touch and taste.

Eagerly, I nodded, my breath mimicking my happy heart.

My fingers tangled in his hair as his tongue lovingly showed me how kisses to the breast were supposed to feel. His mouth didn't resemble a sexual act; it was pure affection. Every single gentle caress and lick spoke of how much he treasured me.

So, as his kisses started to drift to my ribs, my anticipation grew. Beautiful eyes peered out from underneath dark eyelashes, reading my responses, which were screaming of need. More. I wanted so much more. My sexual desires had been lost in the violent storm Kenny had me trapped in, even from the grave. Now, they begged to be set free.

Maverick's beard deliciously scratched at my inner thighs while he kissed the panty-covered place that had been violated. Until that moment, I hadn't realized that I felt detached from the juncture that should still have been untouched. She and I had to separate ways after I had failed her. It was a defense mechanism that needed to be laid to rest. Forgiveness was also needed, but different processes can take different timespans for healing, for different people, and sometimes different traumas.

His soft lips felt like an outsider looking in, reading the past, and an apology for what she had endured before he was there to treat her with respect and love. During these intimate moments, more trust bloomed. So, I said yes as he silently asked if he could remove the silk between him and me. In that tiny ounce of time, I regained ownership my femininity and chose to give her power. I chose to let her enjoy sexual endeavors again. I chose to not make her think she was dirty when being touched. I chose to feel liberated when becoming wet with excitement. I chose to let her enjoy every swipe of his magnificent tongue. I chose to let her be what she is. A part of me that has wants. And those wants are connected to mine. And just like that, *we* became connected. Once again, the part of me that had been mistreated and damaged was whole, with healthy desires.

Maverick hadn't needed permission at all. It was *me* who needed to be permitted to move on. I had to give *myself* the power to let go and move forward in a sexual manner. The more I let go, the more room Maverick had to explore.

Sensations below, especially one spot in particular, had me absolutely breathless. His hot mouth was bringing me such pleasure I was confused and kept calling out to him.

"Delilah," his husky whisper spoke through the night, "have you ever come before?"

Orgasms.

My books had described the sexual highlights, but what Maverick was doing seemed so much more. Sparks kept setting off inside my body as if a fuse had been lit and a bomb was about to explode.

Bewildered to what I was internally experiencing on a physical and mental level, I shook my head as a reply, hoping like hell he was going take me to the orgasmic land I had never known.

When Maverick's mouth started to own me again, my head thrashed on the pillow. My hips rocked, craving more and more of his tongue. Metaphorically, I felt like I was wearing a glider and was running full speed for a cliff's edge, desperate to leap for a brand new view—perspective—on the subject of oral sex.

I had once been tainted on the subject, but now I was the recipient of a master's art. Maverick's technique was exquisite. His tongue slid in and out of me with just enough strength to have me panting, running faster toward that cliff. Then the wet perfection swiped up my slit and sucked on my most tender spot. That tongue pulled so hard it literally drew my upper body forward, forcing me to prop up on my elbows and watch him feast. Maverick appeared enthralled as he worked between my shaky thighs.

Sweat dripping down my chest, I thought I had finally reached the top, the cliff's edge, seeing life from a new set of eyes... until his ravishing tongue changed course and proceeded to rapidly flick the spot he had drawn all my blood to. Incredibly sensitive to any touch, the flicking of his tongue was like a gust of wind lifting the wings of my glider and propelling me into the sky.

In the air, all the sensations fluttering through my body felt like I had found the best sunrays during my flight. I closed my eyes and let my head fall back to soak it all in, every sparkle under my skin, and every blinking light sending signals throughout my euphoric body.

As my glider wisped through the mountain valleys, it also felt like the best freefall imaginable. Slowly being brought back to earth was fantastically wonderful. Every part of me, my heart, my soul and body, was beautifully and perfectly spent. My elbows slid out from under me as my body slipped into a trance, so relaxed I felt drugged.

Once I was somewhat coherent again, I asked Maverick how he

was such an expert with directing my body into bliss. Lying next to me, he spoke of an older lover he met during spring break in Daytona. I marveled at the fact that Viola had a picture of him dancing with this older woman he was referring to.

Maverick smiled so big at my reaction to his story. "What's gotten into you, girl?"

I touched the lips that had just touched mine. "Loving that some dreams do come true."

Headlights suddenly shined against his bedroom ceiling, reminding me I had turned off my phone's ringer so that Maverick could sleep. Maverick jumped up to peer out his window while I checked my cell. I had many missed calls and one from Dad. I was already returning the call when Maverick ran out of his bedroom.

Getting up to follow him, I held my cell to my ear. Dad answered, "Hey, baby, you okay?"

I walked to the hallway. "Yes. Did Tuck fill you in?"

"Yes, and this is what I recommend. Take the bottles and dump them, hide them, whatever. Tomorrow's Saturday, so no doc in this small town will be open to refill her prescriptions. I'll be over in the morning with your brother and breakfast. I take it Maverick is crushed and there will be no hanky-panky?"

I stopped at the top of the stairs. *Oops. His beautiful face was just between my thighs.* "No, sir. No hanky-panky."

Getting off the phone, I met up with Jaz at the bottom of the stairs. In awe, she was watching something in Maverick's living room. Following her line of sight, I saw Maverick, holding little Bailey to his chest and rocking her in a rocking chair. *Be still my loins.*

Maverick having the most talented tongue on this earth held nothing against the sight of this burly man being as gentle as possible with his little sister.

Jaz giggled through a whisper, "You have *got* to have this man's babies."

I side-mouth-whispered in return, "No joke. My ovaries are aching right now."

"Viola would tell you to finish college then trap this bastard."

I elbowed her through more giggles. "Well, she's sick. Never happening."

Maverick and I disposed of the prescription medicine that his mom was abusing. I remember it clearly because I stood over Maverick's toilet with a full bottle in my hand when Kenny entered my mind. I tried to imagine what it must have felt like, what he experienced after swallowing so many. I wondered if there was peace in the high.

Overwhelmed, Maverick rushed in with more bottles. "Damn. I wish my mom knew what it was like to have to watch someone swallow their life away, one pill at a time." He clutched my face. "Hey." His eyes bored into mine. "Thank you for being here."

My hand tilted and emptied the bottle. I flushed every damn pill.

Maverick and I went through another very special bonding time as his mother began her recovery. Jessica was impressively brave through her struggle. She wasn't addicted to the point that she needed to be hospitalized or go through detox; she just needed another outlet for the pain. She found it in the meetings my father still occasionally attended. Those counselors got her in touch with professionals, and Jessica was finding her way to recovery.

Time. Everything has its own span of time needed.

And time started picking up speed. New Year's Eve had arrived, and Maverick and I spent it sober in support of his mom. Doesn't sound like a teenager's dream while at a river party, but it was important to us. Due to our pasts, Maverick and I had already shown signs of maturity. Dad said this alcohol-free decision was another example. I wonder what Dad would have thought if he knew, most of that party, I stood by the river where I had released Kenny's ashes instead of giving them to his own mother.

The residue of abuse had become a spider's web. Everywhere I placed my foot, there was a spiral of silk trapping me. And I was never sure which of my steps was going to alert—awake—the spider to come devour me from the inside out.

I recognized the sound of Maverick's work boots settling on the river's embankment, then I saw two shadows from the lights of the party to the darkness I was in. He whispered something to someone. I heard V reply, "Sometimes," before she walked away.

Again, Maverick's rough voice soothed the turmoil stirring within. He was more than willing to clutch me from the hungry spider with a kiss.

The kiss stirred a whole different storm to life. On the way home, I dared to cross another barrier. After Maverick gave me my first orgasm, I had tried to replicate the high but was clueless with what to do, and every time I closed my eyes and touched myself, I kept seeing mean green eyes. I had talked to V about wanting to learn, but she teased, "I'm not telling you shit."

"What?" I had squawked.

"Hell-to-the-no. Your brother is right. Let those innocent train wrecks take place with my bestie. Have Mavy teach you. He sounds brilliant in the hooha department." She moaned in delight. "What a fabulous crash that will be."

"What if... What if I panic... Because of what happened with Kenny."

"Then panic."

"V! Help me!"

"I am! If you have a *much-deserved* meltdown, then confide in him why." She begged, "Talk about it."

I started to sweat. "No. No way." I tried to explain. "V, no shower cleanses me anymore."

"Do *you* believe women who have been raped are dirty?"

"Jesus! No!"

"Then why do you think that about yourself?"

"No, I didn't say I did—"

Viola delivered a why-are-you-trying-to-bullshit-the-bull-shitter expression."

My eyes welled. "Okay. There's a film of filth I can't scrub away."

Sitting on my bed, she had twisted to face me, looking directly in my eyes. She had grabbed my face and choked on words. "You. Are. Not. Dirty. You are hurt. Huge difference. Let him in."

I was nodding and crying before I could stop myself. "I don't want to feel so... wrong."

With me in her arms, she cried with me. "You won't always. Someday, you will see the treasure you are."

Now, in Maverick's truck, my palms were covering my face and I was chanting in my head, "*I'm not dirty. I'm not dirty.*"

Driving down a road, Maverick tried to see my face. "Lilah, look at me. Why so shy about an orgasm?"

Not shy, just confused and distracted, seeing Kenny when my eyes close.

"Delilah, you haven't masturbated yet?"

I've tried but... "Maybe I just don't know how. Do you?"

"Masturbate? Hell yeah!" cheered Maverick. "I do it all the time!"

I'm not dirty. I'm not dirty... "No. You know, on *me*. Do you know... how... I should?"

"God, I love you."

Perfect response. I exhaled.

His truck turned a corner and raced down a dirt road. "Where are we going?"

"The train, baby."

I thought *Viola is a psychic* as Maverick and I raced to our very own train wreck.

I could feel every bump his tires experienced as Maverick raced down the dirt road. My bare thighs rubbed together, yearning for the release coming under my skirt. My eyes caressed the gorgeous young man gripping the steering wheel as if hungrier than me. His stare left the road when I absentmindedly licked my lips. The truck revved faster toward an empty dark field alongside the active railroad tracks.

His fingers felt delightful as he gripped my waist, lifting me into the bed of his truck. Maverick crawled in behind me with a blanket. After leaning his back against the cab of his truck, he patted between his legs. Crawling toward him, my heart thundered in excitement and reservation. I was desperate for his touch, but I was desperate for it without haunting green eyes.

As my back rested to his chest, his warmth sizzled my skin. The blanket was laid over my legs. When his fingers lifted my chin, I let my head fall to his chest. The heat of his lips was tranquilizing. His tongue? Mystifying. His wet mouth had me panting and we had yet to begin.

"Open your legs."

I gasped, so overwhelmed with a buzz under my skin.

His kiss took back over my senses... and my legs parted.

Callused hands seductively slid down the outsides of my thighs, gripped the hem of my skirt, then lifted, exposing me to only the blanket but it felt like to my future of hope. As those same hands found their way over my thighs and in between, our breaths mixed together in an innocent passion.

It was epically raw.

It was epically delicious as he stole me from the haunted eyes I had become to detest.

My upper body sagged against his while a finger slid inside me. However I felt to him had Maverick's lips pulling from mine to bite my shoulder through an animalistic groan. In such a state of focus to what was happening between my thighs, my head lulled to the side as I pushed on his thighs, hungry for more penetration from his hand.

A deep moan escaped me as his finger dove inside me. My legs widened, pressing against his, begging for more. Maverick's free hand shook as he reached for my right one.

Jolting from the sexual haze, I stuttered, "No, I d-don't think I can." I didn't want Kenny to taint this erotic moment.

"It's just you and me. Private. A special moment for only us."

Those words rung loud in my head. *Private... only us.*

So, my eyes closed, and I dared it to be true. It was. Only his heavy breaths were heard, and only his eyes were what I imagined. Reading me perfectly, Maverick slid another finger inside me. I sighed being cradled by his gentle affections. I didn't even fight him when he moved my own hand under his, causing me to touch myself... without shame attached.

What a relief to know I could be experimental and not feel the filth normally attached.

Maverick's fingers guided mine to touch a sensitive nub. Eyes still closed, I gave permission for my body to enjoy every sensation. I was wet and silky. His two fingers pushed mine inside me. I whispered, "Yes." Black and white clouds danced in my mind, and this volcanic eruption grew down below, building and climbing my inner self.

After pulling my wet fingers out, he moved them up. His husky voice vibrated against my shoulder. "Right here. This is where you are most sensitive." There was a pleasurable ache, an intense need, and I loved every minute of the journey of masturbating. "You can rub harder... softer." His fingers had mine picking up speed and then slowing, exampling the desirable freedom that was literally at my fingertips.

So enthralled, I didn't slow my pace as the train in the distance started to barrel toward us. The energy of the train was a metaphor of my own tracks to ride. As I reclaimed every swipe between my folds and gave myself immense pleasure, I was traveling my path of independence.

"Open your eyes, baby."

The light from the train shined into my eyes as Maverick's fingers followed mine, picking up speed and determination. I gasped through my breathlessness, my body jolting through the intense sensations. Maverick's fingers slipped away from mine as he offered liberty to my very first self-inflicted climax. His mouth ravaged my neck. His hands massaged my breasts as he told me, "You're free, Lilah. Let go... come in my arms. Get as loud as you want."

I moaned in the best torture ever while the train roared past us, shaking the truck. And when my orgasm plowed through me, I screamed, "Maaaaaaaverick!"

Maverick was unaware of another monumental step I was trying to take when I served carrots for dinner. Dad and my brother, sitting with Maverick and me at the dining room table, stared at the vegetable on their plates. It was the first time I had fed them this side dish since middle school. So, when Maverick commented on the fact he didn't like carrots, I became somewhat unreasonable, starting an argument with my boyfriend.

One of Maverick's most attractive qualities is he's not a pushover. He's a fighter in more ways than one. So, our argument grew. I pushed. "I bet you make Bailey eat them."

He pushed back, angrily shoving a carrot in his mouth. "Yep, and I *eat* them. I just don't *like* them."

Desperate for another to suffer with me, I pushed again. "So, what else do you not like?"

"Sitting here and listening to your crap."

My brother interfered, "Whoa," but Dad shook his head no, stopping Tuck.

I took my fork and squashed the damn carrot. The significance of that action had me quickly reevaluating my circumstance. *Am I losing it?* I stared at my boyfriend. *Will I ruin our relationship? Have I already?* "What's happening to us, Maverick?"

Maverick rushed to stand in front of me and yanked me from my chair. In his arms, his voice soothed me even though his words were not reassuring. "I don't know. I don't know."

How *could* he have known? I was still hiding so much.

The old saying, "One step forward, three steps back" is how it felt.

From Maverick's chest, I watched Dad numbly push a carrot around on his plate with his fork. "Another stage of healing. You two will see your way through. Just try harder to be kinder to each other in the process." He peered up from his plate, and his questioning eyes locked with mine. I knew he was catching on.

Maverick had already gone home to put Bailey to bed by the time I was putting away the last dish dried by Tuck. Maverick had let Bailey stay home and eat stew with Jessica. It was a big step. Counseling was helping Maverick's family. So, I had no buffer—Maverick —when my dad was standing in the kitchen, saying, "I'm sorry to have been so hurt by Kenny's death that I missed some key details."

My brother set down the dish towel. "I will give you two privacy to talk."

He got only two steps from the counter when we heard a surreally stern voice exit Dad. "Take one more step and I will lay you down."

Dad was kind, helpful as could be, practically carrying Jessica through her healing process, but Diesel told no lie when he warned Dad was also one scary ass motherfucker when pissed. Hence my brother being a frozen statue not sure what to do.

I swallowed. "Daddy, calm down."

"Don't daddy me, baby. Not right now." Dad wiped his hand across the kitchen island, observing his own actions as if trying to gain control before murdering his children. "That little argument with Maverick got me to thinkin'."

Tucker ran his palm over his face. "Fucking carrots." He leaned his butt against the counter next to me, away from Dad.

Dad braced his hands on the granite as if hoping for it to be strong enough to keep a firm barrier between him and us. "Lilah, what was Kenny to you?"

I grimaced at the loaded question, not knowing where to begin or whether I should at all.

"I see you're ponderin' whether or not to lie to me, but hear this. My eyes are peeled wide right now, so I will see the truth, like I am right now." He inhaled then exhaled. "I'm askin' again. What was Kenny to you?"

I crossed my arms. "A brother."

Dad's head leaned back as he glared at me from the corner of his eyes.

I held up a hand, begging for patience. I could only whisper, "And boyfriend." My eyes started to well immediately, just wording that out loud.

Dad moved his feet back and leaned his upper body forward, hands still firmly planted on the counter while his head hung forward. I'm not sure his lips were moving when he groaned, "Mother-fucker-Goddamn, I need to hurt someone." His fingers gripped the impossibly hard stone. "Lilah, get in front of your brother. Protect him from me."

Tucker stood up straight, looking like a lost deer in headlights. He was as big as my daddy but had yet to put on the powerful girth, nor did he have the disrespectful ways of not honoring my Dad's beating on the horizon.

Dad continued, "'Cause there ain't no way in hell I'm ever gonna believe my dimwit son, Kenny's goddamn best friend, didn't know what was going on under my goddamn roof." When Dad started sidestepping to come around the island, I got right in front of my brother. As Dad stalked forward, Tuck knew I was his best line of defense and stayed behind me. Daddy would *never* raise a hand to me.

As Dad stalked forward, I could feel Tuck's labored breathing against my back.

Dad's eyes found mine, and they were tortured as he slowly kept approaching. "You were hurtin'? From the loss of your very first boyfriend," his glare went back to Tuck, "and you didn't think to tell me?"

Tucker's shaky exhale blew against my hair. "Yes, sir."

Dad's eyes slammed shut as if someone just kicked him. His hands were in the air and his face was contorted, slightly turned to the side as he replied, "Now is *not* the time to come clean."

It was time to save my brother's life, so I let the pain in and tears fall. "He didn't know, not 'til it was too late. Kenny was so happy with the misunder—believing—uh, knowing that I cared for him like that."

My dad went eerily still, and my brother jolted against my back. *What did I say?*

Dad's head tilted. "So... he was a brother to you *and* a boyfriend?" I wiped my wet face, nodding. "Yes."

In complete dismay, Dad slowly covered his mouth and uttered, "You're lying."

My mouth gaped. Then I blinked. "No. I'm not. You're wrong."

He gripped the front of his own shirt. "Baby, brothers and sisters don't become romantic relationship material. You saw him as your brother... or you didn't." With fear in his eyes, he glanced at Tuck behind me then back to me. "Lilah, what was Kenny to you?"

Air was seeping from my lungs at a rate I can't explain. It was as if someone had punctured a hole in each of my lungs and I couldn't contain the oxygen needed. So, my shoulders bounced with every gasp I took. I even grabbed my chest as alarm started to race through me.

Tucker's head leaned to the back of mine. I could feel pity race from his heart and into my chest. I shook my head, the floor I was staring at going incredibly blurry. "No. You guys are misunderstanding me. He was both. He was both."

Tears fell from my father's eyes as he came to me with open arms. His strength wrapped around Tuck and me as if we were his little babies again. In a way, we were. Tuck and I had hidden things from him, which we should never have done, and were desperate for guidance. He squeezed us tight and we both melted to him and his unconditional fatherly love. Tucker was hugging him in return, gasping through his own tears.

If it wasn't for them wonderfully smothering me between their big chests, holding me up, my legs would've buckled. I was in shock, the whole time I kept muttering, "He was both..."

Dad's voice broke as he cried, "Fuck." He clutched the back of

Tuck's neck, forcing them forehead to forehead. "You should have told me."

I felt dizzy. "He was both. He was both..."

My brother sobbed. "I'm so sorry. I'm so sorry."

Dad told him, "I don't know what happened, but we'll stand strong by Light's side. You feel me?"

He sobbed, "Yes, sir. Yes, sir. I swear it."

I was dizzy. "He was both. He was both..."

Admitting to Viola that Kenny was only one—a brother—while I was in a numb state, didn't allow me to feel the magnitude of the situation. Admitting what Kenny was to me, to my brother and father, brought me far too close to the volatile circumstance I had been trapped in. With Maverick in my life, I had become open again, or at least I had thought so. But as these two men held me, I realized my haunted roads were long, they were wide, they were dark, and they were swallowing me.

CHAPTER SIXTEEN

Dad greeted me in the hallway, leaning against Kenny's doorway. I froze. He observed. Then licked his teeth. "I see." He pointed. "I never see you go in here. Why is that, Lilah?"

I swallowed. "Because he's gone."

"Who is gone? Boyfriend or brother?"

"Stop it."

"I love you. I can't." He pointed again to the closed door. "Let's go in there, together."

I stared at the entry I had been dragged through many, many terrifying nights.

Studying me, Dad turned the knob.

I took a step back.

He didn't enter but pushed the door open.

My back slammed against the wall. My fingernails dug into the drywall, like a scared cat clinging to a tree branch, trying to stay out of reach of danger.

Tuck turned the corner from the stairs and stopped when seeing my body language. "Light, what is it?"

My chest rose and fell... "I am not of light."

Dad's jaw locked. "Don't you say that."

Tears dripped. "Then you are asking me not to speak the truth." With my wounded heart reinjured, I left the two stunned men in the hallway. I shut my bedroom door and headed for my bed 'til I a memory of the rape assaulted me all over again. Stumbling backwards, I fell into my corner and slid down the wall, melting into a ball of sobs.

Tuck and Dad rushed in, appalled at the sight of me. They both dropped to their knees, but I wouldn't let them touch me. I kept crying, hysterically, swatting away their offered arms of comfort.

Finally, Dad stopped trying and sat back on his butt. With his arms folded over his knees, he stared at me. He exhaled in some sort of surrender, then asked my brother, "Mav still going to those group meetings?"

I cried, "Daddy, please leave me be."

"Already told you, my love for you won't let me." He ran his strong palm over his exasperated mouth. "Tuck, call 'im. Have him stop by tonight."

Drained, I stood in the kitchen as Maverick walked in. He suspiciously eyed Dad, Tuck, and me. "Hey, everybody." Then he came to me. Reading me as he did so easily, I was wrapped up in his arms. Moving my long hair from my shoulders, he asked, "Talk to me?"

I shook my head in his chest.

Tuck said, "We, uh, got some ghosts from the past happenin'."

A sigh escaped me as Maverick began to rock me, side to side. It was so gentle, I wondered if he knew how perfect he was.

Dad popped open a beer. "How're the meetings going?"

Maverick rubbed my back. "Amazing, actually. Thanks for pushing me to go."

After a couple of gulps, Dad hesitantly asked, "I was thinkin' it would be great if Lilah could go with you."

My boyfriend leaned his upper body back to see me. "I would love that."

I stared at him so he could see I was dead serious. "I don't need counseling." I was never going to tell what happened. I just wasn't going to ever cross that line, in fear I wouldn't find my way back.

Dad said, "But I think it would be really good for you."

"I don't need counseling!"

Maverick tightened his arms on me. "Easy, babe." He told my brother and dad, "Delilah has to want to heal before—"

Pulling away from him, I threw my hands into the air. "Oh, *great!* You agree with them?"

He reached for me. "Lilah, will you hear me out?"

Crossing my arms, I nodded.

Maverick studied me then took a step backward. "I'm at a time in my life where I need to learn how to cope with my pain. I personally need help. If you don't think you do, then by all means, don't go to counseling."

"But you're not saying I don't need it!" It felt like it only took one second to regress one whole year, but in truth, I had never truly progressed.

And everyone pushing me pissed me the fuck off.

Marching out of the kitchen, I heard Tuck tell my boyfriend, "I'm sorry. Shouldn't have dragged you into this."

"Bullshit!" Dad yelled. "She needs help, too, and *he* is my only chance. You know that just as well as I do, Tucker!"

As probably recommended by a therapist, Dad and Tuck gave me space for my denial. And as I continued to ignore my remaining issues with Kenny, Maverick and I found ways to heal other aspects of our lives, like his boxing career. Some months prior, I had tricked him back into his gloves with a kiss. Now, with more encouragement from me, his gloved fists were finding courage to get back into the ring. Had I known that boxing would be the 'other woman' in our relationship, I might've convinced him to take up knitting instead.

Maverick became so preoccupied with boxing that I missed him terribly. We still saw each other every day at school, but alone time was not nearly as often. Viola gave me brilliant advice. "Use sex to gain his undivided attention. No boxing ring can compete with that."

With flirty innuendos being tossed in Maverick's direction, I think he got the hint. He planned out a romantic night that ended up almost setting a barn on fire and killing me in the process. It was such a hilarious story I told my girls. They told the guys, who told Tuck, who, in turn, gave my boyfriend a black eye.

After that, if we did manage to find alone time, Maverick would fall asleep in two seconds flat because of his intense routine.

Round two! Maverick's boxing workouts took over again. To see him more, I started running with him as he built up his endurance. That only complicated my sex efforts. As soon as Maverick would lay down, we *both* would fall to sleep.

V pondered over my dilemma. "I've got it. Burn the sweatpants, wear tight running shorts on every run, drink a Red Bull, and seduce the bastard."

The perfect night finally arrived when Jessica and Bailey went to the movies. Maverick fell onto his back in his bed preparing for a snooze. "Five minutes, babe. Just five."

I grinned to myself. *Operation Vixen commences now!* I crawled into bed with him. His eyes were closed as I kissed his cheek. He smirked. "I love you."

I softly ran my lips over his. "I love you, too." Then I kissed his still bruised eye. "Sorry my brother is an asshole."

His little smile grew. "Nah. He's just takin' care of his girl."

Seductively as possible, I kissed his neck. "I thought I was *your* girl."

Maverick exposed more of his skin for me to have easy access. "Ya know how you would never try to get in between me or Bailey?"

I nodded. "Never."

"I feel the same. That big fisted bastard loves you like crazy. That's why I wouldn't even dare returning the punch. Be downright disrespectful."

I sighed, thinking how Tuck felt the same when my dad came at him.

"If somethin' ever happened to me, who would have my baby's back?"

My brother. No doubt.

I flirted. "You planning on leaving me, Maverick?"

Chills broke out over his skin as I placed another kiss. "Not a fucking chance. Ever, Lilah." His voice deepened impossibly low. "You hear me?"

Now, I was the one breaking out in chills. "I hear you."

Not giving up, I moved Maverick's hair that was getting longer and nibbled on his ear. I grinned as his chest started to show labored breathing. "Maverick, I'm willing to do *anything* to keep you awake."

Without opening his eyes, his mouth searched for mine. "Gonna have to be good. I love my naps."

I teased with only a lip to lip caress. "Maybe we can finish what you started in the barn?"

His Adam's apple bobbed through his heavy swallow.

I licked my hungry lips. "What made you choose that barn?"

"You said it was your favorite." His eyes opened. "Why is that?"

Not sure how to tell him a special biker friend kissed me there once, I kissed Maverick with passion, loving that no one could compare to what he did to me. Maverick opened his mouth wide and let me have him. As our tongues met and danced, his beard scraped at my lips, lusciously marking me.

I knew the nap idea had been dismissed when Maverick grabbed the back of my head and pulled me impossibly closer, and a moan rumbled in his chest vibrating against my tongue. Inhales and exhales rushed out of our noses because we refused to separate our mouths. It was erotic to hear our struggles for breath while choosing passion over air.

Slowly, while lost in his kiss, my right leg slipped over his body. His hand raced to my thigh and squeezed his approval. Loving his hunger for me, I slid completely on top of him. He absolutely *groaned*, wrapping his arms around my ribs and holding me tight. His erection demanded space between us, and I loved how it felt against my pelvis. I even let my hips rock forward because another part of me wanted to feel it, too.

When his mouth suddenly broke from mine and he gasped for air, I thought... "Did I hurt you."

From under me, his brows bunched. "*Hurt* me?" Then he stared at me while pushing hair behind my ears. His voice was husky but kind. "Babe, I've never asked because it's not important to me, but have you ever had sex before?" My eyes averted to his shoulder so quickly he said, "Never mind. As I said, it's not important. It's just you and me right now." His finger tapped my chin. "Look at me, Lilah." Timid, I did. "You didn't hurt me. You stole my breath. The way you just rubbed on me, wanting me... damn, girl, best thing I've ever felt." He whispered, "Do it again?" Daring myself to live on the wild side, I pulled my hips forward, pressing into his. "Yep." His eyes shut and he winced as his mouth opened for a gulp of air. "Best feeling ever. Lilah, you're making me see stars." That earned him a chuckle. His face relaxed into a smile as his eyes opened. "Us guys are pretty simple creatures, huh?"

My smile faded... as did his. I whispered, "Never known uncomplicated 'til you."

His expression showed shock that transitioned into honor. But he didn't ask questions. Instead, he tapped his lips. "Please." My breath shook as I lowered my lips to his. There was no tongue during this union. Just two lovers taking their time to feel simple touches. My lips explored how every angle of his mouth felt. I learned him that night.

When his tongue gently reached into my mouth, my hips pushed forward again. He tasted that good, making the rest of my body jealous. His hands found their way to my hips and tugged, sending rolling sensation up my body. Fingers put pressure on my hips as if trying to control the need to travel to other parts of me. Hovering face to face, I told him, "You never need permission to touch me, Maverick. I trust you, implicitly."

His hazel eyes bored into mine as his hands slowly left my hips and circled around to cup my ass. They never left mine as he pulled me closer to him while gently surging his hips forward. My head rolled to his shoulder, causing him to chuckle through pants. "You haven't masturbated like I taught you, have you?"

Heady, so pent up for relief, I shook my head.

"Tell me why you can't bring yourself pleasure."

I lifted my head and stared at him, unable to speak my truth. In my bed, I never slept alone, always haunted with memories.

Expecting him to push for an answer, I was floored when he demanded, "Take off your pants."

"W-What?"

A crooked smile appeared. "Stopped comprehending English?"

I smacked his chest. "Being rude, don't ya think?"

"Not at all. Just want to make you come."

My eyes felt as if they were popping out of my head, but I tried to cover it with a *pff* and a very witty comeback. "You take off *your* pants."

"Not yet."

Imagining what he was going to look like totally naked, I sat up on his hips, nervous and excited. His eyes rolled as the movement caused friction against his groin. I giggled.

He tickled my sides. "Torturing me is funny to you?"

"I think so."

Maverick shrugged. "Fine." He closed his eyes. "Back to my nap."

"No!" I yanked at the elastic. "I'm stripping."

Eyes still closed, he smiled. "Don't forget that silky G-string."

"How the hell do you know I'm wearing a G-string?"

"You gave me unlimited permission to feel up your ass."

That had me laughing so freely I forgot I was nervous as I removed clothing. When I sat back down on him, I teased, "Now what cha gonna do?"

He stared at my nakedness against his own sweatpants. "I'm gonna beg myself to stay in control and not flip you over and take you—"

My body seized.

His stare immediately shifted and burrowed into my soul. "But I'm in complete control of myself."

I tried to not exhale relief, but it forcibly slipped out of my lungs as my shoulders sagged, heavy with gratitude. I whispered, "Thank you."

His hands gently touched my bare thighs. "Anything you want... and need." His hands tugged again. "Move forward." Tilting my head, I then gasped, understanding what he was asking. Maverick quickly tugged on my thighs again. "Don't overthink it. Just come here." I didn't move. "Babe, do you have *any* idea how many times I've lain here dreaming of you holding onto my headboard," his voice went back to husky, "while sitting on my face?"

The last time his mouth was between my thighs, I came so hard I thought I was soaring to heaven. I could feel heat rushing downward and becoming wet as I panted with more need.

He was struggling to breathe, also. Nodding, he begged, "Please?"

Maverick was far too strong to not force me upward, but he didn't. He was giving me control, and I was shocked to learn how much I wanted that control. How much I wanted to be fearless. With much reservation, I moved forward.

It was kinky and arousing to watch him lick his lips as if dying to taste me. Absentmindedly, he tapped the part of his pillow to his left before moving his arm out of my way. "Knee here." As I followed instructions, his arm lay over my calf and the tapping hand now fiercely gripped the pillow. He groaned, "Your other leg, straddle my neck."

Peering down, I swallowed, not sure if I had the guts.

"My dream, babe."

Blowing out a shaky breath, I exposed myself in a way I never thought I could, placing my left knee above his shoulder. But the way he lay under me, staring at me as if I was what he needed to live yet wasn't rushing my hesitations, a sexuality arose in me.

His ribs expanded against my calves and feet. "S-Shirt, babe. L-Let me see all of you."

I lifted my long-sleeve T-shirt over my head and removed my bra. Enthralled, he swallowed. "Thank you."

With a new sense of empowerment, I reached down and touched his face. My fingers caressed his cheeks as he lay, lungs exasperated, eyes savagely hungry. Then I gently grasped the side of his face and lifted. As if Maverick were suddenly drugged, his eyes went half-mast while opening his mouth. As soon as his lips touched my private ones, we both moaned in ecstasy.

His tongue gently slipped from his mouth and into me, feeling so incredible my upper body fell forward. Strong arms gripped my thighs, his tongue never missing a beat. I let go of his face and grabbed onto his headboard, needing the extra stability. Breathless, I smirked when his groan of approval vibrated into my vagina.

His mouth worked me to a state of oblivion. My body took over, needing this release so damn bad. On their own accord, my knees bent, searching for even more pressure from his mouth. His arms tightened as our frenzy built. I arched my hips to give him better access to the spot that was begging for focus.

Jesus, this bearded young man latched on and took absolute charge of my clit. My head fell back as my fingers dug into the wood I was gripping with all my might. I couldn't even get air in as the intensity surged through my body, informing me a climax was seconds away.

As a light explosion happened behind my closed eyelids, I screamed out his name. I couldn't restrain myself. He knew how to draw out an orgasm that I'm sure would challenge any of Viola's sexy books.

As the beautiful fall after an orgasm took over, my strength began to fade. My upper body leaned against the headboard, my forehead to my hands, and I panted my sexual bliss.

Maverick kissed my left inner thigh before lifting it to move out from underneath me. I was barely aware of being partly in his arms as he helped my body lay down. In a naturally drugged state, my eyes felt lazy, but I watched as he knelt between my spent thighs and removed his shirt. I barely found the strength to reach up and touch his bare, muscular stomach.

As he pulled down his sweatpants, I involuntarily licked my lips as my vagina pulsed. His penis, once freed, stood at attention.

He was gorgeous.

Every single part of him.

Achingly hungry, I asked, "How can I want more?"

He bent over and kissed my stomach. "Some have a stronger sexual appetite." He kissed my breast. "Yours is the most beautiful thing I've ever seen."

Actions speak louder than words. His actions spoke of how honest he was being, and how much he treasured my desires. Instead of demanding his turn for a climax, he continued to show amazing self-control, and his sensational kisses licked every inch of my body. Maverick didn't need to take possession. My flesh was his and he knew it. His tender actions were as if he were mystified—every part of me seemed magical to him. He was just as magical to me. I found myself slowly rubbing my legs and feet alongside his muscular thighs and calves, wanting to feel every part of him simultaneously. Every bit of contact was with wonderful, sincere intentions. Pleasure... and *love*.

The heat rising from his body entranced me even more as his skin slid effortlessly over mine. Maverick no longer asked permission as he roamed and explored my every curve, as if I were utterly edible—a private gourmet delicacy for only him to devour. And I had no hesitation to enjoy his hands when fingers slid inside and out of me with ease. I was so wet, so content, so completely at ease that when this gracious, young man slid another part of his body into mine, I knew I was *never* letting go.

It's amazing, but when you are ready to share, you will.

Immensely joyful tears dripped as I softly said, "I was with him, once... It was the worst." Cautiously and understandably, Maverick started to retreat from inside me. My thighs held tight. He slipped back inside but didn't move; he only stared at me, waiting.

Daring to touch the angel before me, I reached out and held his face. From the bottom of my heart and soul, I said, "Thank you for showing me how beautiful lovemaking can be."

CHAPTER SEVENTEEN

"Sounds like birth control time has arrived," announced V while sitting with me on my bed.

I laughed and smacked her. "Are you hearing the *romantic* part of my story?"

"Are *you* hearing the horrid baby wails that are in your near future?"

I was so happy, and V toying with me made me even happier. I was being a normal girl, having normal girl talk. Another wish had come true. "I told you he wore a condom!"

She eyed my bedroom door. "You're about to tell everyone in this house if you keep hollering like ya are." Then she looked back at me. "Here's the thing, Pretty D, a man as stallion as Mavy Wavy can*not* be contained by some sheer material. He's like your brother—"

"Uh, gross?"

V's eyes shut as her imagination took over. I watched in horror as she growled, "A beast I want to tame, but *hope to hell I can't,* so he will continuously ravage my body and—"

"V. Seriously. I'm about to vomit."

Her eyes opened and she grinned. "Sorry, baby, but your brother is utterly *fuckable*."

"Yep, my lunch is about to come spewing from my mouth."

She stood and admired herself in my full-length mirror. "Speaking of mouths, what are you wearing to the fight?"

Shaking confusion from my mind, I replied, "Not sure what *mouths* have to do with my attire, but I planned on wearing this." I gestured to my jeans and T-shirt.

"Mouths are for eating, and you must dress so Mavy wants to continue to do so."

"You are bound and determined to make me gag today."

Heading to my closet, she blew me off. "Too cold tonight for a slutty dress." Her voice bounced off my closet walls as hangers moved about. "Which, apparently, you don't own." Her head leaned back and peeked out the doorway. "FYI, every girl needs a hooker outfit."

Walking past my open bedroom door, my brother halted. "What?" He entered. "V! Do not corrupt my Lilah."

She came out of my closet with an arm full of clothes and pushed past him. "Mavy likes what he sees. Let's give him a show."

Tuck followed her to my bed. "No. Goat Boy can look elsewhere."

I hissed. "Elsewhere?"

V laughed. "There she is! Paying attention now?"

After a run-by to Viola's house since none of my wardrobe was 'edible' enough, I was in a pair of the sluttiest boots, ever, and the shortest skirt, ever, and the most cleavage revealing blouse, ever. My very displeased, grumbling father and brother followed as V and I entered a warehouse type of building packed with people. Many rows of folding chairs surrounded the square boxing ring, and they all seemed to be full. Not one empty seat in sight. Everyone was buzzing with excitement, talking, laughing, and sipping on beers in plastic cups.

Tuck mumbled, "Holy shit."

Walking down an aisle that led to the ring, I saw Diesel stand up, towering over seated folks. He called out to my dad, "John. Got ya covered over here." Then he saw me and my attire. "The fuck?" *Then* he saw his sister's. "The *fuck?*" *Then* he glared at my brother because V's getup was even skimpier than mine.

Tuck yelled over the tops of people's heads. "She's impossible."

Diesel pointed at him. "Grow some balls, Little Man."

Viola rubbed salt in the open wound by teasingly gyrating against my brother's thigh. Smiling, he swatted her away. "Behave!" Then he playfully shoved us in front him and passed sitting patrons.

Getting closer to our saved seats, my eyes widened. "*Everyone* is here." Hu, Bryce, Cole, the twins and Jaz, even a couple of Diesel's bikers and Cole's parents; Ashley and Buck had driven to Atlanta to show support. After arriving at our saved chairs, I reached to the row in front of us and started delivering hugs. I kissed Cole's mom's cheek. "Mrs. Genner. So, so nice to see you."

Her smile beamed from under her strawberry blonde hair. "Wow. You look stunnin'." She wasn't the beauty my mom was, but this woman had a tale-to-tell behind her green eyes. She was so young to have a son almost through high school, but her story was the same of many in small towns. Diesel wouldn't share the details, only admitting, "They floated into town one night." I didn't understand 'floating' at the time, but I did know teen pregnancies were frowned upon, so Ashley was kicked out of her home before finishing high school herself.

Viola hugged the kind spirited country woman. "Doesn't she?"

Bryce checked out his girlfriend. "Viola, damn. Delicious."

Tucker took a seat next to hers. "She needs to put on some damn clothes."

Sitting back down, Diesel sat next Dad, "Uh, I think we're in for a treat. Hype that our boy is back in the ring is thick. Feel me?"

"No shit?" asked Dad.

Cole's dad, Buck, who looked like a big ol' country boy who *should* be named Buck, turned around in his seat. "I heard about the kid in Atlanta who was quite the up and comer 'til his daddy died. Had no idea it was Delilah's boyfriend."

V polished her nails against her chest. "My bestie is famous." When her nails stuck to bare skin, she laughed, "Oops. I forgot my girls are practically naked."

Tuck took off his jacket and laid it over her chest with a firm warning. "I'm done. Take that off and I'm beating your ass."

She stuck her tongue out but kept the jacket in place.

The overhead lights went darker and spotlights focused on the ring. An announcer lifted a ring rope and slipped under it. He grabbed a mic hanging from the ceiling and spoke of the different fights for the night, but when he mentioned Maverick Hutton, the whole place erupted. Viola gazed around at the cheering people, mumbling, "Oh my God." She stared at me as if I'd been holding back.

Dumbfounded, I uttered, "I run with him. Then he goes to the gym. I've never even seen him box. Only jump rope."

She suspiciously peered around. "I'm not thinkin' he's gonna be jumpin' rope tonight."

The first fight was a bit disturbing. The second even more so. I didn't even know the young men but winced with every hit that landed against their flesh. Managers and trainers were yelling at the fighters, things like, "Uppercut! Body hit! Light on your feet! In-out. In-out!" I had no idea what all that meant, but by the next fight, the guys were bigger and their punches were causing blood to flow. I knew Maverick was next, and I was suspecting his competitor would be just as strong. My stomach soured immediately. "V, I don't think I can watch him get hurt."

She sat up after observing me. "You're pale." She elbowed Tuck. "I need to take her for fresh air."

He leaned forward to see past her. His brows bunched, then he gestured. "Come on."

After a few cleansing breaths outside the building, the nausea started to fade slightly.

My brother smirked. "If it makes you feel any better, I've seen the kid swing. He ain't no joke, Lilah. I believe he will hit more than *he* hit."

Maverick getting punched in his beautiful face raced through my heart, making me panic.

Viola smacked his gut. "Will you *always* be a dumbass?" Cheers erupted from inside, announcing the last fight before my boyfriend's had ended. I jolted with the loud screams. She grabbed my hand again. "Listen, as much as I want to see Mavy in those shorts and watch him sweat, I will stay out here with you if it's too much."

Tuck cringed. "Watch him sweat?"

She eyed him up and down. "I like men hot and in the moment. Feel me?"

He swallowed.

After a deep inhale and exhale, I said, "Thank you, but I want to be supportive for him."

The announcer's voice echoed over the microphone, "... Maverick Hutton!" By the time we made it back inside, one boxer was already in the ring. He was of impressive size, making me sweat with nerves. Music was blaring and Maverick was being escorted through a crowded aisle way. He had on a blue silk hooded robe and was bouncing on his feet, fists in fighting position. He was looking at the floor all the way to the ring. People were cheering and I was stunned, standing in a different aisle, not able to move. It was... surreal.

My brother had me by my arm and was trying to move me along, yelling over the music. "Let's go sit."

Stunned, I blinked my eyes. "Uh, okay."

As I continued down the aisle way, Maverick entered the ring, completely focused and quiet, until he spotted me. The bouncing on his toes stopped and his eyes bugged out of his head.

Viola squealed, "Yay! He loves your outfit!"

Maverick's jaw locked, right before he rushed across the ring, toward me.

My brother moaned, "Aww, fuck me."

Irate, Maverick held on to the top rope and screamed over the music, "Why'd you let her out of the house all smokin' like that?"

Now, my eyes were the ones popping out of my head. He needed to be paying attention to his upcoming battle, not my clothing. I peered around to see *everyone* staring at me. "Oh my God."

Tuck yelled back to Maverick, "Why am I the one in trouble tonight?"

"Because you're doing a shitty job watching over her when I can't?"

"This whole conversation going to be in questions?"

Maverick roared, "Put your jacket on her!"

Tuck thumbed V. "Already covering the less of the two evils!"

V—busy twerking against my thigh—opened Tuck's jacket to expose her practically exposed boobs. "That's me! You like, bestie?"

Diesel yelled from his chair, "Viola! Zip that shit up!" He took a sip of beer in a plastic cup. My dad was trying to do the same but laughing too hard to, wiping his chin.

The audience was laughing hysterically while managers and trainers scurried over to Maverick and escorted him to his stool. It was mortifying.

My boyfriend yelled over his shoulder, "Grow some balls!"

Tucker grumbled as he pushed us toward our seats. "What the fuck is it with you two and my balls tonight?"

I sneered to V, "Thank you very much, Vixen. That went well and wasn't humiliating in the slightest."

We sat back down as Diesel rubbed his silver-ringed hands together. "Atta, girl, Delilah. Get him all riled up. I've got money on this fight. Now, he's so pissed he'd give Tyson a run for my money."

I winced. "Betting? Isn't that illegal?"

He shrugged. "Who the fuck *el* care-os?"

"Maybe I'll nark on you."

Diesel busted out laughing. "You'll be too busy calming down your jealous boyfriend."

Maverick was still brewing on his stool, staring at me. I slunk down in my seat to avoid the heated glare. I couldn't hear what was being said, but a man spoke to Maverick while sticking a mouthpiece up against his teeth. Next thing I knew, fighters were standing, stools were being removed from corners, and a referee was speaking to the gloved men staring each other down as if pit bulls waiting to be freed from their leashes.

I sat up on the edge of my chair, ready to run to the bathroom if I needed to vomit.

The ref asked the fighters to go back to their corners. When a bell rang, I held my breath watching the fighters aggressively approach each other, fists held up by recoiled arms ready to strike. All of a sudden, I could see the dance, the art form of this sport. It was cruel but demanded respect.

Maverick's fist struck out so fast and so impressively hard, I gasped. In horror, I watched as his opponent's jaw went slack, his fist fell to his sides, and then, in slow motion, his body plummeted. The fighter's eyes were closed and his cheek smashed against the mat.

Out. Maverick had knocked the big bastard out cold.

The ref rushed in, pushing Maverick back before doing a count-down for the unconscious individual at his feet. Maverick backed away, unfortunately toward us, then turned around. He found me in a split second. His mouthpiece was still in, but his point and glare said volumes.

I was in deep shit.

I shrunk in my chair again. "I'm going to kill you, V."

Viola held her chest. "Mavy keeps getting hotter and hotter."

"Now *that* is having some balls, Little Man," howled Diesel. He, his biker buddies, and Dad were all laughing so hard they were spilling their beers. Tuck didn't respond to the dig. He was too busy staring at all the folks staring at us. Some looked pissed. I guess Diesel wasn't the only one betting.

The twins were practically huddling around Jaz as if they suspected her to be in a dire situation. Houston, laughing and pointing to us in the row behind him, announced to the audience, "We don't know them. Please do not jump *us* in the parking lot."

Cole's dad laughed over his shoulder. "Diesel, you happen to have more bikers around?"

Bryce teased, "Make it stat. We are going down. I repeat, we are going down."

Viola never did get her outfit back. It turns out that Maverick liked it. A *lot*. Just didn't like anyone else seeing me in it. *Score!*

Our senior year of high school got sucked into the whirlwind of life. Far too quickly, we were all needing to make decisions for our next step of schooling: college. Jazabelle opted to take a year off. No one said anything but suspected it was due to the twins. Viola's college wasn't Bryce's, but they decided to try a long distance relationship. Cole and Hu wanted to take on the world, together, and both got into the same college elsewhere. Maverick had a scholarship waiting for him in DC.

I followed him. Always will.

Dad wanted me closer to home but helped me chase my boyfriend across the country. All he asked was that I live in a dorm, with girls. I didn't want to. Suspicions told me it was the wrong decision, but I met Dad's compromise and tried because Maverick thought it wise to listen to our elders. Most of the time, they were right with their wisdom. This time, they were wrong.

In college, Maverick and I experienced some hard, lonely times. He says they were our worst because we fell so far. He doesn't know the depth of that fall for me, but he was the one who stopped the downward spiral, eventually.

It's probably the same for all college sports students on full scholarships, but Maverick's schedule was quite grueling. He earned every penny of his free degree. If he wasn't sparring in a ring, he was fighting in one. Some reporters went as far as to say Maverick was partly responsible for the rise in college boxing again. With that type of momentum, there was no room for me. I was left farther and farther behind as he rose to his dream.

I spent most of my time with my roommate Sadie, a cute young girl from a podunk town in Kansas. Our small-town vibe wasn't the only thing we had in common. Her boyfriend, Pete, was also a boxer and happened to be Maverick's roommate. Pete was a kind soul. He was quite taller than Maverick and much lankier. He was from Nigeria and had the prettiest dark skin I'd ever seen on a black man. Sadie and Pete had only met in college so, as she and I found ourselves alone again on a Friday night, she wasn't longing for him like I was Maverick.

Sadie actually enjoyed the freedom. Not from Pete but from her parents that were quite strict. Her daddy was some sort of pastor, so partying had been new for the innocent girl, and it quickly became a favorite pastime. Lucky for her, there was always a party happening in the big city college.

I met many people. Guys who wanted to fuck me and girls who hated me because of it. So unfair. All I wanted was Maverick. Nightmares of Kenny, without Maverick's deep voice keeping me level, returned. About two a.m. I woke, drenched in sweat. Memories were hunting me down, and I felt like lost prey in the night separated from her herd. Needing to feel I belonged somewhere, and knowing Maverick would be fast asleep, I called a hero of mine. When he answered, I heard lots of voices and loud music quickly fade as his office door shut. "You need my cavalry?"

Grabbing my pounding chest, I whispered, "No. Just you."

"I'll start riding up tomorrow. Have some business to take care of anyways up there. I need to talk to your pops?"

"I'd prefer not."

"You safe? I'll fly one of my boys out there right now."

"Physically safe, yes. Mentally? Starting to be unsure."

Diesel made it to me in two days. Flanked by two other bikes, he roared into my dorm parking lot. The sun was setting, and I had just finished class. I had been so anxious for his arrival that I stood outside waiting for him. I needed family and didn't want to worry Dad or Tuck. As soon as Diesel stepped off his bike, I rushed to him, shocked to find myself crying. He held me. The big, burly biker actually rocked me while kissing the top of my head. "I'll kill someone if I need to, baby girl."

That made me laugh and wipe tears, unaware of how deadly serious he was. I stepped back. "Nah. Just having nightmares and losing sleep."

"Boxer Boy?"

I shrugged, looking away. "Boxing."

He lifted his chin with awareness. "I see. Where does that leave you?"

Exhaling, I pointed to his leather-vested chest. "Calling you."

I waved at his guys still on their bikes, keeping a distance but watching their president's back. They both smiled and waved back as if I were their adorable little sister. "Hey, JB."

It was wild to remember how long they had been watching me. I wasn't jailbait anymore. I was almost twenty. I asked Diesel, "Do I still have any of them following me?"

"Not right now. Your distance is good. Any new threats wouldn't be aware of your connection to me."

"V?"

"Too intertwined into my world not to be covered at all times."

I nodded heavily. "Sounds like a lot of pressure for you."

"No lie there, but it's everyday life for us."

"How do you, uh," my shoe played with a pebble, "handle the constant pressure of your past?"

He eyed me as if he was starting to understand my call. "You got demons huntin' ya?"

I peeked up to him. "Do you?"

His chest filled with air before reluctantly nodding. "Yeah, I sure do. And I'm thinkin' that's why you called."

Just then, a roar of another Harley had Diesel looking over his shoulder. We both watched as it rode by. The driver was too far away, so I couldn't recognize him. "One of yours?"

He mumbled to himself, "Motherfucker." His voice was harsh as he told one of his guys, "Handle that shit. I'll call Austin's Chapter." A biker nodded and roared out of the parking lot.

I asked, "Everything okay?"

He put his arm around my shoulders. "Hungry?"

I leaned my cheek to his chest. "Yes."

On the back of Diesel's bike, like in Daytona, I took in the city. So many lights and so much traffic had the rides similar, but this time I wasn't searching for new experiences. I longed for the soul that had become a much-needed stability in my life. The move to DC felt as if it robbed me. I ached to go back home and bask in the simplicity of being loved by Maverick.

At another hole-in-the-wall establishment, I scarfed down the best bacon cheeseburger ever. Licking my fingers, I talked around a mouthful. "How? How do you find these places?"

"I get around." He winked.

"You a typical slutty biker, Diesel?"

His laugh was boisterous. "Define slutty."

"Sex with a different girl every week."

He choked on his sip of beer. Wiping his mouth, he chuckled, "I, uh, may be in a whole different category if a little warm-up to my engines is what you consider slutty." He leaned forward. "Can you keep a secret?"

I looked down to my empty plate, thinking of my countless secrets.

He nodded. "Yeah, if the answer were no, I wouldn't be here."

That comment is exactly why I had called him. How could someone in his profession not comprehend what I was going through?

Tiredly, he sat back in his chair. "Truth is, I fuck a lot of girls, babe. I'm searchin' for somethin' that feels right."

"Maybe you're going about that search wrong."

He twisted his beer mug in its condensation. "True. Maybe I'm actually runnin'."

My eyes raised to his.

"It can get tiring, that's for sure."

I eagerly nodded. "So tiring."

"Got any advice for me?"

Surprised, I grasped my chest. "Me? Uh, well, okay. When having sex, what feeling are you searching for?"

He grinned. "Besides the obvious?"

Giggling, I replied, "Yes, besides the orgasm."

Diesel thought for a moment then threw his hands in the air. "Fuck it." He pointed at me. "You are to never *el* repeat-*o* this to anyone."

"Never." I got excited and wiggled in my chair. "Diesel, we're girlfriends now."

The expression on a biker's face when you tell him he is acting girlie is one everyone on earth should experience. "The fuck?"

I fell back in my chair, grabbing my stomach as laughter rolled through me.

"You about done?"

Out of breath, I leaned in. "Yes. I'm done. Spill."

"I want that feeling of someone ready to have my back. No matter what."

"Er, what about your brothers?"

"Not the same."

My head tilted. "You about to go deep on me?"

"*El* fucked up-o, I know, but what a woman can bring a man is like nothing else on earth. Knowing your bitch has your back, no matter what, that is what makes our world go round."

Stunned. I was stunned to hear him wanting a woman, and I don't know why. Beyond his tough exterior, he was one of the best men I had ever known. "You sound as if you've had this before."

He only nodded, staring at me.

"Jesus. With who?"

"To tell you could get you killed."

I couldn't move. "Why is my heart pounding?"

"Because I don't exaggerate."

"Why are you telling me all this?"

"So you will talk to me."

My eyes closed. My throat tightened. "But, only one person knows."

"Probably the same that knows my secret."

My eyes opened. "Viola."

Eyes piercing me, ever so slowly, he nodded.

I did, too. Diesel and I were making an epic, life-changing, life-risking pact. "Tell me who."

Barely audible, he said, "The mother of my son."

I stopped breathing.

Another very slow nod while staring at me. "And you know him. Well."

The sound of my inhale rung in my ears. *Those blue eyes...* "Artist."

A tremor started in my toes, then it moved its way up my legs, into my stomach, my chest... "But... But he sounded so lonely. He said he was searching for the feeling of belonging."

"I guess you and I are not the only ones."

"Why was he not with you earlier?"

"I didn't know about him. She was taken from me."

My heart bled for him. "How? Where's his mama now?"

Diesel continued his stare... then shook his head, with much caution.

"More danger for me to know?"

"Yes."

"Wait, you said only one other person knows."

A nod.

"Art doesn't know?"

A head shake was what told me that Art had found his dad, and he didn't even know it. "I'm limited what I can share with you, but I can tell you this. As I said earlier, I never overreact. If I have you guarded, I've got good reason. Feel me?"

I swallowed. "I feel you." And I also knew something was tragically wrong. If Diesel loved Art's mama, why wasn't he with her? Why was he searching for the same love in a bunch of meaningless sex?

"Something went down tonight. You're back on watch, but I'll keep him in civilian clothes."

I was surprisingly happy with the news. Distant family would be nearby. That is how epically lonely I had become. I was technically in danger, but being back on watch took the edge off. "Diesel, I hate to break it to you, but none of your scary looking guys can be hidden by a plain T-shirt."

He stared.

Oh shit. "No. No—"

"You can trust him, Pretty D."

"It's, it's complicated."

"Because he loves you?"

I winced. "Now knowing who he is to you—Oh, God. Loves me?" I wanted to crawl away in shame. "Jesus. I'm so sorry. He-I-I just don't feel that way for him."

"Boxer Boy is your man, no one is disputing that. Breathe."

I did and then exhaled. "I am sorry though. I do care for him."

"He's got time to find his girl."

I frowned. "You don't?"

"Dangerous lifestyle. My days are numbered, don't ya think?"

I blew out a shaky breath. "Don't want to think about that."

He grinned. "Love you, too, girl."

Swallowing fear, I changed the subject. "Why am I back on watch? What happened?"

"Unexpected company. Now, hold up your end of the bargain."

I blinked, mind spinning. "Bargain?"

"I'll take your secret to the grave."

"Oh." I swallowed again. "Bargain. Right." I kept feeling my breath being stolen. "Uh, shit." I peered around, wanting my business private, and wanting to run.

"See how my back is to the door?" Having it pointed out to me, it did seem bizarre since Diesel had the vibe of always needing to be on guard. "We are on safe grounds, no one minding our business." He stayed quiet while talking. "You guys told me of Kenny's possible mental illness."

"Possible?" My hands gripped the table. "I was there. I know what I saw."

"Is that why you won't speak of what happened between the two of you?"

I patted my hand against my mouth, trying to convince my lips to work.

"V always complained about him looking at you wrong."

I rubbed my hands together.

Not answering seemed to prompt more words from Diesel. "Your dad says there is confusion to what kind of relationship you and Kenny had."

"The confusion was one-sided."

His tongue sucked at his teeth while Diesel studied me. "The mental illness remark tells me it was *his* confusion."

I rubbed at my chest as I nodded.

"Can you understand I'm pushing because I love you?"

"I have no doubt of that fact, hence why I'm not running out the door."

"Like you want to."

I nodded.

"When I speak of Kenny's mental illness, your shoulders seize."

"They do?"

"That usually, in my experience, means guilt."

My stomach started to turn like I was on a ship out on a rough sea.

"Knowing you like I do, I can't imagine what you should feel guilty about. So, I'm guessing, as you have guilt for not loving Art—"

My shoulders seized. I felt it that time.

"You have the same shame in not lovin' Kenny the same as he wanted."

As if preparing to go under water and hold my breath, I kept panting, lips in an O shape.

"Someone who is mentally unstable may not have taken the ego hit very well."

I choked. "He was a good person."

"I believe you, but was he a good man when he wasn't... himself?"

The tears began to fall as I shook my head.

His ring fingers rubbed over his mouth. "If I gave you an easy out, one word to describe the worst he did to you, would you take it? If I promised to stop pushing?"

One word. Could I really wrap up all the torture with one word?

Diesel stayed silent, giving me the chance to ponder.

The fear Kenny caused was earth-shattering, but my heart kept repeating one word. That word said volumes and did much more than physical damage... I whispered, "Rape."

He tried to hide his sharp intake.

Felt like forever and a day, but Diesel finally said, "I keep my word. I won't push anymore, but I'm coming over there to hold you. Feel me?"

My chair scraped against the floor as I stood, so wanting to be held. "I feel you."

In an old dilapidated bar, it was a biker who finally got me to speak out loud the one word that was owning my world.

CHAPTER EIGHTEEN

Outside the gym, Maverick kissed me. "I love you, Lilah." His eyes and smile spoke the truth, always. But it still hurt to watch him walk inside, knowing I wouldn't touch his lips again that night, or possibly in the next few days. In fact, each kiss became rarer as the days passed.

To the empty air, since I was alone, I whispered, "I love you, too." I stared at the keys in my hand, the keys that belonged to the car Maverick convinced me to get, and prepared myself to grab some dinner and go back to the dorms.

Walking past a dark car, I saw blue eyes watching me through the windshield.

Exhausted, I walked to the driver's window. He rolled it down. A chuckle echoed inside. "Was it this awful family car that gave me away?"

I leaned my elbows in the opening as I bent over. "Nah. It was your stealthy spying techniques."

That earned me a laugh.

"Diesel make it home safely?"

"All good."

"How ya likin' DC?"

"Ain't."

"Not being very *artistic* with your words tonight."

"Not inspired." He stared to where Maverick had just kissed me.

"Wanna come meet my roommate, since you're my stalker and all?"

His eyes met mine. "How you gonna explain me?"

Walking into my dorm room, I saw Sadie lying on her stomach, doing homework, her feet wrapping around each other in the air. I threw my backpack on my bed. "Hey."

She tapped a pen on her chin. "Why am I putting myself through this?"

"Because the world has convinced us we will live in despair without a college education."

"That's right." She looked to the door. "Hey! Who's your friend?"

I thumbed behind me. "Transfer student. Art." I faced him. "Art, this is my roomie, Sadie. She is the girlfriend of my boyfriend's roommate, Pete."

He chuckled, saying, "Not too complicated," and held out his hand. "Nice to meet you."

She sat up all bubbly. "You too! I just ordered some pizza. Hungry?"

He smiled. "Always."

Sadie didn't ask questions and she didn't judge. Art became my friend again. He didn't try to kiss me, nor talk of feelings for me. It was nice. It helped with the loneliness, immensely, but it couldn't take away the nightmares. Kenny's eyes would find me in my sleep and silently threaten me. That is why I was so shocked when he suddenly became kind in one of my nightmares, pushing hair from my sweaty face, while whispering, "You should tell."

I sat up in bed, clutching my chest in the dark, sweat dripping from my forehead.

The dorm room was pitch black and Sadie was sleeping.

Grabbing my cell, I called Maverick. It was just after midnight and he wasn't answering. Desperate, I called another number. Art answered, "You okay?"

I whispered to not wake Sadie. "You sound like you're running."

"I am. To you."

My heart felt pings of gratitude. "No, I'm okay. Just a nightmare."

"Want me to come up?"

Yes. "No. I'm going to go back to sleep."

"I'll be in the horrid family car. Call if ya need me."

At a party, Sadie and I were doing another shot of whiskey when Art suddenly appeared in our friend's backyard. Sadie slurred, "Arrrt! Hev fun wit us!"

"Hey, Sadie girl. What ya celebrating?"

"Winnning!" she cheered in the backyard that was lit by street-lamps instead of a bonfire I would've paid high dollar for. I'd never lived in a city and was shocked to learn of Fire Ordinances.

Extremely intoxicated, I could still see Art's evil glare to the surrounding guys. "Oh yeah? What cha win?"

Sadie fell into him when trying to point at a table. "Beer pong."

Holding her to his side—so she wouldn't fall on her face—he took the cup I was raising to my lips. I whined my objection, "Nooooooo," and tried to get it back but failed. Possibly because I wasn't sure which of the four solo cups I was seeing, to grab.

Art sniffed the cup then yanked his face away. "Jesus." He asked the guys, "No mixers? Don't need them conscious later?"

The guys started shifting their weight but, Sadie explained, "Art, dees are ourrrrr new friends."

"Friends, eh? Did your new friends explain you only drink when you *lose* at beer pong?"

"Er." *Hiccup.* She covered her mouth. "I durn feeeeel sur good."

Art nodded. "Pure whiskey can do that to ninety-two-pound

girls."

I slurred, "Stop saaaayin' gurl." I patted my chest. Okay, so I patted my shoulder by mistake, but I was trying to make a point. "We are women."

He winked. "Don't I know it, beautiful."

He was smart. Stroking my ego was the best way to keep my drunk ass calm. I did some sort of bashful smile and ended up spitting on my bottom lip. "Art?"

"Babe?"

"I mey beee a teeny weeny drunk."

He teased, "Get the fuck out of here."

"Where?" Sadie clung to his waist while trying to look around but resembled a one-legged duck.

Art told our new friends, "FYI, Sadie girl is the girlfriend of Pete. Ya know him? The badass boxer attending your school? Maybe I should give him this address?"

Heads shook no as Sadie sighed, "Dat big guuuy, just a swveet hert." *Hiccup!* "Bu' he suuuure like'im sum Sadieeeee!"

Art guided-dragged us to his car. As he stuck Sadie in the back seat, she asked, "Cheeeeeseburger time?"

He buckled her in. "Now you're talkin', Sadie girl."

I was still struggling with opening the passenger door by the time he came to help out the challenged and intoxicated. "Yur handle ees broken."

"Again? I just had it fixed."

I shrugged, which for some reason meant fall-into-car-now. As I bounced off, I offered much sympathy. "Dern no wha' to tell yur."

He opened the un-broke door. "How about Sadie is right? It's cheeseburger time."

"Cheeeeeesebuuuurger time," sung Sadie from the back seat, her head already drooping to her shoulder for *pass-out time.*

Art was in front of my face, buckling me in. I thought of Maverick, and how he had done this once while I was trying to kiss him. "An' Freeench fries?" My lips reached forward.

Artist yanked back. "Sure. And fries." The door shut.

A sting punched my gut. Guilt had me sobering up considerably. I was stunned at my actions and regretted them to the deepest degree. Maverick was why I was even in DC. But alcohol and loneliness were a very powerful combo, and I was its victim of the night.

Art didn't talk to me in the car except for asking about my order of food. After answering him, I stayed quiet in my shame. With bellies full and Sadie sleeping safely in her bed, Artist tried to lead me to bed, folding down my blankets. "Your turn. Crawl in please." My bottom lip started to tremble. "Ah, shit."

I was still very drunk but was more coherent. "I'm so sorry I tried to kiss you."

"That was pretty fucked up."

Nodding, I wiped my cheek of tears. "Yes. You have every right to be mad at me."

"I know that." He exhaled. "But I'm not."

My eyes widened. "You're not?"

"No... I just know how much you'd hate yourself in the morning. I know you love him, babe. Like mad."

Bursting into tears, I sobbed more shame. "I do. So much. But he doesn't seem to love me anymore."

"Babe, I wish that were true. Maybe then I'd have a chance."

I almost hissed. "I-I..." I blew out air that was trembling in my lungs. "I'm so sorry."

He smirked. "Twice in one night, huh?"

I stared at the floor. "If I had control over my heart—"

"Please don't lie to me."

Closing my eyes, I nodded regret. I covered my mouth. "He takes away my nightmares."

A sharp inhale had me opening my eyes, but Art was already covering his reaction. "Then let's get you to him." Pain crossed Art's face as he forced a smile.

I wanted to apologize for the third time that night, but there was no need. Artist was being strong, so I decided to do the same.

Standing in front of Maverick's closed dorm room door, Art had his back against the hallway wall to not be seen. I whispered, "Thank you... my friend."

The son of a biker who dared to love me from afar, swallowed and forced another smile. "Knock, babe."

Feeling awful for mistreating the one who drove me to my boyfriend's, tears dripped as I knocked. When Pete answered, clearly just crawling out of bed, he almost yelled, "Delilah! What's wrong?"

I looked to Art's back as he walked away and cried harder.

Maverick yanked me against his chest. "Lilah, what is it?"

"I'm lonely." I melted to him, the nightmares already feeling farther away with his voice comforting me. He held me that night, and I slept like I hadn't in months. But by morning, Maverick was back to his schedule. He was so distracted, he never asked how I got there that night, nor did he ask if I needed a ride home. He packed his bags for a fight, kissed my forehead, and left me in his bed.

Feeling as if I had no more rope to cling to, I called Art. "Can I have a ride?"

"He doesn't know you're without your car?"

Embarrassed, I bit out, "Can I have a ride or not?" I had come to Maverick, needing him in so many ways, but was left behind, once again. And I was over it. Completely.

Art's sigh was loud and forgiving. "Yeah, babe. I'm sorry this is happening to you—"

"Got your bike?"

I could almost hear him, mentally battling with himself. "Fuck. Yeah, babe."

"I need a shower. I need a day away from school then need to meet up with Sadie at a party tonight. You down?"

Art was down. Reluctant, but down.

In the parking lot of my dorm, Art eyed my clothing from his bike. "A skirt?"

I was showered and ready for trouble. "The problem?" My old anger had returned and was happy to be free again.

"Easy, Pretty D." He started the engine. The rumble matched the roar burning in my soul.

After hiking up my inappropriate riding attire, I slid on the back. "I've never seen you on your bike with your vest."

"Cut."

"Oh."

"It's never happened before. Be honored and stop bustin' my balls with your attitude."

Someone handling me was far too attractive because I felt out of control with no desire to gain it again.

I didn't miss the gun tucked in the back of his jeans as we rode around for a while. I think he was giving me time to cool down before pulling over for a quiet breakfast. I didn't 'bust his balls' so we got along real well.

We rode for a while again and then had a nice lunch together. We fell back into conversation quite easily. It was nice. Sadie was great, but this company and laid-back conversation were needed.

We rode... Then we had a wonderful dinner together. I smiled. I laughed! I felt somewhat human again by the time the sun was telling us to enjoy our evening. And that's exactly what we did. We made another stop so we could keep talking and have a few glasses of wine. It was... enchanting. We had managed to ride a motorcycle into the sunset and into a delusional Cloud Nine. It made me think of Maverick.

Not wanting to remember my boyfriend, who I could no longer hold on to, I stared at the empty glass and said, "Maybe we should get going?"

The behavior was unwanted yet uncontrolled. After being abandoned by the sweet Kenny—when he would switch to someone else—and after my brother had abandoned me—for college to escape—I was no longer able to handle the sensation. It was at that very moment, right there at a little table in a dark bar, that I recognized the feeling. And, I finally understood when it all began: the night my mother died.

Memories of sneaking into my brother's bed as a little girl passed through me.

Memories of crawling into Kenny's bed, the first night he was angry with me, also breezed through me. And memories of the prior night, slipping into Maverick's bed, silently begging for love, had me recognizing a pattern. Now, I was silently begging Art for love, all along *still* not loving myself.

With a knowing nod, he replied, "Yeah. Yeah, babe. I hear ya."

At the party, we both got off the bike. I could barely look Art in the eye because I had been lying to us both. Deep down, I think he knew it but allowed the betrayal. I took hold of his hand. "I want... to go home, with you. I don't belong in the big city."

Even though I was making it clear he was my second choice, he still appeared sympathetic for me. "Not without him?"

Still not able to look up from the ground, I shook my head. "Home is the only place I can be... without him."

He kissed my hand. "So fucking sorry, babe."

I swallowed down tears.

"We'll pack your shit and haul ass."

I whispered, "Tomorrow."

Quietly, he agreed. "Yeah, babe. I'll make it happen."

The party was at a duplex that was clearly being rented out by college students—who had many friends. Sadie was already inside, seeming to be having a fun time. When she saw me and Art, she cheered, "Cheeseburger time!"

Art laughed. "I will miss Sadie girl."

Smiling at the bubbly sweetheart, I sighed. "Me too."

She ran up and hugged Art, then me. Then she asked, "What's wrong?"

I touched her little freckled face. "I gotta go home, girl."

She stilled and paled. "You mean home-home."

It wasn't a question so I didn't answer. "One more party?"

She faked through her evident pain. "Yeah. Of course. One more for my roomy."

A peace came with my decision. I had finally surrendered to what I couldn't change; Maverick and I were done. I wasn't sure how he would take the news but was sure he wouldn't follow or try to bring me back. I was convinced he might actually be relieved. And I believed it would be days before Maverick even knew I had left with my tail tightly tucked.

Imagine my surprise when not even two hours had passed before Maverick charged in like a wild stallion claiming his turf. Standing in the kitchen with Art and a guy we had just met, I instantly became annoyed that Maverick dared to screw up my plan and make me look desperate, pleading him not to let me go. So, I snarled through the hefty buzz I had kickin'. Sadie stood in the kitchen doorway, mouthing, "I'm sorry," to me.

"Lilah, I need to talk to you."

Liquid courage had me saying, "Sorry, I'm *busy*."

"That's not even close to being fair. Talk to me."

Just his energy being present had my skin buzzing beyond the alcohol. I was so in love with him but replied, "I'm having conversations *elsewhere* at the moment."

Art was snarling, too. "Yeah, she's a little occupied." He wasn't interested in my not leaving with him the following day.

But my Maverick was one-track-minded that late evening and wasn't exuding much patience. "Delilah, I'm tired as hell and don't want to argue with you, but—"

"Maybe you should head home for a *nap*," said my ballsy new acquaintance.

Maverick's jaw locked tight. "I'm two seconds away from—" He glared at me. "Lilah, I'm *going* to talk to you—here, with consequences to strangers, or in that pantry for some privacy. Your choice."

In horror, I watched Art reaching into the back of his pants. So, I quickly replied, "Pantry."

As soon as Maverick shut the door, he started in on me, accusing me of cheating, which I almost had, and practically still was. And I was adamant that it was his fault. So, I smacked him. *Slap!* I felt he had chosen his career over me. I felt betrayed. I think I wanted him to feel some sort of pain, just like I was feeling. "You moved me out here and then left me to—" I was going to say, "find my way back home."

But Maverick yelled in the pantry, "No! You moving here was *your* choice!"

He was absolutely right, but I didn't want to look into the mirror of truth.

Slap! I smacked him again. I had only smacked one other person in my entire life. Kenny. Kenny's reaction was horrifying. Maverick's expression showed shock, emotion, and best of all, humanity. But he growled, "I guess the truth hurts."

Slap! Was I testing him? Oh, yes. Without a doubt. I wasn't aware of it at the time, but I most certainly was needing to see if he was what Diesel had described; someone to have my back no matter what. At that point, my back felt exposed to anyone and everything, and I felt I was losing the only man I had *literally* ever wanted.

I shouted, "How dare you say that to me when you have been ignoring me!"

"I'm not ignoring you. You know I'm preparing for fights—"

"Prepare for this fight." *Slap!*

The fight I was speaking of was the one I needed him to commit to when it came to loving me. With every strike to his face, I saw devotion. I knew it was wrong, but desperation can make you do crazy things.

He growled, "I never asked you to—"

Slap!

His emotional responses weren't matching his words. His silent reaction showed allegiance. Maverick asked, "What is it? You want out? You want those guys?"

Slap!

Fidelity.

I warned, "Don't talk to me like that."

"What if this new guy can't touch you like I can?"

Slap!

Desire.

"That all ya got, little girl?"

Slap!

Dedication.

His hand slipped under my skirt. "Have you forgotten who taught you how to come?"

I slapped his chest and saw *faithfulness.*

Yes, Maverick says we fell...

I say we rose.

I may have bit and marked the man I treasured most, and he may have fucked me and begged me never to leave him, but it was one of the final pieces toward our ultimate commitment to our lifetime of love. Some may find these details disturbing. I say don't judge unless you have been internally twisted from a horrid past.

It had been Artist that opened the pantry doors after I screamed through my orgasm. He thought I was being hurt but quickly evaluated the situation, me with my legs wrapped around Maverick's waist. Maverick had only met Art while incredibly intoxicated and never remembered it. And he never saw the palmed gun at Art's side.

The next time I saw my biker friend, I had already moved into a place with Maverick. Dad and Tuck admitted their mistake and had no qualms with me living with my boyfriend. I think, deep down, they were relieved to hear how happy I finally was. None of Maverick's schedule bothered me anymore because, when he was in town, his nights were all mine, and the beautiful lovemaking was enough to feed my soul and keep the nightmares away when my boyfriend was on the road.

Standing in my college parking lot, Artist was saying goodbye. He swore he understood my decision to stay in DC. I apologized. He did, too. Art wouldn't let me take all the blame. I guess true friends never do.

He said, "I would be lying to say I wasn't happy when Maverick was fucking up."

I hugged him. "My spring break tattoo."

Art squeezed me in return. "The girl who reminds me I want more."

Thinking of his dad's words, my eyes welled with gratitude. "I can live with that."

"You and Boxer Boy will make it, babe."

"Oh yeah, we're more solid than ever."

"That's quite the dump he's moved you into."

Playfully, I smacked his chest. "Don't be hatin' on our castle."

Seemingly lost in thought, he smiled. "Guess what? No more watch. You and Maverick can enjoy your roach motel in peace."

That won him another smack while my cell rang. "Hello?"

"Lilah, I planned on surprising you with dinner but, well, your pan may never be the same."

Art kissed my cheek and got on his bike. As he roared off, I watched him and wiped a tear. *Bye, Artist.* "I'll pick up some tacos for dinner."

"I love you, Lilah."

That very night, after Maverick housed thirteen tacos, he eyed me suspiciously. "Why do you want me to hold on to this railing above my head?"

Our warehouse apartment had exposed plumbing and should've been condemned, but I loved every square inch of the dump. "Because I asked you to?"

With his back against the makeshift wall, Maverick reached over his head. His hands gripped the pipe. "Now what?"

In front of him, I lowered to my knees. "Don't let go."

Maverick was already panting, his jeans tightening against his growing erection. I had never given him oral sex, and he never asked why. Another sign of how much he loved me.

As I unbuckled his jeans, I peered up. "Your hands on that pipe is crucial."

His eyes showed concern but he nodded, breathless.

"I trust you, Maverick, but my mind may not."

"You don't have to do this."

"Nope. But I really want to."

"C-Can I watch?"

Pulling his jeans down, I giggled. "You want to see my lips on your dick."

His head shot back and hit the non-wall. "Do you want me to come before you even get started? Dirty talk? Shit, babe! Think!"

Laughing hysterically, my hand took hold of his erection. His whole body jerked but he didn't let go of the pipe. I laughed again. "You good?"

"Never better."

He groaned as I slipped my mouth around him. I was expecting to get apprehensive through the event but ended up quickly loving the feel of him. My head kept bobbing as my mouth begged for more. My tongue swirled and sucked with a passion and hunger that was blowing my mind. Metal creaked above us while he fought for control, but he tasted so good I couldn't let up. I found myself moaning. Every time I did, the creaking pipe got louder. His pleasure only spurred me to suck even harder.

Just then, I could hear the train approaching. It was time to pay Maverick back. I gave him all I had to offer, working my mouth and hand as if possessed.

"D-Delilah."

I groaned.

"Babe. Ah, shit, that-feels-so-good."

Groan!

"Imma, Imma, Imma gonna come any second."

I sunk him deeper into my mouth, daring him to release inside me.

The train charged past our bug-infested hellhole that I adored with all my heart while Maverick roared, "Lilaaaaaaaah..." and came in my mouth.

I guess I really knew what I was doing. Within a few weeks, I was engaged.

We finished out our college years madly in love.

CHAPTER NINETEEN

Once college graduates, Maverick and I moved back home. We were surprised to be a little shell-shocked, trying to get reacquainted with the small-town mentality. We had grown into adults and had done so together. That is why I was shocked to be struggling with the sinking feeling of going backwards. I hadn't had a nightmare in a couple of years, but they were now returning with a vengeance. Whenever Maverick was out of town due to a fight, I would wake up sweating. Being back in my old room was proving to be more than I could handle. The walls were covered with issues I had ignored for years.

One night, I woke, panicked and all alone. Gazing around my dark room, I felt his presence. Kenny was there. Not physically but his spirit. I was sure of it, and it terrified me.

Sneaking down the hallway, trying not to wake my dad and his new girlfriend, Savannah, I slipped into Tuck's room. It was eerie that he no longer lived there, but I was so happy for Viola finally getting her man. She had packed his stuff in an hour flat and took him to her house. Diesel was so happy to have them both living with him while they designed their dream home.

I could still smell my brother though, and that was enough for some comfort. Quietly, I got under his covers. When I realized I was back to old habits, lying in a bed searching for love... I cried myself to sleep.

"You're late?" shrieked Viola. "But I have you on the pill!"

I paced her room, tripping over my brother's shoes. "Maverick and I were getting ready to buy property. Build a house. What have I done?"

"Well, the little rodent *will* need a home, so I suggest you don't cancel those plans."

I stopped and faced her, sitting at her desk that had my brother's clothes draped everywhere. "Rodent?"

Viola held a T-shirt of his to her nose, her eyes closing as if drugged. "Yes, rodent. Infant. Child. All the same."

"Bailey is a child and you adore her."

Viola and Tucker took Bailey to the movies and out for pizza all the time. So, she blew me off. "Bailey is related to a gorgeous freak of nature, AKA, my bestie. Of course, we're going to bond. Very different."

"Er, you have not thought this one through."

"Explain."

"The possible baby in my belly would be your bestie's spawn."

Her jaw dropped. "Holy shit. I bet this baby will walk on water just like JC."

I couldn't help but burst out laughing.

Tuck strolled in. "Two of my three favorite girls."

Viola winked at me. "See? He gets Bailey, too."

After pushing V to a lying position on the bed, he got on top of her. "I want a Bailey."

"Please don't start the process with me still in the room," I begged.

"A rodent?" scoffed V. "And ruin my rockin' body? Fuck that

noise. Besides, only one of your favorite girls should be making a baby at a time."

My brother froze, and my palm smacked my forehead. "Vi-ola!"

"What?"

Tucker rolled off her. Then he sat up. *Then* he laughed! "Dad is going to *beat* Goat Boy's ass." He slapped his hands together. "That's what he gets for wanting to give me a black eye."

When moving Maverick and me to college, not letting us live together, Maverick promised my brother a black eye if it was a mistake. Dad thought the arrangement was well planned.

I hollered, "Tuck! You gave him one first."

"Your point?"

The three of us went to the drug store and bought a test...

I had been so scared to tell Maverick about the baby, but he was one-hundred-percent ecstatic. I don't know why it surprised me. While away at college, he missed Bailey to the point I thought it would make him sick. Unlike most young men, being a father figure was ingrained into his soul to a degree that he didn't know how to shut it down.

Dad was thrilled with the idea of building his baby girl a home, but not so thrilled that a young man had knocked her up. He chased Maverick around the front yard. It was humiliating to me but comical to my brother. The only thing that simmered Dad was the now rushed wedding and being incredibly busied with building my house in supersonic speed. All his connections were being used, and all favors were being cashed in. Night crews made around the clock construction happen, and permits seemed like a walk in the park. Having no neighbors kept anyone from complaining of all the late-night racket.

As my belly grew, the nightmares faded. The baby girl in my belly was filling a hole in my heart, and I had yet to even hold her. Have you ever heard someone say, *"My life is perfect"*? It's incredibly rare, I know, but that is how I felt. A part of me dared to believe I had paid some unwritten due and was now being allowed to truly reap my rewards.

Powerful. It was such a powerful time for me.

With only six weeks left of my pregnancy, boxes and furniture were being moved into my brand new home. Maverick felt so guilty but had to jump on a plane and leave me to unpack. We were newlyweds; we hadn't had time to acquire many belongings, so I wasn't overwhelmed in the slightest. He had been gone a couple of days and was due back in one. The sun was already down, and I was in the kitchen chopping vegetables for my dinner. It felt so good to finally be in my own home that my hips swayed to the music I had playing over the surround sound system Diesel bought as a housewarming gift. I'm sure I looked ridiculous with my big ol' belly swinging in the wind, but I didn't care. I was free and happy. Popping a carrot into my mouth, I froze when seeing a shadow outside my back sliding glass doors. I was sure it was a man wearing a hooded sweatshirt.

I called out, "Tuck?"

He didn't move.

More timidly, I asked, "Daddy?"

He still didn't move.

I whispered, "Art?"

His hand laid on the glass.

I sighed.

He slowly backed away into the night.

I couldn't help but think, *Am I in trouble? Is that why Art is watching me again?* I touched my belly. Suddenly scared of her being in danger, I picked up my cell.

"Hello?"

"Daddy?"

"What's the matter, Light?"

I looked out the glass, into the dark, knowing I couldn't explain. "Uh, hormonal I guess."

"Get your ass in your car and come to me, baby girl. Savannah has cooked up some good cookin'. Your brother, V, and Diesel will be here shortly."

Smiling because that sounded perfect, I ended the call. My phone had only three percent of its battery left. *I'll charge it in the car.* I never did. Had I, would that awful night have gone differently? Would I have heard that gravelly voice over my cell announcing his surprise and rushed back home to my husband's loving arms?

Had I not bought those damn pills, would Kenny still be alive?

Questions like that can make someone go mad. Maybe that is why the rest of the night is foggy when trying to remember. At Dad's, the house phone rang, so I answered it.

I can't describe what it sounds like to hear a mother scream for her son.

There are no words.

Jessica was trying to tell me what happened to Maverick, but my mind kept reminding me he was out of town, that this was all one huge, godawful, mistake. But it wasn't. All I could do was visualize the tree, the one that had been part of Kenny's death, and now my husband's.

Tucker's cell phone started ringing...

Diesel's phone was going off with alerts...

My mind started to... splinter.

Next thing I could comprehend was being in Dad's truck. Viola was in the back seat with me, Savannah in the front with Dad. Diesel's Harley raced off ahead of us. My upper body lurched forward, and I vomited on the floorboard. Viola handed me a construction rag from my Dad's work stuff for my mouth. "Keep breathing for that baby. We're almost there."

Holding my hand, she pulled me through the emergency entrance's sliding doors while Dad and Savannah parked his truck. I watched Viola's mouth move as she talked to the woman behind the desk, but I couldn't hear over the ring in my ears. A buzzing noise was making concentrating so challenging I felt numb. Aware, but not really there. I was more of a spectator than an active member of the travesty taking place in my life.

Past Viola's shoulders and through swinging hospital doors, I saw the back of a leather vest I knew well. It read: *Redemption Ryders*. It was disappearing, walking farther into a hallway.

My steps felt as if walking on traumatized clouds when I stepped around Viola and toward the doors. It was an out-of-body experience as I slipped through them, searching for the vest. I knew Diesel and his boys would be using their connections and checking on Maverick. Emergency room employees were scurrying from one set of hanging sheets to another, working on patients. My slow operating mind would simply watch them rush past me.

My arms hung at my sides and my feet continued their eerie cloud walk. I think I didn't rush because I was terrified of what I would see—Maverick's body without his soul in it. Or maybe it was because of the utter shock that was riveting my body and mind. Losing Maverick was one haunted road I knew there would be no surviving.

There will never be a Delilah walking this earth without her Maverick.

I knew I would soon be a Johnny Cash following his June.

Next to a nurses' station, in another hallway of partitioned white curtains, I saw the back of more leather vests. Many of them. Diesel was livid, his arms waving in the air. "He has to be transferred now!" he demanded.

If I wasn't in a zombie state of mind, I would've hissed at the absurd idea. Even though I had yet to see him, I knew Maverick was in no condition to be moved to a better facility. Bringing in more supplies, nurses were rushing in and out of the partition Diesel and his men were gathered around.

Just then, alarms starting ringing, partly snapping me out of my shock. Someone shouted, "We have a Code Blue! Code Blue!"

I grabbed my chest and whispered, "No."

More employees ran past me again but not to where Diesel was. I panted relief until I heard a nurse ask another behind the counter, "Who's crashing?"

"The burn victim."

Heading in the opposite direction of Diesel, I went to where I had seen the professionals enter. There weren't curtains. This was a room walled by mostly glass. Doctors and nurses worked frantically around a victim I couldn't see. But I recognized a work boot laying on its side on top of a small metal table on wheels. The leather was incredibly charred. The fact that there was only one boot had air rushing from my lungs. It doesn't seem rational, and maybe it wasn't. Doctors were resuscitating my husband, but I was desperate to see the other boot. Why it wasn't there, making a pair, was too gruesome. I needed to see the fucking boot. I needed to hear a gravelly laugh and voice apologizing for putting me through this insensitive joke, but, with only one boot staring at me, I knew that apology wasn't possible, nor was it going to ever happen.

I jumped when Viola touched my back. Gently, she guided me backwards and out of the way of fast-moving employees. "He's going to pull through. That bastard won't leave you." Her voice trembled with so much raw emotion she captured my full attention.

I met her hysterical eyes. We both stood there staring at each other, clinging each other's hands to our chests, shaking as if we might both fall to the ground at any second. But our eyes never let go of one another.

"We got him back," a doctor announced before rushing more instructions. It was more than clear Maverick wasn't out of the deep waters drowning me, but he was alive. He was deciding to fight, so damnit, I was too.

Tears finally found their way from my eyes and flowed down my face. I whispered to my dear friend who just begged me to hold on and not die. "You knew."

She nodded, tears mirroring mine. Her voice broke as she repeated words from the past. "Scarred. Irrevocably marked, seared. Someone has left such a fingerprint on your soul that you will forever be labeled his." Her hands tightened on mine. "You've done the same to him... Light."

I fell into her and cried so hard my heart was shedding tears, too.

Diesel yelling broke us both from our distress, and we turned to see him. "He shouldn't have been there!"

A nurse, who seemed to know him well by her demeanor, was resting her hand on his chest. "Listen to me. Moving him is not an option. The burns are severe."

"Who?" whispered V.

A biker I didn't recognize pushed past the nurse and got in Diesel's face. "He saved the boxer!"

Viola and I gasped, especially when Diesel came absolutely unglued. "You don't know who he is to me!" He started attacking the daring stranger that dared to stand so close to him. Bikers jumped in, trying to pull the two apart as Viola and I ran toward them.

Diesel was enraged as he was separated from a man he wanted to kill. "I don't care what he did! He was not supposed to be here! You don't understand who he is."

There are only a two people Diesel would let Maverick perish for. Viola and his son.

"No." I felt my heart was going to dissolve in my chest.

As Viola got in front of her brother, trying to tame the beast, I nervously pushed past the curtains, terrified at how badly Art was burned. Bikers were in the way, and beyond that were doctors. Nurses kept slipping past the standing bodies, not having time to argue with them all and asking them to move. Security was even in the mix, demanding bikers leave.

They didn't.

In fact, when they noticed me behind them, they purposely blocked me. "No, JB."

I covered my mouth. "Is it that bad? Oh, God, please let me see him!"

Heavy footfalls ran up behind me. "What the fuck happened?"

My shoulders seized before I slowly turned to see Art completely unharmed.

Eyeing the biker at my back, I timidly faced him. "Who are you keeping me from?"

The voice was shaky as if in pain, but I heard it from the center of all the gathered people. "Let her see me."

I swayed back.

I swayed forward.

Invisible emotional waves were attacking me.

My feet could barely stay under me as my mind tried to comprehend what I was hearing.

Like the sea in the Bible, it parted. Bikers moved aside to show me a sight no one could have ever prepared me for. The remainders of the dark hoody that had been cut from his body and arms hung from his shoulders. His hair was much longer, and he had a full long beard, but I would recognize those deep-seated green eyes anywhere.

As doctors wrapped his hands and arms with white cotton bandages, he winced in pain from the hospital bed. He appeared full of sorrow as peered up to me and said, "Hey, darlin'."

DELILAH

I don't think it's possible to hate someone you love...
I should.
I should tell...
I should scream!
But I can't.
I love him.

Delilah

AUTHOR NOTE

Okay, so, I kinda left you guys with another cliffhanger. I am a bad girl. I know. I tried not to do it (yes, that was my excuse with Steal Me) but as these stories grow, they get too big to be squished into one book. Kenny has a lot to say and wishes to tell you himself. So, bring on the pissed posts because I know that *you* know Mama loves ya, and I'm so sorry you have to wait, again, to learn more from these characters' pasts.

Oh, as you rant and rave at me through social media, can you be sure to add #INeedBleedMe

Yep! The next Haunted Roads Novel is Bleed Me.

You guys are the best!

Now, for those of you who were rocked by the heavy scenes in this novel, please know that your feelings and emotions were heavily considered during every process of creating this story. There were discussions about the explicit details, and fear of creating a bad environment for any readers who may be victims of similar violence, but, in the end, the final decision was mine. I am the author. I am a victim who sometimes wishes others could be more sympathetic to those who have experienced any form of sexual assault. It is a horrendous act, no matter the depth of the abuse. It is violating to the heart as well as the body. Maybe, if someone reads this story and all the gruesome details, they will be more empathetic when someone is asking for help. Maybe they will be more willing to step in and protect or at least hold the hand of the one in tears... because damaged souls are worth saving. #DamagedSoulsAreWorthSaving

~India

National Sexual Assault Hotline: 1-800-656-4673
National Suicide Prevention Lifeline: 1-800-273-8255
Crisis Text Line – Text NAMI to 741-741

SONGS THAT INSPIRED INDIA FOR SCAR ME

(Most of this novel was written years ago, to the original song list
mentioned in Steal Me.
The songs below include inspiration for new scenes, old scenes, and
rewrites.)

"Head Above Water" by Avril Lavigne
"Sentence" by Chasing Jonah
"Something Just Like This" by the Chainsmokers
"Space Cowboy" by Kacey Musgraves
"Drive" by Ben Rector
"Boys Like You" by Anna Clendening
"Be Alright" by Dean Lewis
"Back to You" by Selena Gomez
"Butterfly" (featuring Mimi Page) by Bassnectar
"More Than Life" by Whitley
"Wild Horses" by Natasha Bedingfield
"Delilah" by Florence and the Machine
"Feels Like Home to Me" by Chantel Krevillazuk

"Hostage" by Billie Eilish
"With You" by Andrew Chastain Band

INDIA'S THANK YOUS

As some novels are, this was another tough write for me. Due to my personal experiences with sexual abuse, this was quite the private process. I thought I was running behind with preparing the manuscript for my editor, not having time to have betas give me all their incredible advice that I treasure, but now see how wise the Universe is. This novel is as much of me on the path to healing as is entertainment for some readers. With only my Alpha reader (and book life support/PA) Cat Imb, and my exceptionally caring editor, Kendra, this story is from my heart and soul.

Let the gratitude begin...

Thank you, Cat, for being so much more than a personal assistant. You stand by me and keep pointing up, reminding me to reach for the stars. There are no words to describe the gift you are to me.

Kendra, thank you for not only editing my work but being a support system. Your heart and kindness, not to forget excellent editing advice and guidance, are so otherworldly that I am in awe and so thankful and honored to have you in my corner.

Jay, my cover goddess, once again you have magically brought soul to the first thing readers see of my work. I bow to you.

Lyssa, my proofreader, and Tammy, my formatter, you guys bring the last step to making my work all it can be for my fabulous readers. Thank you for all that you do!

Lindsay, my post/tag master, you are a truly magical unicorn that is unstoppable, even by Facebook police.

To my Purple Flames, India's Igniters, and India's Embers, India's Sparks, and ever-loving Bloggers, thank you for all the comments with updates to this novel, and all the posts you guys shared showing me endless support. I love you guys to infinity!

To my readers, it is simple; there is no me—"the author"—without you. That's it. No me without you. You are the air needed for my fingers to type. Thank you for being such a force of nature.

To my friends and family, I may have had some very hard times in my life, but you continue to show me the true beauty in this world. Forever will I be grateful.

To my kids, you have never made me feel guilty for following my dream, even when it meant you had to cook for yourselves. Love you so much it hurts!

To my husband, the multi-leveled alpha/sweetheart, every time I'm spiraling down, I see your open hand reaching for me, always a reminder I won't be down long. I wish for every woman to find a man like you.

ABOUT THE AUTHOR

www.indiaradams.com

www.indias.productions

Purple Flames

Empowering Perfect Imperfections

f facebook.com/IndiaRAdams

🐦 twitter.com/TheIndiaRAdams

📷 instagram.com/indiaradams

📌 pinterest.com/indiaradams

BOOKS BY INDIA R. ADAMS

Tainted Water

Blue Waters

Black Waters

Red Waters

Standalone

My Wolf and Me

Haunted Roads

Steal Me

Scar Me

A Stranger in the Woods

Rain

River

Mist

Forever

Serenity

Destiny

Mercy

All books can also be found and purchased on India's website:

www.indiaradams.com

Made in the
USA
Lexington, KY